A Brush with Death

Rachel McLean writes bestselling crime and mystery books with characters you'll be rooting for and stories that readers can't put down. Originally a self-publishing sensation, she has sold millions of copies digitally, with massive success in the UK, and a growing reach internationally. She is the author of the Dorset Crime novels and the spin-off McBride & Tanner series and Cumbria Crime series. In 2021, she won the Kindle Storyteller Award with *The Corfe Castle Murders* and her books regularly hit No1 in the Bookstat ebook chart on launch.

Millie Ravensworth is the pen name of two authors who have been writing entertaining novels together for more than ten years. The Millie Ravensworth books focus on their shared love of crime stories and charming characters who readers love spending time with.

Also by Rachel McLean and Millie Ravensworth

The Lyme Regis Women's Swimming Club series

The Lyme Regis Women's Swimming Club
A Brush with Death
The Mystery of the Runaway Reindeer

The London Cosy Mysteries series

Death at Westminster
Death in the West End
Death at Tower Bridge
Death on the Thames
Death at St Paul's Cathedral
Death at Abbey Road

THE
LYME REGIS
WOMEN'S
SWIMMING CLUB
BOOK 2

a BRUSH with DEATH

RACHEL MCLEAN
MiLLiE RAVENSWORTH

ACKROYD PUBLISHING

Ackroyd Publishing

ackroydpublishing.com

Printed and bound in the UK by CPI Group (Uk) Ltd, Croydon CR0 4YY

Chapter One

Annie Abbott stood barefoot on the pebbles, her dry robe fluttering in the breeze as she sipped her first coffee of the day. As usual, she'd delayed her first caffeine hit until after the group's morning swim. It added to the enjoyment.

Annie loved her swims in the waters of Lyme Regis bay, in that sheltered sweep between sea wall and beach. But even now, at the height of summer, the water was cold first thing in the morning, and she knew that what she really loved wasn't so much the swimming but the having swum.

And now, having swum, she had a lovely day to look forward to. Time later with her three grandchildren – Poppy, Louis and brand new baby Daisy. And right now, a cup of coffee from the Kiosk in her hand, the Dorset sun shining down on her and the company of the other early morning swimmers.

"Cakes!" declared Figgy.

A plastic tub appeared. Figgy peeled back the purple lid and Annie peered inside.

"What are these?" she asked, eyeing the wobbly loopy icing on top of each of the cakes.

"Coffee and walnut cakes."

"Cake for breakfast?" asked Rosamund Winters.

Rosamund was a key member of the group. She cherished the company, especially since her husband of many years had run off with his PA or something, but at times her tone could seem a little judgemental, an impression that wasn't softened by her piercingly blue eyes.

Figgy's expression wobbled.

"Never turn down good cake," said Annie, picking up one of the soft cakes. "It's always tea time somewhere in the world." She thrust it into her mouth.

It was moist, light and delicious. Figgy's kitchen might inhabit the cramped corner of a static caravan along the beach, but it was clear she didn't need space to produce baked wonders.

Helen Cruickshank stepped forward and grabbed a cake. "When I was in Brazil, it was *bolo de fubá* with coffee every morning!"

The plastic tub went round. The elderly twins, Sally and Peg, took one each (Sally declaring that despite her type two diabetes, she could have the cake because she had 'been good this week'). But when the box was passed to Juniper, the young Australian waved it away.

"Coffee and walnut. Allergic to nuts, mate."

"I didn't forget you," said Figgy. She dipped into her bag and pulled out a similar but much smaller box. "An individual lemon drizzle cake."

Juniper took it, opened the lid an inch and looked inside. "Oh, lovely." She looked at the lid. "Figgy Edmunds 7B?" she read.

The words were painted on with what looked like nail varnish.

"It was my old lunchbox at school," said Figgy. "My grandma did it. Never scraped it off."

Juniper gave her a polite smile, closed the box and put it down by her things. "Thanks, Figgy. I'll have it later if that's all right."

Juniper raised her hands over her head and began some post-swim stretches. She was one of the few members of the group who treated the swim as serious exercise.

Annie enjoyed an invigorating dip and a splash about before getting quickly wrapped up in her dry robe. Juniper would do half an hour's hardcore aerobic swimming between the beach and the end of the Cobb and then stand on the beach in just her cossie, stretching.

This was the Dorset coast, not Bondi Beach. It was a wonder she didn't get a chill. But then again, if Annie was a tall, willowy twenty-something, maybe she'd spend more time standing around in just her cossie.

"This is very good," said Rosamund, chewing cake.

And it was. Annie leaned against the sea wall, enjoying her cake and drinking the last of her coffee.

It promised to be a warm day, which wasn't always guaranteed, even in July. Lyme Regis thronged with tourists in the summer months. The narrow streets frequently became gridlocked. And during Lifeboat Week at the end of the month, the place went absolutely bonkers. Annie's old friend, Tim Cromwell, who ran the lifeboat station, was working non-stop in preparation. Annie had offered a hand with some of the minor tasks, like organising tombola prizes.

Annie wasn't one to bemoan the annual influx of holidaymakers. They were the very lifeblood of this town. But locals who wanted a bit of peace and quiet either needed to be out super early in the morning or to seek their peace and quiet far from the heart of Lyme Regis. Tourists were drawn to the beaches and to the Cobb, where a wide path on top of the rock harbour wall allowed them to stride out right into the sea. The Cobb was wide enough to support buildings along its middle section, including a small aquarium.

But for now the Cobb was quiet, with just a few morning walkers. Sitting at the very end was the familiar figure of Clifford Muldoon, the elderly local painter renowned not only for his paintings of the local area, but also for the fact that he sat with his easel at the end of the Cobb every day of the year, rain or shine, his mustard-coloured scarf either draped around his shoulders or wrapped around his neck, depending on the weather.

"You reckon he gets lonely?" Annie mused.

"Not all of us need to fill our days with chaos and noise," said Helen, with a raised eyebrow.

Juniper grunted. "That man loves his own company."

Juniper was an art student and had some sort of grant or dispensation to use the flat and studio at the end of Muldoon's garden. She knew him better than any of them, except possibly Helen, who displayed and sold his canvases in her gallery.

Annie licked the last of the icing from her thumb. "Good cake, Figglington," she said.

Figgy grinned.

"Makes me want another drink," said Rosamund, squeezing her empty cardboard cup.

Annie nodded. She looked around at her companions. "Coffee? Coffee?"

"Mocha for me," said Figgy.

"I'll go," said Juniper. "I need to talk to Cam anyway."

She picked up her phone from her pile of things. She whipped round the group, confirming from memory each of their orders, then strode off barefoot along the sand to the Kiosk café that faced directly onto the beach.

The cake box had done a full circuit and returned with a couple of pieces still in it.

"Anyone want another?" asked Figgy.

Sally, the supposedly well-behaved diabetic, began to raise her hand, but her twin sister thrust out an arm and lowered it.

"I might take a piece over to Tim at the lifeboats, if that's all right with you," said Annie. "That man always looks like he could do with feeding up."

The women began gathering their things and drifting off to begin the rest of their day. Annie relished being able to set about her morning in the happy knowledge that with her swim out of the way, she'd already achieved something. Soon there was only a handful of them leaning against the sea wall, enjoying the sound of the waves, the sight of the rounded clouds and wheeling seagulls in the sky above and the warmth of the rising sun on their legs.

Annie released a contented sigh. All was well with the world and nothing could spoil it.

Chapter Two

Peering around at her friends, Annie noticed Figgy staring towards the Kiosk.

The Kiosk's counter faced the beach, where deckchairs were arranged for customers to enjoy their drinks and food, provided they were mindful of greedy, divebombing gulls.

But Figgy wasn't watching the gulls. She was watching Juniper, at the head of the small queue, laughing and chatting with Cameron behind the counter. Cameron Winters was Rosamund's son and, as far as Annie could tell, Figgy's boyfriend.

"Everything all right, Figgy?"

Figgy dragged her gaze away. She pointed at the little plastic pot with the nut-free cake she'd made for Juniper.

"She hasn't eaten her cake."

"I'm sure she will."

Figgy's expression tightened. "I don't think she likes me."

Helen turned to look. "She's Australian. She just comes across as a little blunt at times."

Juniper's loud laugh carried across the beach.

"Very confident, your average Aussie," Helen added.

From where she sat, Rosamund craned her neck to see. "Not jealous are you, Figgy?"

"No."

"Cameron is allowed to talk to other girls, you know."

"I know."

"And it's not like you two are a thing, is it?"

Figgy looked at her. "We're planning to go wild camping on Exmoor."

Annie grunted. Did wild camping mean they were 'a thing'?

Juniper had been given a carry tray of drinks but still seemed to be loitering at the Kiosk counter.

"Meaning no offence," said Rosamund, "I can't help but be glad that Cameron is popular."

"Not helpful, Rosamund," said Annie.

Rosamund shrugged. "Que sera sera. That's what my mum used to say."

"Twaddle," said Helen. "There's no destiny. We're all just happy little snowflakes in the blizzard of life. Seize happiness while you can and don't think about tomorrow. I've lived my life as an untethered free spirit and it's served me well."

Annie stifled a snort.

"Does Harper agree with that sentiment?" asked Rosamund.

Harper was Helen's girlfriend. The pair of them lived together, and Harper worked in a metal-sculpture workshop behind Helen's art gallery in the centre of town.

"Harper gets me," said Helen.

"Thinking about it," said Rosamund, "my mum used to say, 'If your chosen train's in the station, don't wait for the

7

whistle to blow before getting on board.' She had a similar aphorism about the last parking space at Waitrose. Very much a woman in favour of seizing the bloke she wanted."

"Is Cameron the last parking space?" asked Figgy. "Or am I meant to be a happy snowflake?"

Annie patted her hand. "Figgy, dear, I think you should pay less attention to so-called 'words of wisdom' from a bunch of middle-aged women."

"Who are you calling middle-aged?" said Rosamund.

"We're hardly relationship experts," replied Annie. "No offence, Rosamund, but your David buggered off last year. I'm all alone, current house guests excluded. And is your mum still happily married, Rosamund?"

"God, no," said Rosamund. "Dad cleared out years ago. The pair of them couldn't stand each other."

"There. See?" Annie straightened her dry robe around her. "Now, young Juniper is coming back with our hot drinks, so enough of this nonsense." She took the cake box from Figgy. "And once I've got my cuppa, I'll take these up to Tim if that's alright with you."

Helen nudged Rosamund. "Tim," she said with a smile.

Annie blinked at her. "What?"

"Oh, don't think we haven't noticed you finding excuses to pop in on Tim every now and then."

"Tim Cromwell and I go way back," said Annie.

"That's what I'm saying," smirked Helen.

"He does a lot of good work for the town, work I'm keen to support, and I want to show the grandkids round the lifeboat station next week. Doesn't do any harm to be nice to people who might help you in turn. I've already promised a hand with organising the tombola."

"Organising the tombola, eh?" said Helen. "Not heard it called that before."

A look passed between Rosamund and Helen.

"Fine. Yes." Annie gave a defiant pout. "If things had been different, maybe Tim and I might be whatever. No need for you to be all childish about it."

Helen giggled.

Annie pushed herself away from the wall. "Ah, Juniper!" she said loudly. "A well-timed return. Is that one mine?"

Juniper looked from one woman to the next. "What have you lot been talking about?"

Figgy swallowed hard. "Annie's boyfriend, Tim," she said.

Annie gave Figgy a pretend scowl. "Thought you and me were on the same side," she said, before marching off with her coffee in one hand and the cake box in the other.

Chapter Three

After a brief visit to Tim at the lifeboat station, Annie walked up from the beach towards her house. There were a multitude of alleyways and shortcuts on her route back to Anning Road and she made good time, avoiding the busy roads.

As she approached her house, she heard music.

A neighbour?

No, it was coming from Annie's house. And it wasn't hard to guess who was playing the music.

She put her key in the door and pushed it open. It vibrated with the boom-shakalak of the bass-heavy music inside.

"Dante!" she shouted.

No response.

"Dante!"

She went into the living room to find him dancing around the coffee table, eyes closed, oblivious to her presence.

Despite herself, Annie smiled. Dante Legg was not a young man, but he moved in a manner that suggested he wasn't quite ready to accept that. His hat was jammed onto his head, as always, and he stepped around the room in a style that sat somewhere between polished Northern Soul dancing and the 'Nutty Boys' phase of Madness. It was carefree and stylish, a bit like Dante himself.

Dante was the father of Mike, Tina's husband and Annie's son-in-law. That probably meant they were related, but Annie had no idea what the name of that relationship was. They shared two grandchildren, that was the main thing. And none of the family had seen Dante in a very long time. Especially Mike.

"Dante!"

He turned to her and grinned. He lifted his arms, encouraging her to dance with him. "Why you shouting, Annie?"

Annie matched his moves, enjoying the opportunity to dance without any reason. "So I can make myself heard."

"Been swimming?"

"I have."

"Morning workout, a bit like this." Dante lurched into a funny stepping, crouching dance, moving across the living room in slow motion and encouraging Annie to copy his motions.

Annie laughed, picturing what the two of them must look like, then remembered they were shattering the peace of the summer morning.

"We should turn it down a bit."

"Why would we do that?"

"Because of the neighbours. Not everyone wants to hear loud music so early."

Dante went over to the turntable he'd brought with him and lifted the needle from the vinyl. The silence that followed seemed shocking, after the energy and pounding volume of the music.

Annie straightened. "Thank you."

Dante pouted. "It's good for the soul, you know? Music makes us all better people."

Annie shook her head.

How had she ended up with this crazy senior staying with her? Supposedly, Dante had come to see the new baby, Daisy, and there was no other logical place for him to stay, what with Tina, Louis and Daisy all crowded into Naomi's house. Tina and Naomi got on as well as any two sisters, but that house was definitely full.

Annie also wondered whether Tina had been quietly keen to keep Dante at arm's length because of the strained relationship between her husband Mike and his dad. With this arrangement, when Mike came over to Lyme Regis to see his family, he could do so without running into Dante.

And on top of all that, there was the undoubted fact that Dante was a handful.

Since he'd turned up, Annie's house had become a very different place. She'd be the first to admit that she'd always lived a somewhat chaotic life, and that her house reflected that. But it was her own chaos.

Dante had brought with him the chaos of someone who thought nothing of frying potato pancakes at three in the morning and then leaving the plates, smeared with chilli relish, in random places around the house. He always tidied them away when asked, but it was like having a child in the house again.

"What's happening today, Annie?" he asked. His eyes

were bright with expectation, and Annie felt a weird pressure to provide fun and excitement.

"We'll be seeing Tina and the kids very soon," she said. "So, think of their delicate hearing before you put any more records on, eh?"

Dante nodded. "Musical education, yes. Full volume, no. Gotcha."

"You could just do some colouring with them?" she suggested. "Or we could put a film on, maybe? All watch something together."

"We got that lovely open space over the road," he replied. "Nice day like this, we could go and make a festival."

"A festival? Sounds lovely."

Annie left Dante and went to perform a sweep of the house. If Poppy came across a plate of Dante's chilli relish, things could get messy. She found four plates, six mugs and two home-made cassette tapes with scribbled labels. She returned the crockery to the kitchen and handed the cassette tapes to Dante.

"Blast from the past, these," she said.

"Forgotten formats. Someone has to keep them alive."

Annie wasn't so sure. She had clear memories of the tapes coming unspooled within the machines, the tangling and resulting damage forming some of her earliest sources of stress. And even worse, trying to record songs off the top forty countdown without the DJ speaking over them. She still resented some of those DJs for deliberately spoiling her teenage attempts at piracy.

Annie went to get showered after her swim, and when she came back downstairs, found Dante quietly absorbed with some paper crafts at the kitchen table. At last, some peace. She left him to it.

She needed snacks for the visiting grandchildren. Figgy's baking efforts had inspired her; there was time to make cookies before Tina arrived.

"Chocolate chip?" she asked herself.

"Yes please!" she replied.

Chapter Four

Tina pulled up outside her mum's house on Anning Road. It was a glorious day, a fine way to enjoy these last couple of weeks of her maternity leave, especially as she was spending the time at the seaside.

Truth was, Tina loved her job. Motherhood brought with it a lot of stresses, not least the zeal with which her mum had attacked being a grandmother, a zeal which had doubled since Daisy's arrival.

Tina hoped Annie would be distracted by her house guest, Dante.

"Come on then, everyone!" She helped to unbuckle her three-year-old son Louis and her seven-year-old niece Poppy, then lifted Daisy's car seat out.

Annie was already there, beaming at them all as she dived in to deliver hugs.

"In you go, littlies! Need a hand, Tina, love?"

"I've got it, thanks."

Annie put the kettle on, and Tina followed her into the

kitchen. Dante was sat at the kitchen table. Poppy and Louis went over to see what he was doing.

"You want to set Daisy down in the lounge?" Annie asked. "Be a bit quieter in there while she's asleep."

Tina carried the car seat through and plonked herself down in an armchair. Nobody would mind if she sat here for a moment.

"Here's your tea," said Annie, appearing in the doorway. "We can leave Poppy and Louis in there with Dante for a minute."

Tina nodded. "How's he been?"

"A constant surprise and delight. Honestly, I'm never bored."

Tina laughed. "Sounds like just what you needed. You get bored too easily, that's your trouble."

Annie frowned for a moment, then shrugged. "Well, it's only right that he should have a fair crack at being a grand-dad. Even if he wasn't the greatest of dads."

Tina pulled a face. "Yeah. I don't know if Mike will want to see him at all, while he's here."

Annie looked crestfallen. Tina knew that in her mum's world, people would all somehow get along if they'd only try. "Is that a definite 'no'?"

Tina shook her head. "I asked him if he was coming over. He said the house repairs are at a critical point, and he can't possibly get away."

"Wait, what? He's not doing the plastering himself?"

"No. There's a contractor doing the work."

Annie scowled. "He can't keep pretending though, can he?"

Tina shrugged. "He doesn't need to. He's made it clear that he doesn't want to see Dante." She lowered her voice.

"It's non-negotiable. If your dad walks out on you as a kid, it's not easily forgiven."

A shout came through from the kitchen. "Did I hear my name being taken in vain?"

Annie rolled her eyes. "He does like to be the centre of attention, doesn't he?"

Tina smirked, wondering if her mum realised how alike she and Dante were in that particular respect. "Come on, let's go and see what they're all doing."

The two of them went into the kitchen, where Louis's head was adorned with a paper fedora.

"Look!" shouted Poppy. "Louis got a hat. I'm having a blue one."

Louis jigged excitedly, showing off his hat, which featured glitter princesses.

Dante was busy with a pencil, glue stick and scissors, making a second copy of his own hat from a large sheet of colourful paper.

"Is that my wrapping paper?" asked Annie with a frown. She peered under the table, where there was a carrier bag holding several bright tubes. "Good grief, Dante."

"It's for the kids though, isn't it?" replied Dante, flashing a grin as he traced round the brim with a wide sweep of his pencil.

Tina caught the look on Annie's face. 'It's for the kids' was a cast-iron defence for doing just about anything as far as Annie was concerned, but she still looked annoyed about her wrapping paper.

"We going to make a hat for Daisy as well?" asked Poppy.

"We can do that," said Dante. "It'll need to be a really small one though, yeah?"

Poppy nodded solemnly. "Daisy's head is forty centimetres all the way round."

Annie and Dante exchanged looks at this unexpected revelation.

"Poppy's been doing measuring," explained Tina.

"I see," said Annie. "Well, you should tell her mum that she's been very thorough."

"Want to put some glue on this for me, Poppy?" asked Dante.

Poppy picked up the glue stick and carefully dabbed it where Dante pointed.

Dante looked up at Tina. "How is that son of mine?"

"He's doing fine," she replied. "Getting the house back into shape. It's taught him a lot, this project."

"Yeah? Practical skills?"

She shook her head. "No. Mostly it's taught him to call in the professionals."

"Well, send him my best, won't you?"

"You should make him a hat," Poppy told Dante. "He might like that."

Tina stared at Poppy. It was easy to forget that a seven-year-old could be so clued into the dynamics of a discussion.

"Make him a hat? That is a very fine idea," said Dante. "What do you think his favourite colour might be?"

Tina felt a brief moment of sadness at the fact that Mike's own dad knew so little about him.

"I think he wants an orange hat," declared Poppy.

"Maybe you can measure his head next time he comes around?" said Dante to Poppy.

"Yes!" said Poppy, thrilled to have another measuring job.

Tina's eyes narrowed. Had Dante just recruited her

niece as an unwitting spy, to report on Mike's next visit? He must have forgotten that Tina was a detective and would see a ruse like that from a mile off.

She sighed, hoping there wouldn't be any unwanted family drama.

Chapter Five

As the week continued, the weather went from 'pleasantly summery' to 'downright glorious'.

For most of the year, the early morning swimmers could be out and dry by 7am and feel that the rest of the world hadn't yet woken. But on bright days like these, even as they waded into the water, it seemed as if the day had got up, had its first cup of coffee and put on its trousers for work.

Warm weather meant longer in the water for some. Rosamund, who took her swimming almost as seriously as Juniper, tried to match the young Australian in her front crawl lengths out to the buoys and back. Annie was all for proper exercise, especially after those cakes earlier in the week, but she thought some people were inclined to overdo it.

On Saturday, Annie had her usual splash, paddle and moment of inner tranquillity. Then she came out to dry, enjoying the snuggly warmth of her dry robe and a coffee from the Kiosk. Helen and Figgy were comparing peculiarly shaped pebbles and discussing which animals they could paint them to look like.

Helen enjoyed artistic whimsy, and Figgy liked the introverted cosiness of small-scale art, which meant this was a common topic of conversation between them.

Annie was on her second coffee and giving everyone an update on Dante's slightly chaotic influence on her home when Rosamund finally emerged onto the beach, out of breath, and reached for her towel.

"You still got Tina's father-in-law staying with you?" she said, pulling a face.

Annie nodded. "For the foreseeable. He's not that bad, really."

Rosamund grunted. "One of the attractions of moving here years ago with David was that it was too far away for relatives to drop in unannounced. I've never understood people who want their mum or dad just around the corner." She shuddered and towelled herself down.

"Cake box," said Annie, clicking her fingers.

"Pardon?" said Helen.

"Just remembered." The talk of family had made her think of Figgy's grandmother. "I left Figgy's cake box at the lifeboat station," she said, gathering her things and standing.

"Oh, no," said Figgy. "No hurry."

"You need it back before Lifeboat Week swings into action. It'll be bedlam down there. It'll end up as a prize on the tombola stall they're running out of the lifeboat station."

Helen tutted and tapped Figgy's arm. "What you're witnessing here, Figgy, is Annie creating another subtle excuse to visit Lifeboat Tim."

Annie stuck her tongue out at her friend. "I don't need excuses, Helen Cruickshank. I'm a grown woman."

"Debatable."

Annie grinned as she made her way up to the promenade and along towards the lifeboat station. This end of the promenade, things were quieter. The shutters were going up on Breaststrokes café bar. The Cobb Arms overlooking the harbour hadn't yet opened its doors.

The harbour was an uneven horseshoe shape, the short sea wall to the left side and the wide sweeping Cobb on the right. Lyme Regis lifeboat station was just to the right of the Cobb's entrance, with access both to the marina slipway and to Monmouth beach further to the right.

It was a compact building with a high sloping roof that made it look a bit like a chapel. Tim Cromwell kept it well maintained, inside and out. He was a tidy-minded and conscientious soul, that was for certain.

Wellington, a statue of a dog made entirely from wellies, stood on guard outside the visitors' centre door. Annie patted him before going inside. There were information panels on the walls, and various model boats, fluffy toys, key rings and such like on the shop shelves around the room.

Tim was behind the counter, counting out RNLI pens in a wicker display box. He greeted Annie with a gentle smile.

"Good morning. Thought I'd have a minute to myself before the first visitor of the day."

"I can go and come back again."

"Don't you dare, Annie Abbott." He put down the last of the pens. "I'm only saying I'm gearing up for a busy one."

Tim was the same age as Annie, and they'd been in many of the same classes at secondary school. The years had weathered his thin face, and etched lines in his cheeks that often made him look mournful when he wasn't smiling.

Maybe that was why he smiled a lot. Although Annie liked to think he just smiled a lot around her.

Tim's Dorset accent was stronger than hers. He dropped 'h's all over the place and pronounced 'r's where most people would drop them. That, along with his penchant for woollen jumpers and round caps, gave him the air of a traditional sailor or fisherman, which must have gone down well with the tourists.

He passed her the display box. "Pop those down over there for me, would you?"

She put them in the space on the shelf.

"While you're here." He reached below the counter and produced the larger of Figgy's cake boxes. "Tell your Figgy it was delicious. Very moist."

"Ah. The very reason I came over," she said, taking it.

"Oh, not popped in to ask me out to an art class?"

"Art class? Really? I can do that, too."

He tilted his head, one eyebrow raised. "My diary is mostly empty. Aside from a load of prep I need to do for Lifeboat Week. Tombola prizes that need organising, that sort of nonsense. It'll fill up most of my time."

"Well, if that's the case—"

He abruptly held up his hand to stop her.

Annie was confused; it wasn't like him to be rude. "Tim—"

The hand turned into a single finger. His expression was tight.

He stepped round the counter, past her and hurried outside.

As the door opened, Annie caught what he must have already heard: high panicked shouting.

She followed Tim outside.

A woman was running down the highest path on the Cobb. She waved her arms and pointed. It took a moment for Annie to hear the words.

"In the water! In the water! There's someone in the water!"

It was still early and there were few people by the harbour or on the Cobb. Most of them either hadn't heard the woman or were just staring.

Tim was already running. Annie hurried after him as quickly as she could.

She didn't have to go far before she spotted what the woman was pointing at.

Over the eastern left-hand side of the Cobb, across the harbour, there was a figure in the water. It was no morning swimmer.

It was a man, floating on his back, fully dressed.

Chapter Six

Annie caught up with Tim to stand on the Cobb.

Even at a distance, she'd recognised the white hair and the touch of mustard fabric at the man's neck. A glance to the end of the Cobb confirmed her suspicion.

"That's Clifford Muldoon."

Tim nodded and pointed in the same direction, towards Muldoon's usual painting spot. "Go to his things. Grab anything important."

"Important?"

"Medication. Phone." He was already running back to the lifeboat station. "I need you to be my eyes and ears!"

Annie hurried along the Cobb. She could hear a siren wailing from the lifeboat station. Tim had put the call out.

Clifford was still in the water, still floating. His only movements seemed to come with the rise and fall of the waves.

She felt an urge to rip off her dry robe, jump into the water, and swim across the harbour to him. She was a fair swimmer, but it would be quicker to run to the end of the

Cobb and, either way, any launched boat would be faster still. Besides, she'd read enough news stories in which a person, almost always a man, leapt into water to save someone only for the rescuer themselves to be the only casualty.

She forced herself to continue along the Cobb to Muldoon's usual spot. A canvas folding chair lay on its back at the end of the Cobb. In front of it sat a wooden adjustable easel with a canvas in place. It was the early stages of a painting of the view looking east, along the coastline towards Portland Bill. Only the rough outline of the land and the shape of larger clouds had been filled in.

By the side of the fallen chair was a large over-the-shoulder leather bag. With another glance back to Clifford Muldoon, floating in the water, she opened it and looked inside to find two more canvasses. They too were paintings of the same scene at different stages of completion, although neither seemed completely finished.

Beside them was a soft leather wallet and...

"Hmmm."

There was a little plastic pot with a purple lid and 'Figgy Edmunds 7B' painted on it in fading nail varnish.

Figgy's other cake box. The one with the non-nutty cake for Juniper.

Juniper knew Muldoon, of course, but the presence of the box here didn't entirely make sense. Annie pushed the box into the pocket of her dry robe and dug deeper into the bag.

"Ah-ha!"

Below the wallet was a grey and blue plastic tray of tablets. The lids along the top were marked with the days of the week, and there were several little pills in each compartment. She looked deeper in the bag. There was no further medication.

There was no phone either. Maybe Muldoon had it on him.

She didn't know for sure, but Clifford Muldoon had looked like a guy in his eighties. Not the sort of age where someone might carry their phone at all times.

Had. She was already thinking of him in the past tense.

With Clifford's pill tray and wallet in hand, along with the large cake box she'd carried from the lifeboat station, she looked to where Muldoon floated on the water. Further along, on the beach, she could see people looking on with concern. Was that Rosamund and Juniper down at the water's edge, probably debating whether to swim out to the man?

She looked up to see a small inflatable boat approaching. There were two figures on board. The one steering at the outboard motor was Tim.

A tall round figure in lifeboat yellows was jogging down the Cobb. She recognised the bushy beard: Lachlan Fellows, barman at the Cobb Arms and lifeboat volunteer.

It had seemed like an age had passed, but in less than five minutes from the shout going up, the lifeboat crew had been mobilised and were attending to the man in the sea. And yet, looking at that motionless figure, its face turned to the sky and mouth hanging open, Annie felt in her heart that it was all far too late.

Clifford Muldoon was dead.

Chapter Seven

Tina was making herself useful at Naomi's. She knew Naomi and Dougie welcomed her extended visit, but it couldn't be easy, having three extra people in the house. So she was doing the shopping and meal planning for the coming days. Dougie was taking her to the supermarket in the patrol car and had promised to run her back when she was done.

They drove down Sidmouth Road with Daisy in the car seat in the back.

"I know Naomi will have said you should get the healthy brown bread, but can we have some white as well?" Dougie asked.

"She told me you'd do this."

Dougie's face dropped.

Tina smiled. "In Naomi's own words, 'nice try sunbeam'."

"Flipping heck. Maybe Naomi should be a detective."

Tina chuckled. "I think it speaks of a strong marriage. She knows you well."

The radio burst into life.

"Incident at the Cobb in Lyme Regis. Person in the water, status undetermined."

"I'm going to need to – you know." Dougie twirled a finger in the direction of the Cobb.

Tina sat up straighter. "Yep. Off you go. I'm coming along for that."

"You've got the baby with you," protested Dougie.

"Daisy will be fine. It's not as if there's a live shooter or anything."

Dougie pulled a face but drove down Cobb Road and pulled up outside the lifeboat station.

Tina was about to stride into the crowd that had gathered there when she remembered to get Daisy from the back seat. She hooked the car seat onto her arm and followed Dougie towards the Cobb.

"Right, I need you all to stay clear of the Cobb!" Dougie shouted to the crowd. "Please don't make it any harder for the professionals to do their job, eh?"

Tina could see her mum's swimming group among the people shuffling back at Dougie's words. But there was no sign of Annie herself. Tina looked around, knowing that her mum was almost certainly in the thick of things.

She approached Helen Cruickshank from the art gallery. "What's happened?"

"Clifford Muldoon. He was in the water right there. The lifeboat went out to him."

Tina frowned. "Who's Clifford Muldoon?"

"He's an artist. Celebrated local talent. You'll have seen him at his easel on the Cobb."

Tina had seen him. Her gaze was drawn to the easel, still standing in the shelter of the wall.

"Is my mum here?"

A nod. "She was with Tim, the lifeboat guy."

Tina spotted her mum near the slipway, where the lifeboat team were leaning in over the person they'd pulled from the sea.

A siren approached.

She walked over to see what was happening. Dougie continued to shoo onlookers back from the scene as he unspooled crime scene tape to form a barrier.

One of the lifeboat men was performing CPR. Someone hurried over with a defibrillator in a fluorescent bag, but Clifford Muldoon remained unresponsive.

Tina approached Annie. "How come you're here, Mum?"

Annie lifted the cake container she carried. "Went to see Tim after my swim. Collecting this."

Tina eyed it. "Tim the lifeboat guy? I recognise him from ages ago. He's been here since year dot, yeah?"

Annie pulled a face. "By 'year dot' do you mean since I was young?"

Tina suppressed a smile. "Pretty much."

"Then yes."

"Did you see Clifford before or after he went in the water?"

"Yes. I mean, both."

"Tell me. What did you see?"

"He was there on the end of the Cobb doing his painting as usual. We saw him while we were swimming." Annie paused. "He's part of the scenery really, we see him every day. Then when I was talking to Tim, someone down on the beach shouted, saying he was in the water."

Tina turned as she heard another voice.

PC Wendy Sharman was unspooling more crime scene tape as she spoke to Dougie, catching up with events. Tina waved at her, glad of the extra help.

"What happened at that point?" she asked Annie.

"Tim put the call out for the lifeboat crew and sent me up to check on any medication and whatnot that Clifford might have. At that point, it was a medical emergency, I guess."

They both turned to look down at the slipway. The lifeboat team continued to work on Clifford, but it was clear that they were waiting for a medical professional to confirm that he was dead.

Annie looked away.

"Hey, Mum. We can do this later." Tina put a hand on her arm.

"You're all right, love. I'm fine." Annie shrugged off the hand. "I found his pills."

"What did you do with them?"

Annie waved the pill box. "I brought them back, in case they were needed. His wallet, too."

Tina fished in her bag. She took out an evidence bag and held it open. "I'd better take those."

"What are you even doing with evidence bags?" Annie asked. "You're on maternity leave."

Tina ignored the question, holding the evidence bag out. Annie nodded and dropped Clifford's wallet and pills inside. Along the slipway, two people in the uniform of paramedics were approaching the lifeboat team and the still body of Clifford Muldoon.

Tina set the car seat on the ground so she could use both hands to write on the bag. The movement made Daisy stir.

Annie sprang into action, picking up the carrier and

peering at Daisy's face. "Let's get you away from here, shall we?" She looked at Tina. "Want me to take her home with me?"

Tina looked around at the crowd and sighed. At the very least, there were numerous witnesses here, and the police would need to get their details before they grew bored and drifted away. There was a lot of work to be done, and she knew she should lend a hand, even if it wasn't yet certain what kind of incident this actually was.

"If you don't mind. Thanks, Mum."

As Annie walked away, Tina went over to where Clifford Muldoon lay. The paramedics had spent a few minutes talking to the lifeboat team, and as Tina approached, they were exchanging sorrowful shakes of their heads.

Tina looked down at the artist. His clothes had been cut away to expose his chest for the defibrillator.

He was deeply wrinkled. He spent all day out in the sun, so that was to be expected, and he must have been in his eighties.

He wore a pale blue lightweight smock, made of a rough fabric. And trousers that Tina automatically assumed came from M&S. Sensible, sturdy and traditional.

He looked smaller than she remembered.

She pursed her lips. Death did that to people sometimes.

Chapter Eight

Rosamund Winters drove home after the drama at the beach.

She'd assumed she could swim out and tow Clifford back to safety, but she'd been told the lifeboat was the better option. She'd just be in the way.

Then she'd been caught in the foolish trap of wanting to stay and show support for the rescue operation. Wanting to hang on for her friend Annie, who'd ended up stuck in the middle of it all.

Eventually she realised she was just one of those ghastly looky-loos staring at an unfolding disaster. She'd been there so long, with the police collecting everyone's details, that she'd ended up having to pay the higher fee at the Cobb Gate car park.

After her shower, she went to her to-do list on the fridge. She had a post-swim routine of doing a small but irritating job while she was still feeling the afterglow.

Clean oven

Windows – inside downstairs

Tidy away plant pots
Sort wardrobe

Cleaning the oven was no massive chore on a day like today, when she could take the racks outside for scrubbing. As she opened the oven to assess the size of the job, the doorbell rang. She pushed the oven closed and went to answer.

Rosamund's house was full of gadgets, and she could have checked the app to see who was there. But she'd been thinking about removing some of them. They were so very David.

She opened the door, and for a few long moments considered closing it again straight away. The slim, neatly coiffured woman standing on her driveway stared back at her.

At last Rosamund spoke. "Mum?"

Rosamund's mother, Joanna King, was very much a member of the city-dwelling species. She was like a delicate bloom that would drop its petals if you put it in the wrong environment. Yet here she was.

Joanna King, now in her mid-seventies, still presented herself as the stylish and expensively dressed woman Rosamund had known almost all her life. It was not a look or a style that suited rural coastal living.

Surely, her carefully blow-dried blonde hair would be blown askew in the sea breezes? Even her clothes, all pale creamy chiffons, were unsuited for the seaside.

"Darling." Joanna somehow looked both fragile and unapproachable. She smiled and pointed an elegant finger towards the house. "Aren't you going to invite me inside?"

"Mum. What are you doing here?"

"Is that any way to greet me?"

"I mean, hello, Mum, but..." Unable to think of what to say next, Rosamund went to help her mother with the enormous suitcase she had with her. How had she even got here with that?

She put the case to one side and, still stunned, ushered Joanna through to the kitchen. "Why don't I make us a cup of tea and you can tell me what brings you here?"

"That would be lovely." Joanna's smile never looked insincere; it was her greatest superpower. She flashed it now as Rosamund put the kettle on. "Do you have Fairtrade?"

"I do."

"Marvellous. I wasn't sure if you'd get it down here."

Rosamund rolled her eyes. In her mother's eyes, anywhere that wasn't London was small and parochial.

She reached into a cupboard to retrieve the teapot. She didn't bother when she was on her own, but her mother had standards.

"I might not even need to warm the pot, it's so sunny today," she said.

On the rare occasions she actually used it, Rosamund never warmed the pot. But now, with her mother here, old habits and insecurities were rushing back.

"Maybe give it a rinse round with some boiling water, darling," said Joanna.

Rosamund did as her mother suggested.

"You're right, it is sunny," said Joanna. "Humid and windy, too. A very different kind of heat from the city."

"Refreshing," Rosamund replied. "Mum, it's lovely to see you but I wasn't expecting you."

"Doesn't sand get into everything, though? That's the thing I remember most about the seaside."

Rosamund felt her jaw tighten. "Around the beach, of course. But we don't really have a problem with sand in the rest of the town."

She looked up, wondering why her mother was talking about sand.

"Listen, Mum," she said. "Really nice to see you. I know it's been a week or two since we've spoken. But if you were planning on visiting, couldn't you have called ahead?"

Joanna's face was tight with concern. "I heard about you and David, darling."

Rosamund stiffened. How did she know? Was her network of friends connected to Lyme Regis?

"I came as quickly as I could."

"Sorry?" said Rosamund.

"David leaving you. I can't imagine how awful you must feel."

"Um... right."

"But we can sort you right out, I promise."

Rosamund turned to face her mother. Slowly but surely, the utter shock of her mum coming all the way from London to Dorset was turning into irritation.

Chapter Nine

Annie jigged Daisy in her arms as she went to answer the door.

"What d'you reckon, Daisy? Is this your mummy come to pick you up?"

Tina smiled at the sight of them, but then her serious police face took over.

"Hey, Mum, I wonder if you'd mind looking after Poppy and Louis as well?"

Annie looked past her daughter to see a patrol car waiting, Dougie at the wheel. "Of course! Are those little smashers getting a ride in a police car? How exciting."

She went out to exchange greetings with her son-in-law and helped Poppy and Louis out for a one-armed hug with Daisy clamped in the other arm.

"Where are you off to?" Annie asked.

"Clifford Muldoon's place," said Tina. "We need to inform his next of kin."

Annie frowned. "Yes, of course. I don't even know if he was married."

"We'll find out when we get there," said Tina. "We should get a move on, or the grapevine will beat us to it, and that's never good."

"Best of luck." Annie waved them off.

She herded Poppy and Louis indoors, into the kitchen. Dante had gone out for a walk. He claimed he wanted to 'soak up some rays', but Annie suspected he was taking a look at the drama on the Cobb for himself.

She sat Poppy and Louis at the kitchen table and put Daisy into the bouncy chair on the table itself, so she could address them all at eye level.

"Right, kiddos, I'm glad we have this unexpected time to chat. There's a fun project that I have in mind, and you're all invited."

She reached over to the cookery book shelf. These days she got most of her recipes from the internet, which was just as well because it made room for three large hardback journals. She pulled them down and spread them across the table.

"Did I say invited? What I meant to say is that the three of you are at the absolute epicentre of this thing. We have here the Poppy journal, the Louis journal and the Daisy journal. We are going to fill these bad boys with all sorts of fun activities, and I call this meeting to order so we can discuss what those activities might be."

She grabbed a pot of pens and some paper.

"We don't like bad boys," said Poppy, reaching for one of the pens.

"Ah. Figure of speech. And now I come to think of it, not a very pleasing one, if we're empowering young minds. What I meant to say, young Poppy, is that we will be choosing some activities that we can all do, and then we're going to write about them in here."

She patted the books.

Poppy pulled one over, pen poised.

"We can do the documenting together when we have a plan," said Annie, pulling it gently back again. "If you want to do some note taking, have a sheet of paper."

Poppy took a sheet and carefully wrote her name at the top.

"Good work. Now, let me explain how committees work. Committees are one of the cornerstones of getting things done in this country, so you're definitely not too young to learn."

"Ma-mitty," said Louis.

"Committee," corrected Poppy, as if she sat on lots of them.

"The thing about committees," said Annie, "is that we all have a voice in any decisions that are made."

"Even Daisy?" Poppy asked, looking up from her drawing.

"Oh yes. She might not have much input just now, but it's important to include everyone."

Poppy looked at Daisy, who jigged lightly in her bouncer as the other three faces turned towards her.

"A committee usually has a chairperson, whose role it is to direct the meeting. I will do that for now. Another important role is the secretary, who writes down what's been decided."

Poppy put a hand up. "I can do that."

"Then we're good to go!" Annie clapped her hands. "I think our first job is to collect some ideas for the journals. Activities that we can all do together."

Poppy frowned. "Colouring?"

Annie nodded. "It should go on the list, definitely. All three of you can do some special colouring that we will glue into the journal."

"Gluestick!" Louis clapped his hands. He seemed more delighted at the glueing than the colouring, but that was fine.

"Now, we might want to set our sights a bit higher than colouring," continued Annie. "Something like going on a seesaw, maybe? Finding a fossil?"

"Baking!" cried Poppy.

"That's a very good idea indeed," said Annie. "Any others? Louis, what do you want to do?"

"Bricks," Louis said.

"Building a tower? Or a house? I think we can get that in there. Good call."

"Recycling," added Poppy. If Annie's memory served her right, Poppy had been doing recycling at school.

"Great idea, that!" Annie looked around at all three faces. Daisy hadn't added much to the discussion, but she was clearly enjoying being a part of it.

"I'm just going to recap some of our ideas," said Annie, counting them off on her fingers. "We've got colouring, baking, bricks and recycling. I think that's a good number to have a vote on, don't you?"

Three blank faces looked back at her.

"Voting. Let's talk about that. It's where we all choose, but we're choosing for the group, so we want to see if we can agree, don't we?"

Poppy and Louis nodded. Daisy kicked and hiccupped.

"If we don't all agree on something, and that happens a lot, then we have to count up and see which thing gets the most agreement. Sound fair?"

More nods.

"Good stuff. Now, the way we're going to vote is by putting up a hand if we like an idea. Let's give it a try, shall we? Who would like to put their hand up for colouring?"

Poppy's hand went up, as did Louis's.

"And who would like to put their hand up for baking?"

Poppy leaned over to lift Daisy's hand as well as her own. Louis raised his own hand.

"Bricks?"

Louis raised both of his hands. Poppy scowled and kept her hands down in protest.

"And recycling?"

There was a great deal of interest in recycling. Poppy raised both of Daisy's hands with her right hand and put her left one in the air. Louis raised two hands as well.

"Democracy in action!" said Annie, punching the air. "Recycling wins the first round. We might need to come up with some ground rules for future voting sessions, but you all did a good job there."

Daisy kicked her legs and chuckled.

"Now," said Annie, "how about we spend a couple of minutes drawing a picture of what good recycling looks like? Maybe it will inspire what we'll actually do for this activity."

Poppy and Louis attacked sheets of paper with gusto while Annie played peekaboo with Daisy for a few minutes.

"Who's finished a picture?" she asked.

Two drawings were thrust into the centre of the table.

"Ah, I see what's happened here," said Annie, looking at the picture Louis had made. He had latched onto the 'cycle' part of the word by drawing a bike. "You're putting the cycling into recycling. Clever approach. How about you, Poppy?"

She held up Poppy's picture, which showed all four of them in a semi-circle at the rear of what looked like a bin lorry.

"You have us working a bin lorry? Well, I can't fault your passion, kiddo."

Annie put the drawings down, wondering how she could chart a course through the tricky territory she'd created.

"Tell you what, there's a nice way we can do recycling as a first attempt. How do we all feel about junk modelling?"

"Yaay!" shouted Louis. Annie was fairly certain he had no idea what she was talking about.

"Yaay!" shouted Poppy, determined to make more noise than her cousin.

Baby Daisy jigged at the noise, entertained by the outburst.

"Well, that's unanimous then," said Annie. "I declare this meeting closed."

Chapter Ten

Tina and Dougie left Anning Road and nipped along Woodmead Road to avoid going back into town. Clifford Muldoon's place was one of the larger properties further up Silver Street.

Tina put a call through to her boss, Detective Inspector Hannah Patterson, as Dougie drove.

"What's this I hear about you getting involved in police business again while you're supposed to be on maternity leave?" Hannah asked as soon as the call connected.

"I'm just riding along with PC Anderson, that's all."

"Riding where, exactly?"

"There's been a death. We're going to inform next of kin. There might not be anything here for Major Crimes to get involved in. I can support local officers, seeing as I'm here, can't I?"

A pause. "Keep me informed. As soon as it becomes clearer what we're dealing with, we can decide whether I need to send any active officers over there." Hannah sounded stern. But Tina knew how busy the team was.

Tina agreed and ended the call. Her colleagues on the Major Crimes Investigation Team in Winfrith covered Lyme Regis, but it was well over an hour's drive away.

"Blimey, I think I might even be doing this with the boss's blessing."

Dougie smiled. "Well, I'm very glad you're here."

Tina turned to him. "Want me to take the lead?"

He narrowed his eyes. "No. I've got this. But, grateful for the support."

He pulled up outside an enormous Victorian house. "Here we go."

"This place is massive." Tina stared up at the building. "It's got to be one of the biggest houses in the town."

It had four dormer windows, indicating that there were rooms in the attic, and Tina could see opaque windows at ankle level suggesting a basement, too. It had been built in one of those mash-up styles that probably had a name but put Tina in mind of a suburban pub, with stone-framed mullion windows against red brick.

Dougie rapped on the door, then frowned. "Oh, hello."

Tina stepped forward to see what he was looking at. The door was slightly ajar, with rough splinters at the edge.

"Been forced," she said. The paintwork was otherwise immaculate. "We should take care."

They paused, waiting for a response to Dougie's knock.

"Taking care in this instance means calling for backup," he said.

Tina shrugged. "Call for backup by all means."

Dougie stepped towards the car. Tina didn't move.

"If I go and call for backup, are you just going to walk straight in there?" he asked.

She chewed her lip. No point lying. "Yep."

He sighed and rolled his eyes. "Fine. Give me one minute. Just one minute, right? I'll call for backup and we can go in together, yes?"

Tina nodded and waited for him.

Two minutes later, he joined her back at the door and they entered the house together.

The hallway was painted in shades of pale blue. It was empty except for an umbrella stand featuring a seagull perched on the top. The next room was a large sitting room, painted in jewel colours. There was nobody in there, and while the room wasn't tidy, it had the cluttered disorganisation of a creative mind: scattered sketch pads, magazines and squashed tubes of paint.

"Hello?" called Tina.

"This is the police!" Dougie added.

Their shouts echoed faintly back. There was no response.

"What do you reckon?" Dougie said.

"I reckon we should check the rest of the house, see if anyone's here. Then we take a better look round at the state of the place."

Her brother-in-law nodded.

It was a truly enormous house. They walked through a library, stacked floor to ceiling with art books, some piled on the floor, others on various chairs. There was a room that looked as though it was used for painting, and yet another sitting room. All of them had massive paintings on display and bright, vibrant painted walls, but Tina had no time to absorb the details. The kitchen was empty, too.

They went upstairs and checked each bedroom. Only one of them appeared to be in use. Most of the others were used for storage.

"Next floor up?" Dougie asked.

Tina nodded, as their phones pinged.

"Wendy's downstairs," Dougie said.

"Tell her she's our eyes and ears on the ground floor," Tina told him. "We're nearly done up here. Actually, she can start looking for any sign of where we might find next of kin."

They climbed up to the second floor.

"These rooms are massive," whispered Dougie.

The windows on the upper floor made the rooms seem much larger and brighter than Tina had expected. Teak mid-century furniture cluttered the first room, although it might have once been in use as a studio. An easel was positioned near to the window, looking out towards the bay.

"I think we're all clear up here," said Dougie. "Just the basement left."

They went downstairs to find Wendy taking a look around the ground floor.

"Anyone here?" she asked.

"Just need to check downstairs," Dougie told her, "but nobody so far."

It took them a moment to find the correct door off the kitchen and then locate the light switch.

"I'd say the basement doesn't get used much," said Tina as they reached the bottom of the steps. It had vaulted ceilings and raised areas covered in tiles, but all that stood on the tiles were dusty boxes, a few wine racks and rows of home pickles that looked at least a decade old.

There was a pile of equipment beside a dirty sink that looked as if it was an ancient experiment in some sort of printing. Dried ink curled in crusty fragments on a mesh-covered frame.

"Nothing down here," Tina said. "Let's go back up and take a closer look at that break-in, shall we?"

"What you thinking?" Dougie asked as they climbed the stairs.

"A man's dead and someone broke into his house," she replied. "I'm thinking that maybe this does need to involve Major Crimes."

Chapter Eleven

Rosamund's tea had turned cold, but she felt anything but cool right now.

"You're going to sort me out, Mum?"

"Yes, darling." That smile again. "Sort you out."

"How—"

"How? Well, I can show you." Joanna held up her handbag. It was a Birkin, as she would tell anyone who'd listen. She reached inside and pulled out a notepad. "I've been doing some manifesting on your behalf."

"Manifesting."

"I know it's not supposed to work that way, but I thought you'd want to get a head start."

What Rosamund actually wanted was for her mum to put that notepad back inside the bag and go away.

"Here we are," Joanna went on. "Page one. Get Rosamund back on track and get David back home where he belongs." She looked up from the page, which had stickers and sketches embellishing the central statement. Rosamund didn't want to examine them too closely. "What do you think?"

Rosamund turned back to the fresh drinks she was making, and plipped a sweetener into Joanna's.

"Oh, wait, does that have aspartame?" Joanna asked.

"What? No. Why?"

"Reenie Ballantyne says it causes cancer."

Rosamund didn't know who Reenie Ballantyne was, or if she was qualified to hand out fake-sounding medical advice. She chose to say nothing.

She carried their mugs into the living room and put them on the table.

"No coasters?" Joanna asked.

"This table wipes clean."

"Yes, but still."

Rosamund sipped her tea, casting about for the most neutral words she could find. "When you say that I need to get back on track, is that specifically about getting David back?"

Joanna waved a dismissive hand. "We all need to course-correct every once in a while, don't we? Let's look at things from David's point of view for a moment. He was always a man of exacting standards. It's probably fair to assume that something has slipped. All we have to do is find it and fix it." She looked around the room and nodded.

Exacting standards? Something has slipped? Fix it?

Fix what?

David had left her, and it was somehow her fault? The woman had been in her house for less than ten minutes and Rosamund was ready to toss her out.

She took a deep breath. "There are a few things I should make clear. I don't want David back."

"Oh?"

"And I definitely don't want to look at things from his point of view. My standards are the same as they have always been."

"Well, maybe that's the probl—"

"I do not need course-correcting, and I am doing fine."

Joanna gave an indulgent smile. "That's my girl. Of course you're putting a brave face on things. I'd expect nothing less." She flicked through her notebook. "How does this one sound, then? Get Rosamund ship-shape. Tidy house, tidy mind."

Rosamund looked around the living room. It was immaculate. What could her mother be talking about?

"How am I not ship-shape?"

"Pfft! I saw your list in the kitchen. All those things you need to do. We need to whittle it down."

She wanted to explain that the list was an important part of her life, and a very welcome one. But something else snagged her mind. "Wait, you want to clean the oven?"

"Good grief, no!" Joanna recoiled in horror. "But I will help you organise your wardrobe."

"Absolutely not."

"Well, we'll need to start somewhere," said Joanna. "First things first. I'll pop upstairs and select a bedroom for me to use, shall I?"

The giant suitcase.

Rosamund's mouth fell open. "You're staying? How long?"

"As long as it takes, darling."

Rosamund watched as her mother climbed the stairs. That massive suitcase looked as if it held enough clothes for a lengthy stay. How on earth was she going to deal with her mother being here, on some open-ended, overzealous mission?

She sent a message to the WhatsApp group for the swimming club.

I know it's been a weird day, but it's just got weirder. My mother has turned up to 'fix me'. She is staying here for I don't know how long! She's a lot at the best of times. Send thoughts and prayers.

Helen was the first to respond, with a meme showing a doctor's prescription for 'all the wine'.

Figgy sent a hug emoji and Annie responded with *Crikey. Hope it's not too awful.*

Rosamund gave a small smile as she listened to her mother prowling around upstairs. She inhaled deeply and went up to see what she was doing, hoping against hope that the woman wasn't already going through her wardrobe.

Chapter Twelve

The suggestion of foul play meant the boss had advised bringing Detective Sergeant Nathan Strunk up to speed, and Tina was on the phone to the DS.

Nathan was part of the MCIT team back in Winfrith. It seemed obvious to Tina that she, a team member here in the town, ought to be involved, but the boss wanted someone on active duty to lead the investigation.

"Front door's been forced," Tina told the DS. "We're looking around now, see if there's anything obvious missing."

"So, we have a dead artist, dragged out of the sea. He lives locally and someone's broken in." The DS sounded as if he was scribbling notes. "Any indication when the break-in might have happened?"

"Nothing yet. Although if it happened prior to his departure for the Cobb, we can assume he'd have reported it. That would suggest it happened earlier today."

"Which suggests a link to his death." The DS paused. "I'm just googling him now. His paintings go for a lot of money."

"Yeah? There are quite a few here in the house." Tina walked through the living room. "If he lived here alone, and we don't yet know that he did, he had a lot of space. This place is massive."

"Reckon he had a cleaner? Other people with keys to the property?"

"Whoever broke in didn't have a key. They forced the door."

"I meant, we could ask them to see if anything's missing."

"It's a good shout. It's messy but clean. Maybe he did have somebody come in to clean."

"What about his death?" the DS asked. "Anything at the scene?"

"Scene was utter carnage. Lyme Regis Cobb at the height of the season? It was like a circus. Uniform did well to close it off for the lifeboat team and the paramedics. His painting stuff was there on the Cobb, that's all been taken in."

Tina sighed and plonked herself onto a bright green sofa.

"He was pulled out and taken away," she continued. "No obvious signs of trauma on the body as far as I could see. We'll need to wait for the post mortem."

"Any medication in the house?" he asked.

"Actually, he had medication in his bag on the Cobb. It's in the car in an evidence bag. We'll take a look here as well."

"You're going to want the CSI team. I'll sort that."

"Thanks."

"I'll be over as soon as I can get there."

"I've got it for the moment."

"You know the boss won't stand for that," he said. "You're on maternity."

Tina pulled a face. "Still here though, aren't I? You do what you need to do, but I'll keep things going over here."

She ended the call and went through to the kitchen, wondering about that medication. Wendy Sharman was in there.

"You need to take a look at this," Wendy said.

She pointed at the window by the kitchen door. It was a cast iron frame with tiny panes of leaded glass. It looked good but would have struggled to keep out the cold in winter.

"What's up with it?" asked Tina.

Wendy reached over to work the latch mechanism, a small scrollwork lever that lifted up and down to hook onto a catch that was fastened onto the window frame. The lever lifted smoothly, and the window was unbroken. "Take a look at this." She put the lever down, so that it was locked, then gently pushed the window. It opened easily. The catch simply tilted over to release it.

Tina looked more closely. The screws that were supposed to hold it in place were missing. It was possible they'd just rusted away.

"You think it's important?" she asked. "We've got a break-in point at the front door."

"True," Wendy replied. "But then I saw this."

She pointed first at a line of dirt on the edge of the windowsill, and then at the draining board in front of it.

"You have to look at an angle," she said.

Tina bent down and saw what the PC was referring to. The faint outline of the edge of a shoe, marked in grease and condensation, barely visible at all.

"Bloody hell. Well spotted," she said. "You think someone climbed in through here?"

Wendy shrugged. "Looks like it, doesn't it?"

"Huh. This makes no sense." Tina thought about the

forced front door and now this additional sign of a break-in. "We have two points of illegal entry? It doesn't add up."

Wendy shook her head. "What if it's not two points of entry? Look at the direction of that shoe. Maybe our intruder came in through the door and out through the window?"

Tina looked out through the window and across the back garden. It was a long garden, especially for a town as densely packed as Lyme Regis was. At the far end, beyond a drooping tree, there appeared to be another building, some sort of outhouse or maybe a garden office.

"Why would someone break in the front and flee out the back?" she asked. "Why would they do that?"

Wendy shrugged. "Maybe they were disturbed and had to run out?"

Tina texted DS Strunk with the additional information, then returned to the front door, walking slowly through the house with a little more purpose this time.

The first living room was definitely some sort of showcase. The artwork in here was more varied. Maybe they were pieces that Clifford had bought and admired, rather than his own work?

The library featured lots of Lyme Regis paintings. The bay, the Cobb, the cliffs. Everything was a local view, all executed in a similar style. The frames all matched, too.

There was something out of balance, though. The paintings were evenly spaced around the room, but there was a gap.

Tina walked over to the gap and peered at the wall. There was a dark patch, clearly an area that had previously been covered by a painting. There were even wispy traces of cobweb between the painting and the wall. It hung down in ghostly tendrils.

"Dougie? Wendy?" she called. She felt her heart rate pick up as the others entered the room, and she turned to face them.

"I think I might know what's missing," she said. "It was a burglary for sure. They've taken a painting."

Chapter Thirteen

"Right, lovelies!" Annie addressed her grandchildren. "No time like the present. Let's go for a walk and gather some materials for our junk modelling, shall we?"

Going for a walk with the three of them was no small undertaking. Poppy and Louis were happy walking, but there would be frequent breaks to inspect a beetle or deal with a stone in a shoe. Daisy would snooze in the buggy, but Annie still had to load up with changing paraphernalia, snacks, drinks and suncream, even for the short trip into town.

They pottered along in the sunshine, Annie snapping pictures of Poppy and Louis smiling in their bucket hats. She sent the pictures to Naomi and Tina so they could see that the children were having a good time.

"First stop is the gallery, I think," she said. "Helen will have some good ideas about this project of ours. She has the right kind of mind."

Wheeling her small procession through the crowds on

the narrow pavement wasn't easy, and Annie had to concentrate on making sure everyone was safe.

"Annie?"

She looked up to see her cousin Gillian standing on the pavement near Helen's gallery.

"Gillian." Annie felt her previously positive mood sink. Gillian Hewish wore an immaculate two-piece linen suit and had the height and the skinny frame to carry it off. No sticky chocolate fingers would decorate that expensive ensemble.

Gillian's gaze passed over the children, and then she looked at Annie, unsmiling. "What brings you here?"

Annie squared her shoulders. "I'm off to see my friend Helen. How about you?"

Gillian inclined her head towards the closed-up shop next door. It had previously been a fossil shop but had been closed since the death of its owner, Marco Callington. "Taking a look at a prospective acquisition."

Annie felt her hackles rise. No property that Gillian took over retained its character. The woman seemed to somehow sidestep all of the planning regulations intended to protect heritage buildings. "What do you think you'll do with it?"

"Not decided yet, but it's such a prime location, isn't it? A wealth of possibilities."

"Well, I must get these children off the pavement." Annie was conscious of the cars squeezing past. "I'm sure I'll see you soon."

She went inside and closed the door behind her.

"Annie!" Helen came out from behind the counter to give her a hug, then high-fived Poppy and Louis. "What a day, eh?"

Annie nodded. "It's why I've got the kids. Tina's gone off

with Dougie to Clifford Muldoon's house. Is there a Mrs Muldoon?"

"Do you know, I'm not sure." Helen pulled a face. "I've sold his paintings for years, but he was a very private person. I'd have loved to get him in here for a promotional event, but I never managed it."

She gestured to the pieces that hung in the exhibition space towards the rear of the shop. Annie had seen the moody landscapes before but had rarely been drawn to them.

"His stuff was never my style," said Helen. "But he was a generous patron of younger artists by all accounts."

"Ah yes. Juniper's digs. Would it be terrible of me to admit that I wondered if there was something odd going on there?"

"Odd?"

"You know, older man, younger woman practically living in his garden..."

Helen looked at her. "I asked her before. There was no funny business, no mucking about. Those were her actual words. Tea?"

"Oh, go on then." Annie called through to the back of the shop while Helen went through to put the kettle on. "I saw Gillian outside. She's looking at the shop next door."

Helen came back through, the kettle in her hand. "What? Your cousin Gillian?" She shook her head. "Gillian buying-up-all-the-property-in-town-until-there's-nothing-left-but-holiday-lets Gillian?"

"The very same."

Helen scowled. "There's no end to the interest in that place. Honestly, it's like watching dogs sniff round a kebab."

Annie narrowed her eyes. "Am I to take it that you'd like the place for yourself?"

There was a clattering sound from the kitchen.

Helen turned to see Harper, her girlfriend, emerging. "Sorry, love. Was about to make a brew but I got distracted. How's the Pegasus going?"

"Good." Harper's voice was low. "Can really see the character now."

Helen turned to Annie. "Harper's working on some impressive pieces. Larger than some of the work she's created in the past."

"Sounds lovely."

Harper held out a hand for the kettle and withdrew with a smile.

Harper was a solid, practical counterpoint to Helen's ethereal flightiness. She didn't waste words either, which was why Annie knew not to be offended that Harper hadn't done much more than nod in her direction.

"Where was I?" said Helen. "Oh yes! Next door. Of course I want it. It's the natural next step for anyone with a business to want to expand, isn't it?"

"I guess," said Annie.

"But you should see the red tape. It's horrendous. There's a solicitor doing all the admin, and there are marking criteria for anyone who comes forward wanting to take it over. They're doing a scores on the doors thing to decide who should have it. Can you imagine?"

"Marking criteria? What on earth d'you mean?"

"Applicants are scored financially, obviously. But there are also scores against the local plan. Like, does it fit in with 'future Lyme Regis'. You can bet your boots that Gillian's all over that one. I wouldn't be surprised if she even had a hand in making it so very complicated."

That did sound like Gillian.

Harper entered the room. "Here's your tea, Annie."

"Thanks, Harper."

Helen's tea, in contrast, was slammed onto the counter, splashing the paperwork beside it.

"Oh, steady!" said Helen. "What's wrong, darling?"

Harper was quivering. Annie ducked down to check on Daisy.

"You can commit to the business, then?" Harper said, her voice strained.

"What?" Helen asked.

"Expansion. Next steps."

"It's just some possibilities I'm looking at."

"Natural next step, you said." Harper's voice was tense.

Annie stayed down, making sure the children's hats were all still on, despite them being indoors.

"Business is business. There's always a next step," said Helen, her tone placatory.

"Tell me why it's not like that with relationships, then? You're a free spirit, yeah? How d'you think that makes me feel?"

Annie wondered whether she could crab her way out of the shop with the buggy and two toddlers.

"We can talk later," said Helen. "You know I'd never do anything to hurt you."

There was the sound of a slamming door. Harper had gone back out to her workshop, where she spent most of her days welding metal sculptures. Annie thought it must be oppressively hot on a day like today.

"You can come up now," said Helen.

Annie rose slowly. "Erm."

"Pfft. She's blowing off steam. She gets like this."

"Right." It wasn't Annie's business, but it sounded more

serious than that. "Hey listen. I wanted to ask your advice on a project we're about to start. Me and the kids, I mean."

"I'm all ears." Helen smiled, clearly glad of the distraction.

"Junk modelling. What materials should we use, and more importantly, what kind of glue?"

"Oh lovely! Reduce reuse recycle. Very popular. Depends on your definition of junk."

"Very loose," said Annie. Her vision hadn't stretched much beyond cereal boxes.

"I have some nice cardboard tubes. Strong ones. I can get Harper to run them through the bandsaw so they're in usable sections."

"Perfect!"

"And the beach is always a good place to source random discarded junk. You could try that."

"Again, very much the sort of thing we can build into our day," said Annie. "Beach sounds good, doesn't it, kids?"

There was agreement from Poppy and Louis.

"As for glue, I'll get you some of the stuff I have upstairs. Best you apply that, mind, rather than the kids. We don't want tiny fingers stuck together."

Helen disappeared upstairs to fetch the glue, and Annie went over to the window to see if Gillian was still around. So, there was a lot of interest in the shop next door. She just hoped that whatever came next would be a positive addition.

Chapter Fourteen

The moment Tina mentioned the missing painting to DS Strunk, he declared he'd be straight over.

"I might get a lift with the CSIs," he said. "I'll check what their plans are."

"I'm not done looking around here," Tina told him. "I haven't even been outside yet."

"Outside?"

"There's some sort of garden office. It's quite big – I'll see if I can take a look."

"See you later."

Tina returned to the living room, where Wendy and Dougie were discussing the missing picture.

"The cobwebs suggest it's only just been moved," Wendy said, pointing at the wall. "The place is quite clean, don't you think? A person who likes things clean wouldn't leave all that on the wall."

Tina nodded. "Have either of you been outside to look at the building in the garden?"

Wendy and Dougie shook their heads.

"I'm heading out there now."

"It's tucked away down there," Dougie said. "You can barely see it from the kitchen. I'll come out with you, shall I?"

"We'll go out through the front. CSIs might want to take a look at that back door, so we'll leave it alone. And we've already been through the front."

As they went round the side of the house, they had a better view down the garden.

"Hello, who's that?" murmured Dougie.

Two figures stood outside the garden office, which looked a lot more substantial now Tina could see it close up.

This was on the more permanent and expensive end of the garden office scale. It was clad with wood but appeared to be well-insulated, with plenty of natural light from double-glazed windows.

Tina frowned. "That's Rosamund's son, Cameron. And one of the swimmers who was there earlier. Juniper Brown?"

Dougie nodded. "What are they doing here?"

Cameron and Juniper turned towards them as they approached.

Tina took the lead. "Cameron. Juniper. Can I ask what you're doing here?"

Cameron gave a nervous laugh, but Juniper answered immediately. "Do you make a habit of walking up to people when they're at home and asking what they're doing?"

Only then did she seem to notice Dougie's uniform. Her face fell. "Oh. Clifford. Oh, hell. I'm sorry." She gestured around. "I live here."

Tina gave her a questioning look. "You live here?"

"I do."

Tina pointed at the house. "Up at the house or here?"

"The studio flat." Juniper jabbed a thumb over her shoulder. "Clifford has a – wait, no, had – a programme to support up-and-coming artists. A free residency in his garden studio. I was selected, so here I am." She shrugged.

Tina nodded. "And you, Cameron?"

"Oh, Juniper asked me to help her move some stuff. I'm just here lending a hand."

"Can we take a look inside the studio, please, Juniper?" Tina asked.

"Sure. It's mine, though. Clifford wouldn't normally come in here."

"I understand. It would just be helpful for us to understand."

"Understand what?"

"What's happened here. There's been a break-in at the house."

"No." Juniper put a hand to her mouth.

"Flippin' heck," said Cameron.

"Have you noticed anything out of the ordinary?" asked Tina.

Juniper shook her head. "No. I don't think anyone's been in here, if that's what you mean. Am I in danger? Are they coming back?"

"I don't think so. But we might need to treat this building as part of the crime scene, given that it's on the same site."

"Look. I thought the world of Clifford. It's terrible, what's happened. I live here, though. Can I still stay here?"

"We'll have to let you know about that," replied Tina. "Now, maybe while we look around, you could give us some background on Clifford?"

Juniper shrugged. "Sure."

"Do you need me for this?" asked Cameron. He looked uneasy.

Tina shook her head. "I know where to find you. You can leave if you'd prefer."

Cameron disappeared around the side of the house.

Juniper watched him go, her expression unreadable. "Come inside and take a look, then."

Tina and Dougie followed Juniper in through the doorway.

"This part out here is the studio. It's where I work. The other half of the building is my accommodation. Bedroom, bathroom, kitchen."

Juniper waved a hand, inviting them to explore.

It was a pleasant space. The studio had easels, counters and a sink, all liberally splattered with paint, and the other end of the room had a colourful sofa and table. The colour scheme was different to Clifford's house. Here, everything was heavily patterned as well as brightly coloured. It all worked together in a busy and slightly bohemian way that put Tina in mind of a Moroccan market.

The table had several art books open on it, and all the easels were occupied with paintings in progress. They were bold and abstract, very different from the local landscapes inside the main house.

"So, you work in here, and Clifford would have worked in the house?" Tina asked.

"Most of the time, yeah. Clifford would occasionally invite me over there. Sometimes he'd visit me here. If I asked him a question about technique, he might come and demonstrate, or he might bring me a book from his library."

"He passed on knowledge, that kind of thing?"

"Yeah. He knew how lucky he was to be making a decent living as an artist. He wanted to pay it forward. He never used those words, mind. He called himself my patron. I wasn't crazy about that word, but it was a generational thing, you know?"

"Is there anyone else who lives in the house with Clifford?" asked Tina.

Juniper shook her head.

"Any idea who his next of kin might be?"

"I don't know. He was married, years ago."

Tina nodded. "We'll need to look into that. Maybe he left a will, or mentioned a solicitor?"

Juniper shook her head. "Sorry, but we didn't talk about stuff like that. Honest, I'm just the lodger."

"So, what did you talk about?"

"Art. The things we want to say through art. How art speaks to different people." She sighed. "It probably all sounds a bit trivial to a homicide cop."

"No," said Tina. "Homicide cops are human, too."

"I know that."

Having explored the studio, Tina now turned her attention to Juniper's living quarters. "What can you tell me about Clifford's movements today?" she asked, opening a door to peer into the bedroom. It had a bed and a table that held a clutter of makeup products as well as a pile of paperwork.

"I don't see him leaving in the morning," said Juniper. "His front door's out of sight. I know he tends to go out early when the light's good."

"Was it good this morning?"

"Yes."

"What's early?"

"Before six."

Tina could see the attraction of being on the Cobb before everyone else. Clifford would need to claim his space before the crowds arrived.

"Does anyone else have a key to the house?" she asked. "A cleaner, maybe?"

"He did have a cleaner," said Juniper. "She didn't have a key, though. He was a bit of a stickler for security."

"Yeah?"

"Yeah. She was only allowed to come when he was in. I know because she turned up one day at the wrong time and chewed my ear about not being able to get in."

Tina wondered about that window latch and exchanged a glance with Dougie. If Clifford was so keen on security, how could he have overlooked a broken window?

"Juniper, maybe you'd join us up at the house, see if anything looks out of place to you?"

The young woman shrugged. "Sure."

Chapter Fifteen

Rosamund crept around her house, anxious not to draw her mother's attention. She needed to deal with Joanna before she took over, but she was feeling too fragile right now.

She went upstairs to talk to her.

"How are you getting on with your unpacking?"

Her mother had declared that the guest bed wasn't firm enough to support her back, so she was moving into Rosamund's room. Rosamund was filled with a nervous apprehension that her wardrobe was going to get organised whether she liked it or not.

Joanna carried a pile of carefully folded linen and placed it on top of Rosamund's chest of drawers. She patted it gently as she put it down.

"I'd like some hanging storage, obviously. I am nothing if not flexible, though. Here for my darling girl, that's the main thing, isn't it?"

Rosamund smiled. "I wondered what you might like for

supper? Normally it would just be Cameron and me, so I might need to pop out and get something."

"Oh, you know me." Joanna patted her stomach. "Always watching my weight. I can just make do with the veggies and you and Cameron can have whatever you were planning."

Rosamund wasn't going to do that, but she simply smiled. "I might need to pop out and get some extra veggies, then."

Joanna straightened. "Do you know what? That's a marvellous idea. I would love to have a walk around the town. It's been an age."

Rosamund had hoped to use this as an opportunity to escape, but she resigned herself to taking a shopping trip with her mum.

Later, they walked around the supermarket trying to find an acceptable butter substitute. Joanna put down another product, bemoaning the ethical record of the manufacturer.

She pulled her earnest face. "Well, we need to start somewhere with getting you back on track. So, tell me, darling, what was it that made David leave?"

Rosamund tried to keep her composure. "I don't know, Mum. I don't actually want to talk about it."

"You probably have some idea, deep down. Think hard, darling. This could unlock everything."

"If I had to think really hard, I would imagine that it's probably more to do with David than it is to do with me," said Rosamund.

"Of course you'd think that. I think it, too, my sweet, because one never likes to think that one's own daughter might be at fault."

Rosamund rounded on her mother. "I'm not at fault. I did nothing wrong."

"Nothing?"

Rosamund felt heat rise to her face. "Why are you so determined to lay this at my door? Is it all to do with having something you can 'fix'?"

Joanna hesitated. "It's true. I do want to help. I just think that if you can work out what went wrong, then—"

"Tell me this, then," Rosamund said. "What did you do that made Dad leave? If it's always so cut and dried, you can tell me what you did, can't you?"

Joanna gave a small laugh. "Oh, heavens. That was a lifetime ago. I'm not at all sure I can remember."

Rosamund sighed and picked up a packet. "This one's made from olive oil."

"You can't bake with that one."

Rosamund shook the packet. "Were you planning to bake? What do you even want this for?"

"You're right, darling. What am I thinking? You'll need to tighten your belt now David's gone. Can't afford luxuries like this until you've stabilised your financial situation." Joanna took the packet and placed it gently back in the fridge.

Rosamund clenched her jaw. "I'm fine, really. There is no 'financial situation'. I have a job now."

Joanna sucked in her cheeks. "You have a job?"

"You're doing that voice," said Rosamund. "That voice and that face."

"Sorry?"

"The 'what will the neighbours think?' voice. Seriously, it's so very twentieth century, the way you're acting right now."

"I'm a very progressive woman," said Joanna.

"Right."

"I am!"

"Well, then you should have no problem with the fact that I have a job, and I'm delighted to be making a living," Rosamund told her.

Joanna gave a smile that was more of a grimace. All teeth, no upward curve.

"What job is it that you have?" She frowned. "And why aren't you there now?"

Rosamund selected her words carefully. "I am a house-keeper. I maintain standards at several properties in the town. It tends to be one or two days a week. The timing is very specific."

"I see." Joanna narrowed her eyes. "Are these prestigious properties? I mean, it seems like something that's very much beneath you, if I'm honest."

"Prestigious, yes." Rosamund decided that she'd said enough. "About supper, then. Shall we have sausages?"

Joanna looked horrified. "Second rate offal? Is this what you're reduced to now that you're a single mother?"

She picked up a packet of salmon.

"We can have something more nutritious and less abattoir. My treat."

Rosamund picked up a packet of sausages. "It just so happens that Cameron and I are very fond of sausages."

They stood in front of the chiller cabinet, each brandishing their chosen foodstuff like swords.

"Well, perhaps I care more than you do," Joanna said. "Is this why David left? Was he so sick and tired of all the sulphites that he couldn't bear it anymore?"

"David left because he lusted after new meat of a different sort!" Rosamund snapped, jabbing the sausages towards Joanna.

"Mum? What are you – wait, Gran?"

It was Cameron, standing in the supermarket aisle, right beside them.

"What on earth are you both shouting about?" he asked.

Rosamund and Joanna spun on their heels, tucking their food-based weapons behind their backs.

"My sweet boy! How you've grown!" said Joanna, leaning in to dab a kiss onto Cameron's cheek.

"Um, hi, Gran," he said. "When did you get here?" He looked to Rosamund. "Did you tell me Gran was coming?"

"No," said Rosamund pointedly. "Gran didn't bother to tell *me* that she was coming."

"I like to be a wonderful surprise." Joanna smiled. "By the way, Cameron, you're probably of an age where you can call me Joanna now."

"Er, OK."

"'Gran' is such a damaging term."

"Is it?"

"I am manifesting a new future for myself, and in my next era, I have decided not to acknowledge my age."

"I see," said Cameron. He nodded at the shopping items they still had hidden behind their backs. "Tell me the rules of playing rock, paper, scissors with food at the supermarket."

Rosamund rolled her eyes. She put the sausages in the basket and made her way to the checkout.

Chapter Sixteen

Tina led Juniper Brown up to the house.

"I'm going to ask you to step where I want you to step."

"No problem, mate."

"And I don't want you to touch anything. In fact, best stick your hands in your pockets."

The tall young woman wiggled her fingers and tucked them into the pockets of her jeans.

Tina, Dougie and Juniper stepped into the house.

"I assume you're familiar with Clifford's work," Tina said.

"Of course. I mean, he's a traditional painter of the old school, but the man knew his craft."

Tina led them through to the library where she'd seen the gap on the wall where a painting had once hung.

"Did you come up to the house much?" Dougie asked.

"Yeah. Yeah, I did," Juniper replied. "We'd meet and talk and have meals together. But I rarely came up beyond the kitchen."

"Oh?"

Juniper laughed. Tina looked at her.

"A lot of artists get a certain reputation," said Juniper. "Single fella, got a younger woman living on the property. I can tell you that my folks back in Brisbane were horrified at the idea of their girl 'shacking up with a dirty old painter'."

"Are you saying that Clifford made... advances towards you?" Tina asked.

Juniper laughed again, louder now. "Heck, no. Clifford was a lovely guy, we got on real well and..."

She stopped. Her face contorted through a range of unhappy expressions.

Tina put a hand on her arm. "Juniper, we don't have to..."

Juniper waved her away, shook her head and took a deep breath. Her eyes were wet with tears, but she remained controlled.

"I forgot he's dead." She sniffed, blinked and put on a fragile smile. "He was a lovely guy. Clifford. I didn't mean to suggest..." She found some calm. "I'm a lone woman. He's got this big house to himself. I set myself some rules. I didn't want to put myself in any kind of situation."

"But he was old," said Dougie. "I mean, he was really old. The age gap..."

Juniper looked to Tina, clearly seeking understanding. And Tina did understand. It seemed Juniper had her head screwed on. She'd been living on Clifford's land, but she'd kept things formal, professional. Safe.

"He was married back in the seventies," said Juniper. "That didn't work out. I think it ended amicably. She died ages ago, he said. No kids neither." She looked at the art around them. "Yeah, this is him. A plein air painter. That meant he did it outside. He'd use acrylics while he was out there, but he often finished up in his studios. Greens and blues and browns. The man hit his stride thirty plus years ago and didn't think to change it up. Always with a bloody seagull somewhere."

She pointed to a seagull in one of the paintings. Tina could see that there were indeed seagulls, often just bent smudges in the sky, in every one of the pictures.

"And this one?" Tina gestured to the empty space.

Juniper looked in incomprehension for a minute.

"Damn. You're telling me it's gone missing? I mean... that there was a painting here?"

Dougie frowned. "You mean, you don't know if there was a painting here?"

Juniper gave a helpless gesture. "I never come in here. But..."

She stepped around the room and looked at the paintings on display. "These are all older pictures. I mean, at least fifteen years, plus."

Her hand hovered over one.

"Hands away," said Tina.

"Sorry." Juniper thrust her hands in her pockets. "Yeah, this is old stuff, and I guess, from the faded wall and dust, you reckon there was something there. Yeah, I get that."

"But you have no idea?"

"Sorry."

"Are his paintings worth much?" asked Dougie.

"Varies a lot, I think. Helen Cruickshank, with that pokey little gallery in town, she sells some. A few hundred pounds, a few thousand sometimes."

"Thousands?" He sounded impressed.

Juniper grinned. "Mate, one of his paintings, Broad

Street Rain No. 1, I think, like a twenty by thirty canvas, it sold at Bonhams for twenty-two thousand quid."

Tina couldn't hold back a whistle of appreciation.

"These...?" she said, pointing at the paintings around them. "They're worth up to twenty thousand pounds each?"

"Some of them, yeah," said Juniper. "You know, if you really want to know about the commercial side of things, what he painted and what it's worth, that Helen's your best bet. I'm just a struggling artist. We're famously rubbish when it comes to the business side of things."

Tina nodded. If there had been a burglary, possibly a twenty thousand pound burglary, then some expert information would be welcome.

Juniper looked at the police officers.

"Are you saying that this and Clifford's death, it's all connected, then?"

Tina gave her an honest shrug.

"That's what we intend to find out, Juniper."

Chapter Seventeen

At home, Annie cooked fish fingers for the children and Dante before Tina and Dougie came to collect them. Annie had tried to give subtle hints that she'd be interested in any information about Tina's investigation into poor dead Clifford Muldoon. Tina had either not noticed them or ignored them.

Annie and Dante stood at the door waving the family off.

"Fish fingers. I should eat those more often." Dante nodded as they went back inside.

"You offering to cook?" Annie asked. "Your turn next time, then."

"I will demonstrate my expertise." He bowed. "A man of many talents, that's me."

"Is that right?"

"Oh yes." Dante gave her a look. "You'd be amazed."

"Well, Dante, I'm always prepared to be amazed. Bring it on, I say."

"This evening, then. You got plans?"

Annie did have plans, but they mostly involved sitting

down with a book. "I can be flexible. What d'you have in mind?"

He gave a rueful smile. "Karaoke at Breaststrokes bar. You probably hate the idea."

Annie recognised the clumsy attempt at manipulation. "Annie Abbott never backs down from a challenge. Well, almost never. I might point out that a man died today. Does it feel a little disrespectful to you?"

Dante gave the question some thought. "I reckon, times like this, when we get a glimpse of mortality, we all want to do things to reaffirm that we're alive. Karaoke sounds like exactly the right sort of thing."

Annie couldn't fault Dante's logic. "Fantastic! Let's do it."

Annie changed into a spangly top, because if there was one thing that brought stage presence, it was a spangly top. Dante wore a sharp suit, which set off his hat and brought to mind words like 'dapper', although Dante had a chaotic energy that undermined any neatness his appearance might have otherwise suggested.

"The best way to tackle karaoke is to go on a mini pub crawl before we get there." Dante sounded authoritative. "That way, we can breeze in, make an entrance and then knock 'em dead with a confident performance."

"Right." Annie's mind whirled with the logistical problem of taking in various pubs on the way down to Breaststrokes. "Come on, then. Let's head over to Silver Street."

"There's a pub there?"

"The Nag's Head. After that we head straight down the hill and take in The Volunteer Inn and the Pilot Boat. I think that sounds like a decent enough warm up, don't you?"

"It'll do for a start!"

Annie led the way to the first pub, but it wasn't long before Dante took charge.

"We neck the first two drinks," he declared. "It's the rule."

"Who made that rule?" she asked.

"It's a well-known fact that that's the best way to reach the mellow phase. Trust the process! You can go easy after the first two."

As a consequence, they were soon in the middle of Lyme Regis, stopping only as long as it took to buy and knock back a drink in the first two pubs.

"This feels highly irresponsible," said Annie.

Dante gave her a wink. "Great, isn't it? See how it's essential prep for karaoke?"

Annie considered. "I see that the idea of a pub crawl is a nice one. It mixes up the drinking with a short bout of physical exercise."

"Never thought of it that way, but yeah."

"Trouble is, now we're here in the middle of town, the places are too close together," Annie pointed out. "The drink to exercise ratio is all wrong." She illustrated the size difference with slightly drunk hand gestures.

"Wrong? Or just different?"

"Hm. Definitely wrong. I have an idea, though."

"Yeah?"

Annie led the way from the Volunteer Inn onto Marine Parade. "Let's have a running race between pubs."

"Running? Are you joking?"

"Nope. It's the physical exercise thing. We pretend the pubs are further apart than they really are."

"We could just do walking."

"No! A running race it is. To the Kiosk and back. Unless you're chicken?" Annie said.

"Never said I was chicken."

"Good, then go!"

Annie shot off, aware that she had the benefit of a surprise start. She wasn't unfit for her age, but running wasn't something she did very often. She clutched her chest, realising that she was wearing the wrong bra, and charged along as fast as she could manage.

She heard a roaring sound behind her, as Dante attempted to increase his speed with the power of his voice.

"Steady on!" she yelled, still ahead. "You don't want to spoil yourself for karaoke!"

By the time Annie reached the Kiosk, she was still ahead, and she turned to make her way back. Dante spun around on the spot and ran back from where he was.

"Oi! Cheating!" Annie shouted, but she clattered along, certain that she could still beat him.

They reached the starting point at exactly the same time, and both doubled over in laughter.

"You didn't even run the full course!"

"Not a local. Still finding my way around the landmarks," he said with a shrug.

Annie laughed. "I think I won fair and square."

By the time they reached Breaststrokes, the drink and the running had left Annie feeling both exhilarated and confident.

"Right," she said. "Karaoke, here we come!"

Breaststrokes was heaving with customers. As they fought their way to the bar, an elderly gent was battling his way through 'Bohemian Rhapsody'.

They found a seat and picked up a card that told them how to request a song.

"We should do a duet," suggested Dante.

"Oh Lord! What do you suggest? What would you normally sing?"

"Hm. Something ska, or maybe reggae. Not so many duets there, mind."

"Wait, Madness is a ska band, yeah? We could do one of theirs," said Annie. "At least I might know the words."

Dante laughed. "Madness it is, then. Shall we do 'Baggy Trousers'?"

"Yes!"

They had to sit through two more rounds of drinks before their turn came around. Annie followed Dante to the stage area, and they took a bow.

Annie had forgotten how rapidly the words to that particular song needed to be sung and was left standing as Dante rattled through them. Happily, he left her to chip in with the straightforward 'Baggy Trousers!' chorus. Dante's sharp dressing and word-perfect rendition probably carried them both, but Annie was happy to bask in the limelight as they stepped down to thunderous applause.

"That was brilliant, Dante!" she said as they left the bar. "Anyone would think you'd sung on the original."

"Nah. I did play a bit of sax on the B-side, mind."

Annie laughed. "Yeah, right."

"No, I really did. Session musician on all sorts, me."

Annie stared. He was being serious. She had a new-found respect for her uninvited guest. Not only was he a hoot on a night out, but it seemed he had an unexpected and entertaining past.

Chapter Eighteen

On Monday morning, Tina and Dougie headed down to the Cruickshank Gallery on Coombe Street. By nine o'clock, the streets were chock-a-block with cars, tourists attempting to drive through a town that hadn't been designed with so many people in mind.

Dougie parked in the rough little car park that backed onto Helen's gallery, and they walked round together.

The town might have been heaving but the gallery was quiet, almost empty. Helen was checking price tags on a number of the canvases hung in the well-lit display area. She looked up.

"Ah! And for a moment, I thought it might be actual customers." She smiled as she turned to them.

To Tina's eyes, Helen Cruickshank was a collection of beautiful contradictions. She was well-spoken and clearly highly educated, and yet she tended to dress in clashing skirts and tops that looked like they'd fallen off a charity shop clothes rack. Her manner was both charming and formal but somehow seemed to carry an intrinsically disreputable air.

Annie had commented once that Helen always seemed to have either a cigarette or cocktail in her expressive hands, even when she very clearly didn't. Helen looked like a woman who was thoroughly enjoying herself at a lifelong party and didn't give a hoot what anyone else thought of her. Maybe this was what 'bohemian' meant.

"Unless you two fine officers are looking for some artwork for your police station canteen," suggested Helen. She frowned at Tina. "You're still on maternity leave."

"Just helping out," said Tina.

"Helping out with what, exactly?"

Dougie gripped the lapel of his police vest. "We were wondering if we could talk to you about Clifford Muldoon, Ms Cruickshank?"

"Oh?" said Helen, intrigued, and then seemed to remember herself. "Oh. Yes. Sad business. It's a police matter, is it?"

"There has been a possible break-in at his home," said Dougie.

"A possible break-in."

"We believe a painting from his house might have gone missing," added Tina.

Helen gestured to the paintings all around the shop. "And I'm the number one suspect?"

"Hardly." Tina smiled, although it occurred to her that gallery owners selling on stolen works wasn't unheard of. "We hoped you might be able to help us identify the item stolen, and its possible value."

"Ah. That's interesting. Do tell."

Dougie had a manila folder of printed photos, which he held open. The photos were of the walls in Clifford's library, plus other paintings hanging around his house. Tina had suggested that photos of his entire home collection might give valuable context.

Helen looked over the images.

"This is where? Clifford's house?"

"Yes," said Tina. "Have you been there?"

"I have. I have sold a number of his pieces in the gallery. In fact, most of his output in the last five years. He has an agent in London who handles the most significant work. Much less of that recently."

"Significant as in worth more?" asked Dougie.

Helen gave him a tight-lipped look. "Obviously, the worthiness of art can only be measured in currency, constable. Yes, I mean the pricey stuff."

"And what's the difference between the stuff that's more expensive and the stuff that's less expensive?" asked Tina. She hadn't meant to wave her hand at Helen's displays when she said 'less expensive', but it happened automatically.

"Oh, the impact on the viewer, technical proficiency, the capturing of a mood." Helen grunted. "But, in truth, the value of art is wholly subjective. It's worth only what we pretend it's worth. It's a game. In that regard, art is one of the few truly honest industries. We don't pretend anything has actual real value. Finance is a farce and we're in on the joke."

"But these pieces," said Dougie. "Specifically, the one that would have been there..."

Helen blew out her cheeks and chuckled. "I don't remember what Clifford had up in his house. Not even sure I've been in that room."

"Oh," said Tina, deflated.

"But," said Helen, holding up a finger, "do not lose heart. There are ways and means."

"Yes?"

"For a start..." She led them over to a display area and an unframed painting. It depicted Lyme Regis harbour and the cliffs and hills behind it in muted yellows, browns and greens. The sea was a dark turquoise. "A typical Muldoon. Seven hundred pounds it's up for, and we'll get that eventually."

She lifted the canvas off the wall and deftly turned it over.

On the reverse of the frame, where little nails held the canvas in place, there was writing on the fabric.

"He writes the name of the piece in charcoal. Here. 'Lyme in Autumn #34. 10 October 24.' The date is always the date of the initial charcoal sketch. Each is uniquely marked, which is a good thing, because, let's be clear, the vast majority of his works are, shall we say, of a similar type."

"And they've all got seagulls in," said Dougie

"That they have, constable," Helen flipped the canvas back round and hung it on the wall again. She waved her fingers over the simple seagull in this picture, painted with a single brushstroke. "I heard a theory once that Muldoon encodes especial meaning in the position and attitude of his seagulls."

"A seagull code?" said Tina.

"Tosh and nonsense." Helen smiled. "An attempt to give the man's work profundity where there is scant profundity to be found."

"You don't like his work?"

"Like?" She wrinkled her nose. "No. Not really. It's attractive in a purely representative sense. But it's popular. And that's not a negative assessment. People like what they like and if it moves someone, lifts someone..."

She made a gesture and returned to the shop counter. From under the counter, she produced a ring binder.

"Now, I do also have access to a range of art catalogues." She spotted Dougie's frown. "Lists of artworks, who painted them, who owns them and where they can be found," she explained.

"Oh."

"Clifford Muldoon is of sufficient significance that all of his works that have ever gone on sale or been insured should be listed."

"That's interesting," said Tina, seeing where Helen was going.

Helen nodded. "With time and a little information, we could make a best guess as to what the missing piece might be."

"And would you? Would you do that for us?"

There was a twinkle in Helen's eye. "It sounds fun, doesn't it?"

Chapter Nineteen

It was a shame dogs couldn't understand calendars. Or read. Or just talk.

Annie walked her neighbour Marie's dog, Dex, several times a week. Throughout the long spring and summer months, he was confused and irritated by the fact that he wasn't allowed on the beach. The signs were clear enough and even attached to the promenade railings at dog height. But the concept of dogs not being allowed on the sand between April and September was not something she was ever going to be able to convey to him.

They walked along the promenade, Annie hoping that the sight of the sea gave him some sort of pleasure. Dogs were simple creatures, but that didn't always make them easy to understand.

Along the front Annie saw Tim Cromwell, sitting on a bench outside the lifeboat station. He held a piece of wood and a short whittling knife. As she approached, she could see the wood was slowly taking the form of a bear. Or possibly a fat fox. He was working on it with quiet intent.

"Now, are you working on a piece of art, or are you thinking of your enemies as you stab that bit of wood?" she said, approaching.

He looked up and smiled. "A clever man ought to be able to do both."

He scooted along the bench and patted the seat beside him for her to sit down. She did so gladly. Dex pulled on his lead to sniff at Wellington, the rubber boot dog statue.

Annie looked at Tim's whittling-in-progress. "What's it going to be?"

Tim sniffed and wiped his brow with the back of his hand. "I'm like Michelangelo. I just start with the block and chip away everything that doesn't belong."

"Oh, yes. I always thought of you as a Michelangelo type."

He gave a grunt of laughter. "And what are you doing this fine day, Annie?"

She leaned back, feeling the warmth of the sun on her knees. The wall behind them caught the morning sun and made a sun-trap of this spot.

"Oh, a bit of dog walking. Mostly, I'm walking off a bit of a hangover."

"Is that so?"

"A night out with Dante. Karaoke, of all things."

"Dante?" said Tim, then gave an 'oh' of recollection. "How's your new gentleman lodger?"

"Gentleman, yes. Lodger, temporarily. My gentleman lodger? No. Very much doing it as a favour to Tina and Mike. Tina's bringing the grandkids over this afternoon."

"That'll be nice."

Tim let the knife and wood sit in his lap. His gaze travelled out over the harbour and to the sea beyond. The sun made silver ribbons on the waves and even on a clear day like today, the land beyond the bay was a thing of hazy blue and green silhouettes. Tim gazed at it, his eyes unfocused.

Annie wondered if her mention of grandchildren had anything to do with his reverie. She was lucky to have three grandchildren before she'd even turned sixty. Tim had none. He'd been married once, and there'd been a little boy, Simon, who'd drowned when he was about eight years old. It had broken the parents and their marriage. Annie had watched Tim slowly put himself back together and, like so many friends, she had tried to help.

Some people assumed Tim had got into the lifeboat thing as a response to his lad's death, but he'd been part of the crew for a while by that point. And being part of a community group, something larger than himself, had perhaps helped Tim through that dark time.

"See something?" she asked.

"Thinking."

"Yes?"

He turned to her. "About that Clifford?"

"You did everything you could."

He gave her a quizzical frown. "That man was dead by the time we got to him."

"Of course. But still, it must be a shock, to get up that close to death. I know from experience."

"I won't pretend you get used to death. But you do get to know it. I've looked at death." He waggled his whittling knife at the end of the Cobb. "But that old bugger has gone now. Gone. Snuffed out."

"Well, yes."

"It makes you think."

"It does," she said, then had to ask. "Think about what?"

"How life comes and how life goes."

Annie gazed at Dex, who was lying on the ground in front of them, yawning. "I suppose so."

"We don't know how long we have."

"We don't."

"All that... What's that film where him out of Mork and Mindy stands on a desk and teaches boys?"

Annie raised an eyebrow. "I think you're thinking of *Dead Poets Society. Carpe diem.* Seize the day."

"Exactly that." Tim turned on the bench with some energy, still holding the knife and the wood. He put them down.

"So," he said. "Karaoke? Is that what you like?"

This sudden swerve in conversation took Annie by surprise.

"Uh... uh, I guess. Not my actual thing, you understand."

"Only there's one of those 'paint and sip' events on at Oliver's Wine Bar on Wednesday night. They sell the tickets in pairs. I wondered if you fancied it."

Annie smiled. If she understood correctly, this quiet and unassuming man was asking her out. On a date? A romantic date? It was hard to tell.

"And this would be a...?" she prompted.

"They have a prize raffle as well," he said.

This didn't answer the all-important question.

"I mean, you had me at 'sip'," she said.

A peculiar look broke over his face. There was joy in there, definitely joy. But something more. Fear? Did Annie feel that fear, too? She'd been a widow for a while now, and although she had no fear of social situations and enjoyed the company of men, it had been decades since she'd experienced any romantic approach as earnest and tentative as this.

Something fluttered inside her. Her fingers tingled.

But what she didn't grasp was why Clifford's death had sparked this approach from Tim. Yes, yes, she understood the whole *carpe diem* thing and how a glimpse of death brought thoughts of one's own mortality and the fleeting nature of life.

But this?

Tim was a mystery.

Chapter Twenty

Tina sat at her mum's kitchen table. Poppy and Louis chased each other in and out of the garden, shrieking and giggling. Daisy kicked her legs in the bouncy chair.

"Last two cookies," said Annie. "Either we eat them sneakily ourselves, or face ructions if we try to share with the larger group."

"Deprive the children?" Tina took one and munched it. "Save the tears. The noble thing to do."

Annie despatched the other one with equal speed.

"DS Strunk has asked me to be his local contact on the investigation into Clifford Muldoon's death," said Tina. "Would you be alright having the kids a bit more?"

"Would I ever?" Annie grinned. "How's that all going? Did you find the next of kin?"

Tina shook her head. "Juniper's one of the few people who actually spent time with him."

"You spoke to her, then?"

"She was there on the day. Rosamund's son was there with her, helping her move something."

"Cameron?"

"Yes."

"I guess they know each other from the beach."

They both turned at the sound of a low chuckle. Dante was out in the garden. He'd been snoozing in a deckchair when Tina arrived, but now he was up and playing with the children.

"Come on, kids!" he shouted. "Who can go up the slide and down the steps?"

Annie pulled a face and turned to Tina. "Is that safe?"

Tina shrugged. "We can keep an eye on them."

Annie stared belligerently out of the window.

"Sit down, Mum. I'm sure they'll be fine," said Tina.

"How's Mike?" Annie asked, taking a seat, but positioning it so she could stare through the back door at the slide activities.

"He says the house is almost in shape now. It won't be too much longer before it's liveable."

"I should think so, too."

Tina looked up. "He's doing his best."

"Oh, I know. That sounded a bit sharp, didn't it? It's been a while though, hasn't it, love?"

Tina nodded. "Yeah. It has."

"I've not seen him for a while, too. He still coming down to see you?"

"Yeah. He's not avoiding you, Mum. But he won't come here while his dad's staying in the house."

Annie pulled a face. "Do you think he might come around?"

Tina considered the question. Mike had some deep-rooted resentments, and for good reason. Might he be better off if he could move past them? Possibly. Was Tina prepared to push him? Definitely not.

"I'm not sure."

Annie made a disapproving sound in the back of her throat. "What's he doing now?"

Tina leaned over to take a look.

Dante had the watering can and was making a small puddle of mud at the edge of one of the flower borders.

Poppy and Louis leaned over in fascination. Dante gave each of them a small length of stick and invited them to mix the soup. They jigged with excitement as they stirred up the mud, splashing themselves and each other.

"Well, that's just the limit!" said Annie, standing.

"Sit down, Mum," said Tina. "They're having a fine old time."

"They're going to get filthy!"

"We've got spare clothes if we need them."

Annie huffed and pouted. Dante fetched a flower pot and a trowel from the shed and invited Poppy to scoop some mud into the flower pot.

Louis bent over with laughter as the mud slopped from the holes in the bottom of the flower pot. "Let me!"

"He has no sense of responsibility, does he?" Annie said. "If it was him who had to do the laundry, he might think twice about getting them to play with mud."

Tina smiled. "Hello? Is this Annie Abbott speaking?"

"What? What do you mean by that?"

Tina looked at her mum. "You don't see it, do you?"

"See what?"

"The stuff you're complaining about. The irresponsible attitude?"

"Yes? What about it?"

"It's the same stuff you do. All. The. Time."

Annie looked stunned. "That's not true."

Tina counted off on her fingers. "Slightly wild and wayward ways of entertaining the kids. A belief that any amount of mess is justified if the kids are having fun. Squeals of joy are the currency of happiness." She looked at her fingers. "Shall I go on? Because there are more."

Annie sniffed. "I don't think we're at all alike."

Tina eyed her. "Are you envious that you didn't think of making mud-based mess?"

"Oh, stop it." Annie pulled a face.

Tina laughed. "I knew it! You could go and join them, you know."

"No. I think what we have here is a good cop, bad cop setup," said Annie. "Sooner or later, someone's going to have to go out there and tell them to stop having fun in the mud. It looks as though that person's going to have to be me, doesn't it?"

"Oh. My. God. Listen to yourself!" said Tina. "You're annoyed because you think you might have to act like a responsible adult, and you don't like it."

Annie pouted.

Tina needed to text Mike. She leaned out of the door to capture a photo of Dante and his mud-based playing.

"What are you doing?" Annie asked.

"Sending Mike a picture and telling him that if his dad's achieved nothing else at all, at least he's managed to turn you into a responsible adult, very much against your will."

Annie rolled her eyes. "Fine."

Tina couldn't stop herself from laughing as she shared the story with Mike. Would it change his mind about his dad? Probably not. Would it make him laugh? Maybe.

Chapter Twenty-One

Annie waved Tina off as Dougie drove her away. She was going to the police station for a couple of hours. Dougie was also giving Dante a lift down to the town, so Annie was left with the children.

She sent a message to the rest of the Lyme Regis Women's Swimming Club.

If you were going for an evening out and you weren't sure if it was a date or not, what would you wear?

She turned to the children. "A little bit of a clean-up needed, and then we'll see what we want to do next, eh, kids?"

"We don't need to get cleaned up," said Poppy. "We'll just get dirty again."

"You have a point there, young Pops. Still, we'll get the worst of it off. We need to set a good example for Daisy, don't we?"

Daisy slept soundly in her chair. Poppy pulled a face. Where on earth had she learned that?

Annie checked her phone for replies.

Helen had sent a clear response.

You jolly well make sure that it is a date by dressing up to the nines. Hemlines up and necklines down!

Rosamund was more considered.

Something elegant but fun. That would be my advice. Maybe some nice jewellery to accentuate your favourite parts of yourself?

Annie wondered what kind of jewellery would complement an inappropriate sense of humour.

Figgy tried to be supportive.

Is this Tim? Good on him, and good on you as well. I hope you have fun. Wear what you like.

A few minutes later, when Louis and Poppy had washed themselves, they all sat down at the table. Daisy reclined on the top, snoozing in her bouncer.

"It's time to make a start on our journal. What were we going to do, can you remember?"

"Recycling!" Poppy and Louis chimed.

Annie was impressed that they remembered. Daisy hadn't, but that was understandable, given that she was a baby and also asleep.

"And do you remember that Helen in the gallery gave us some cardboard tubes?"

"Yes!" they chorused.

Annie found the bag that she'd carried them back in and plonked it onto the table.

"Here we are." She lifted out the sections that Harper had cut up. They were all heavy-duty cardboard in good, solid chunks, each the size of a biscuit barrel.

Louis and Poppy each picked one up and turned them over in their hands. Annie thought they were very tactile.

"We want to make something with these, yes?"

Louis grabbed another, put one on each forearm, and rolled them across the table in a reasonable facsimile of a miniature steamroller, although the noises he made to accompany the movement were somewhere between a racing car and an aeroplane.

"That's not a dustbin lorry," said Poppy. "There's nowhere for the rubbish."

"Maybe a dustbin lorry is too complicated for our first go," said Annie. "We could make a game instead."

"Yeah!" Poppy seemed enthused by the idea of a game.

"What if we did this? We get three tubes, all different heights. We paint them nicely, one for each of you, and then we glue them together and use them for scoring points in a ball game."

They passed a quiet, studious half hour while paints were sploshed around the table. Poppy covered her tube in pale blue and added stick figures around the base.

Louis added plenty of every colour, then swirled them around with his brush, making a sludgy brown.

Annie painted Daisy's tube green and added a daisy motif but left a large space. She pulled out her phone and took some pictures, keen to document the process for the journals.

"Now, I wonder if Daisy will mind if I borrow her hand for a moment?" she whispered to Poppy and Louis.

She cradled Daisy's hand in her own and daubed red paint across it. She then brought the tube against it and pressed lightly.

"Ta-da!"

Daisy woke with a grimace and reclaimed her hand, immediately pressing it against her mouth.

"Ohh, Daisy's making her face all red!" squealed Poppy in delight.

Annie scrambled to get a baby wipe, removing the paint from Daisy's hand and face while Poppy and Louis chortled at the mess.

When order had been restored, Annie put all three painted tubes in the centre of the table to dry and cleared away the paints.

"Can we play the game now?" Poppy asked.

"Not until the paint's dry. Next time you come round," replied Annie. "Now stand behind the tubes so I can take your pictures. It's all going in the journals."

Poppy and Louis stood for a picture, and Annie smiled with satisfaction. She had spent quality time with the children, and in a much safer way than Dante.

She sent pictures to Tina, Mike, Naomi and Dougie. They needed to see what responsible grandparenting looked like.

While she pored over her phone, selecting the best image, Poppy and Louis had each found a longer piece of tube and started hitting each other with them.

"Oh. No! They aren't for that!" Annie shouted. "Time out before you do someone a mischief, those things are heavy."

She took the tubes and put them away. Poppy and Louis went out to play on the slide.

Annie picked up Daisy and followed them outside.

"Is this workable, Daisy, kiddo?" she asked quietly. "Can we do activities for all three of you without the older ones getting bored?"

Daisy said nothing, but Annie thought she knew the answer already.

Chapter Twenty-Two

Tina sat on a swivel chair in Lyme Regis police station. The office furniture here was the same awful stuff as everywhere else.

Not long ago, she'd sat here with her enormous pregnant belly. Now, at least, she had a working centre of gravity. The chair was only punishing in the regular ways: chunks of foam missing, and no way to lock the back rest into place.

Dougie, Wendy and Sergeant Jim Connor were all present, and DS Strunk had just arrived. It was great to see a face from Major Crimes.

"Traffic out there's horrendous." The DS's face was flushed, either from the weather or hassle of driving through Lyme Regis.

He got sympathetic nods from around the room.

"Right." He wiped his brow. "Clifford Muldoon. We'll have a bit of a recap, yeah?"

"Good idea. Shall I?" Tina stood, grateful to get out of that chair.

"Sure." The DS rolled his eyes. He'd given up questioning why Tina was working while on maternity leave.

Tina supressed a smile. She went over to the board, where they'd attached a picture of Clifford Muldoon seated at his easel. She tapped a finger on the picture.

"Clifford was pulled from the water five days ago by the lifeboat team, after being spotted floating in the sea just off the Cobb. His easel and paints were on the Cobb, in a position where he sat most days, like in this picture."

There were nods of recognition. Clifford was a familiar sight.

"Dougie and I went round to Clifford's house to inform next of kin. So far, we've not found any, but we did find signs of a break-in. In fact, curiously, we found that as well as the front door showing signs of recent forced entry, there were also signs of someone climbing in or out of a rear window. What's more, there was a space on the wall in his house where a painting had been recently removed."

"A lot of paintings in that house," said Dougie.

Tina nodded. "And we've been given a bit of an idea how valuable they are. Thousands of pounds each, the more sought-after ones."

DS Strunk gave a low whistle. "I guess that makes burglary an obvious motive. Anything from the CSIs?"

"They're still on site," Tina told him. "It's a big house."

"We're tracking down the cleaner who used to work for him," added Wendy. "She's local, but she's been away for a few days."

Tina nodded. "Also there's a whole extra building at the bottom of the garden. An artists' studio that Clifford lent out to up-and-coming younger artists. A woman called Juniper Brown is staying there. She says she maintained a strictly arms-length relationship with Clifford. She also said she wasn't familiar with the layout of most of the house, so was unable to confirm any details of the missing painting."

"Could there be other paintings missing?" the DS asked. "Less obvious ones?"

"There could," replied Tina. "But we can at least follow up on the one that we can see has gone. Helen Cruickshanks, who runs a gallery in town, is taking a look at catalogues for us."

"She knows her stuff," said Jim, with a nod.

The DS cleared his throat. "Let's move on to the post mortem, shall we? I went over to Exeter to observe." He pulled out his notebook. "Full report will be with us when the toxicology results come back, but the basic gist is that there were several signs consistent with death by immersion in water."

"Drowning, then?" Tina asked.

He shook his head. "Not necessarily. Clifford didn't have the distended, water-filled lungs that usually come with drowning. Apparently around ten per cent of people who die in the water get cold water shock and suffer cardiac arrest."

"Makes sense," said Tina.

"The pathologist also suggested that his age, clothing and general health wouldn't have made it easy for him to save himself if he fell into the water."

Wendy shook her head. "Poor guy."

The DS flicked over a page. "There were no obvious signs of external trauma. But you'd only see that if he was attacked or if he hit something on his way down." He snapped the notebook closed. "Looks like he just went straight down into the water."

Tina frowned. "He died of natural causes, then?"

"Probably."

She considered. "Do we think we might be looking at an accidental death, and an opportunist burglary off the back of it?"

Dougie leaned forward. "There was all that chaos down on the Cobb, wasn't there? Wouldn't surprise me if someone in that crowd knew he lived on his own, saw their chance and nipped over to do a bit of breaking and entering."

Tina turned to him. "Any way we might track that using CCTV?"

"We can take a look. There were no cameras close by Clifford's house, but we could look into some of those properties on the way up Silver Street, see if they've got doorbell footage."

"Lovely." Tina looked at DS Strunk. "We should brief the DI and maybe catch up with the CSIs at the house."

"*I* should brief the DI," he replied with a sigh, "as I'm the one who's officially working. We're telling her that we're focusing on the burglary, but we don't suspect murder?"

"Yep," said Tina. "No murder."

Chapter Twenty-Three

Annie's phone dinged with a message as she cleared away the aftermath of the grandchildren's visit. It was Rosamund.

My mum's driving me to distraction with her whole 'tidy house, tidy mind' thing. I don't think I live in squalor, but she's going through the place like a minimalist whirlwind. She's got her eagle eyes on David's record collection now. Says it's got to go. She's probably right, actually. Didn't you say Dante has some musical knowledge? Wondered if he might tell me whether any of this stuff's worth passing on, or whether it's for the dump?

Annie shook her head. Rosamund was so house proud. If someone turned up and told her the place was a mess, she'd be distraught. And for it to be her own mother!

Listen bud, you hang on in there. I'll have a word with Dante. Even if he doesn't come, I can pop over for some moral support, if you'd like?

A moment later Rosamund replied.

Moral support would be very much appreciated. Thank you Annie x

Well, that was decided.

Dante had returned from town half an hour earlier. He'd bought himself a pair of cheap espadrilles from one of the beach supplies shops. They had bright palm trees all over them, and he was breaking them in by practising dance moves to a UB40 album. She could hear stomping and thumping over the heavy bass.

"Dante!" She entered the lounge to find him swivelling his hips. "Job for you. We're taking a trip out."

He turned off the music. "Where we going?"

"A friend needs some records sorting. Asked if you might offer an opinion. She's only over the other side of town."

Dante followed Annie out to the car. "When you say records, do you mean vinyl?"

Annie hesitated. "I don't honestly know. We'll soon see."

The most obvious route to Rosamund's house was through the centre of town, but in peak season it was faster to cut through the back roads. She pulled up on the gravel drive.

Dante whistled. "Nice place."

Rosamund lived in a large, modern house with Cameron, her son. And, of course, her temporary guest Joanna.

"Now, behave. Rosamund and Joanna are not as... earthy as me," said Annie as they stood on the doorstep.

Dante chuckled. "You think I might scare the posh people with my antics?"

Annie eyed him. "Yes."

Dante put out his tongue just as Rosamund answered the door.

She raised her eyebrows, but ushered them in, graceful and accommodating as ever.

They went through to the lounge, which was in its usual tidy and tasteful state, but now contained several large boxes. On the settee sat a woman who was clearly Rosamund's mum. They shared the same blonde hair and sculpted cheekbones, but Joanna also had an air of stately disdain. She looked like a woman who'd dined on all life had to offer and was now on a diet.

"Let me make some introductions," said Rosamund. "Mum, this is Annie and Dante. Annie and Dante, my mother, Joanna. Dante has some musical knowledge, so he might be able to help us with this lot."

Joanna flashed a dazzling smile, aimed mostly at Dante. He did have a way of pulling all the focus in a room.

"Can I take a look?" he asked, returning the smile.

"Of course," said Joanna, even though the boxes weren't hers.

Dante squatted down and lifted one of the lids.

Annie realised these weren't the cardboard boxes most people used for storage. These were purpose-made archive boxes, strong cardboard specifically sized for vinyl LPs.

"D'you have a turntable?" she asked Rosamund.

"David's old one, yes." Rosamund opened a discreet cabinet in a corner.

Dante stood up and went over. "Oh. This is a Linn Sondek."

Rosamund cocked her head. "Is it?"

"Expensive."

"Do you think it still works? David was never keen for me to touch it. I'm not even sure how to turn it on."

"Only one way to find out." Dante explored the rest of the cabinet. "Here's the amplifier."

There was an audible plunk from all around the room as Dante turned a large knob.

"Sounds promising," murmured Joanna.

"Want to select something to test this baby out?" Dante asked her.

She gave a playful smile. "There must be something here." She leaned forward, a demure tuck to her legs as she found the nearest box and flicked through the records inside.

"Goodness me. The Boomtown Rats." She pulled out *Mondo Bongo*.

Annie frowned. "Interesting choice. Did you like New Wave stuff, back in the day?"

Joanna looked up. "Oh, they were always on the radio, weren't they? And wasn't Bob Geldof so delightfully disreputable? Before he turned out to be so very wholesome, I mean."

Dante walked over and took the album from her. "This brings back some memories. They recorded it in the Round house Studios, you know?"

He eased out the glossy black disc and held it up to the light, cradling it in his outstretched hand, careful only to touch the edges.

"Is that a famous place?" Annie asked.

"I spent a lot of time there as a session musician," said Dante, placing the record on the turntable and starting it spinning. "Let's have a listen to 'Banana Republic', see if you can hear yours truly doing a spot of percussion and backing vocals." He placed the needle on the track and rocked back on his heels.

Joanna was watching Dante with evident surprise. Her

mouth was a perfect 'O', but any sound that might have come out was drowned out by the Boomtown Rats.

Dante stood up to dance.

Annie wondered why she'd never noticed how heavily influenced the record was by reggae. At the time it had just been another catchy tune on the radio.

Dante held out a hand to Joanna, inviting her to dance. She looked bashful, then stood up to join him.

Annie shared a look with Rosamund as Dante twirled Joanna by her hand. She stepped slowly but gracefully along with his guidance. He sang along with the backing vocals.

As the track ended, Dante went over to lift the stylus away.

"Has an awesome sound, doesn't it?" He turned back to them all. "The turntable, I mean, not just the percussion."

"It certainly does," said Joanna, with another flash of her smile. "You think there's anything here that merits a closer look?" She waved a hand to take in the vinyl and the turntable.

Dante didn't take his eyes off Joanna as he replied, "I certainly do, yes."

Chapter Twenty-Four

Tina, Dougie and DS Strunk returned to Clifford's house. The DS had driven up separately.

The front door now featured a temporary padlock attached to some wooden braces, so the scene could be secured. It hung open and the door was ajar.

"Gavin!" Dougie called as they stepped through the door. "What's new?"

Tina recognised Gavin Larcomb, second-in-command in Dorset's CSI team, and so tall she had to crick her neck to return his smile.

"It's just me here now," Gavin said. "Non-urgent follow-up should be my middle name." He backed up and let them follow him into the lounge. "You can step where you want in here. We're all done with this room."

Tina looked around. "Want to run us through the highlights? Any fingerprint evidence?"

"We focused on those entry points," Gavin said. "Sent the lifts off to the lab, so you need to check the system for any matches. We found some tools in the basement and sent those off to the lab as well, in case they were used. I'd be surprised, given how dusty the toolbox was, but you never know. Photos of the toolmarks on the front door should help determine what sort of tool was used. All on the system, but it looks to me like a crowbar. Brute force prying, using something with a large, blunt blade. Want to see the size?"

The DS nodded. "Yes please."

Gavin led the way back to the front door and pointed to the damaged portion. "See here, where the wood's broken away around the lock?"

They all nodded.

"That took a lot of force. It was created at this insertion point here. See where the wood's compressed? You can see the width of the tool that was used. Two contact points with a gap in the middle, which makes me think crowbar with a notch in the centre, rather than tyre iron. The lab will compare it against a reference library."

Tina could see the mark Gavin was pointing at.

"Useful stuff," said the DS. "Thanks, Gavin. What about the back window?"

Gavin shook his head. "Less to go on there. It looks more like wear and tear. Loose rusty screws. Could have been done deliberately."

"But the burglar came in through the front," said the DS.

Gavin shrugged. "I'm just the CSI."

"So the fact that the burglar left through a window with a dodgy latch might just be coincidence," said Tina.

Another shrug. "I've been cataloguing Clifford's medication today. I found something interesting."

"Yeah?" Tina asked.

"Not quite finished in here, so don't touch anything," Gavin warned. "He had a lot of his medication in the cupboard with his teabags. I guess it makes sense if you're a man who likes his tea."

The cupboard was open. Several unopened boxes of teabags sat inside, an open one on the left. On the right were boxes of medication, and a pill organiser.

"Didn't I see a similar pill organiser in Clifford's effects from the Cobb?" asked Dougie.

"Yes. It seems he used two of them." Gavin nodded. "Use one, one week, while prepping the other for the following week. We'll document all his regular medication. I made a start on that. He had a lot of pills, but he was at an age where that's not unusual."

"What kind of medication was he on?" asked DS Strunk.

Gavin moved some boxes aside. "I'm not a pharmacist, but this one's Atorvastatin, statins in other words. Captopril is an ACE inhibitor, I think. Warfarin, some diuretics. Looks like he had some heart problems. Not unusual in itself." He moved to some other boxes. "Here's something different though. Madopar. I had to look that one up. It's used to treat Parkinson's disease."

Tina pulled a face. "And would the medication mask the symptoms?"

"Once again, not a pharmacist. I don't know."

"Yeah, sorry."

"Shall I show you the interesting part?" Gavin asked.

"Please," said Tina.

"If you look at the counter below this cupboard, there's a very fine dusting of powder. You need to shine a bright light at the right angle."

Dougie produced his torch as they all crouched to see.

Tina could see the residue. She wondered how Gavin had spotted it.

"Is it sugar from where he's made his tea?" asked the DS, straightening. "I make a mess like that all the time. Worse, actually."

"No sugar here," said Gavin, indicating the cupboard. "I don't think Clifford indulged. Quite right, too, given his health problems. Also, the grains are much too fine to be regular sugar. I've bagged some up, but I wouldn't be surprised to find that the composition of this powder matches one of Clifford's medicines."

The DS nodded slowly. "Sounds like we could be looking at tampering."

Tina pursed her lips. "So, if Clifford's medicine was tampered with, then we have to consider foul play after all."

Chapter Twenty-Five

On Wednesday evening, Annie walked through the town to Oliver's Wine Bar in what she considered her finest 'painting and sipping' attire. Tim Cromwell was waiting, dressed in his usual harbourside outfit of jumper, shirt and trousers. Except these trousers were light chinos and the shirt was a pale denim with a buttoned-down collar.

He didn't look all that happy about being dressed differently or being in Oliver's Wine Bar, but his face lit up when he saw Annie approaching.

"Ha! I thought you might not come."

"Really?" She glanced at her watch. She was early. "What made you think that?"

He waved away her question. "You look smashing."

She laughed. "I don't think anyone's used the word 'smashing' this century."

"That's me, a dinosaur."

"Vintage," she corrected.

"Almost as bad." Tim opened the door and ushered her into the bar.

The downstairs bar was full of dark polished wood, brass and glass wall lights, and had a welcoming yellow-orange glow. The bar was along one wall of the narrow space.

"What can I get you?" asked the barmaid.

"We're here for the painting thing," Tim said.

"Upstairs."

"A white wine spritzer for me," said Annie.

"Is it uncouth if I have a pint of stout?" asked Tim.

"Uncouth?"

"I don't know if you're meant to bring beer to a 'paint and sip'. Beer seems more of a 'paint and quaff' type thing."

Annie shrugged. "If you want to quaff but pretend to be sipping, I won't tell anyone."

They took their drinks upstairs. The upstairs was more spacious, with the tables moved to the sides for the evening activity. Annie recognised Mrs Fournier, the artist who lived next door to Naomi. She was centre stage in a white smock, with six other people sitting around her. Little tables of paints were arranged between them.

"Are you here for the couples painting?" asked Mrs Fournier.

Tim nodded.

Couples painting? Annie raised her eyebrows as Mrs Fournier gestured for them to find seats.

There was an array of paints and soft brushes on the table between them. As they put their drinks down, Mrs Fournier gave Tim's pint a stern look. He in turn gave Annie a sheepish 'I told you so' look.

"So, tonight," said Mrs Fournier, "we begin an exploration in art. Be gentle, be bold. Tonight, there are no mistakes. We are exploring ourselves through art."

Several people nodded eagerly. Some looked nervous.

"Art is all about sensation, all about discovering what it means to be human," Mrs Fournier continued.

Tim leaned across to Annie. "Where's the thingies?"

"What thingies?"

He drew a square in the air. "The easels. The, the canvas things."

He was right. There were no easels. Annie looked around the room. There were no canvasses nearby. *Couples painting*, she thought, and a worrying image struck her.

"These paints are non-toxic, obviously," said Mrs Fournier. "But do avoid the eyes. Be sensible."

"Oh, Timmy Boy," Annie whispered to her date. "What exactly did you buy us tickets for?"

He frowned.

"You will be each other's canvasses," said Mrs Fournier. "Be delicate. But be fearless."

Tim seemed to grasp the truth only when one woman pushed her sleeve up to the elbow and a man across the room took his shirt off.

"Oh, my goodness," he said as their fellow participants began to daub paint on one another.

Annie bit back a smirk.

He looked to Annie with fear in his eyes. "I had no idea! Lachlan said I should sign up."

"And I bet Lachlan's laughing his socks off at you right now," she replied.

Tim must have seen that she was amused, not offended. His face creased with laughter.

"I can't believe this," he said. "You do know I didn't do this on purpose, Annie?"

"I know you, Tim," she said, picking up a paint brush. "This is..."

"It's bloody hilarious," he said. "Or will be. What's that they say? Comedy equals tragedy plus time."

"I'm already starting to see the funny side." She dipped her brush in some orange paint.

"You don't expect me to take my top off or nothing, do you?" he asked.

"Give me your hand, Tim."

He held it out. She turned it over and began to paint on the back of his hand. A splodgy orange circle appeared, and she decided immediately it would be the sun. His long fingers were warm against her hand. The hairs on the back of his hand took the paint in unexpected directions, the sun surrounded by spikey lines.

He sat silently, occasionally sipping – not quaffing – his pint while Annie switched colours and painted in hills and fields on his hand.

"That's proper good, that is," he said.

"I've no idea what I'm doing."

His fingers squeezed against her hand, and she felt a shiver run through her.

"When we're done," she said, "we'd better take a photo to show that Lachlan Fellows."

"I've half a mind to give him something more than a photo next time I see him."

She blew on his hand to dry the paint and held onto him when he reflexively pulled away.

When it was Tim's turn, he went straight to the blue paints. He mixed the royal blue with dabs of white and a touch of black, and then, with her hand held in his, painted a sinuous wave along her forearm.

It had a moody tone to it that Annie found attractive. He followed it with a line of white and a band of sea green.

"The sailor painting the sea," she said.

He raised an eyebrow. "Paint what you know. I spend every day looking at it. Half my life spent on it."

He leaned in close and painted with focused intent.

"That's beautiful," Annie told him.

He nodded in simple acceptance.

"You must love the sea," she continued.

"You're friends with that young girl, um, Edmunds."

"Figgy. Yes. Why?"

"I was on the lifeboat when her granddad's trawler went down."

Annie felt her stomach dip. "I didn't know that."

He nodded, not looking up. "Waves taller than I've ever seen in the channel that night. Didn't love the sea that night."

"No. No, of course."

He was switching brushes as he changed colours. Now there was a pink splodge in the sea.

"What's that?" she asked.

He smiled. "That's you. Having a swim."

"I look like Mr Blobby."

"Tssh. Nonsense. You look elegant. Like a porpoise."

"I'm sure that's a compliment."

He sniffed and brought his face closer to her arm and hand, so close she thought he might kiss it. He painted fine strands of hair on her head.

"Course, my eyesight isn't what it once was," he said. "Everyone looks like Mr Blobby when they're out in the sea as far as I'm concerned."

"And all of us as elegant as porpoises," said Annie.

"Nope," Tim replied softly. "Only you."

Chapter Twenty-Six

"You'll promise to behave, won't you, Mum?"

It was at least the third time of asking, but Joanna seemed disinclined to give any answer that would reassure Rosamund.

Joanna had asked to come along to Rosamund's 'little swimming club', and Rosamund had agreed, not least because she didn't think her mum would be capable of getting up that early in the morning. Her heart had sunk when she'd risen at 6am to find Joanna by the front door in a pink tracksuit, a gym bag in one hand.

Three times, Rosamund had asked if her mum was going to behave when exposed to her friendship group, and three times Joanna had ducked the question.

"I just want to see these brave women at play," she said. "Such larks!"

As they made their way down through the park and past the crazy golf to the beach, Rosamund consoled herself with the thought that perhaps it would be good for them to do something recreational together. They had never been friends like some mothers and daughters. Perhaps if Joanna showed an interest in swimming, it could be a point of connection, the starting point for a better relationship.

A couple of the women were already in the water. Rosamund could see Juniper walking down to the sea with Sally and Peg. Helen, Figgy and Annie were chatting by the sea wall, not yet in.

"Morning!" Rosamund called to them.

Helen spotted Joanna. "A new swimmer?"

"This is Rosamund's mum," said Annie. "Joanna, isn't it?"

Joanna did a girly curtsey in greeting. "Rosamund's told me all about you," she said, quickly adding, "Collectively. As a mass. Not individually."

"We met the other day," Annie explained to the others.

"Brought over that Dante chap," added Joanna. "Very handy when it came to shifting David's old tat. I've been organising him on the WhatsApp to take away those old LPs."

"I'm sure he'll find a good home for them," Annie said.

Rosamund noticed that Annie had paint up and down both her forearms, great swirls of blue along one arm.

"Did you walk into a painted wall or something?" she asked.

Annie looked down at herself then back at Rosamund. "Oh, you're admiring it, too?"

"Annie was at a 'paint and sip' event last night," said Figgy.

"'Paint and quaff'," corrected Annie.

Helen had a strange smile on her face. "She was on that date she messaged us about," she said.

Rosamund frowned. "Tim from the lifeboats?"

"The very same," said Helen.

"And you went to bed without washing it off?" asked Joanna, disapprovingly.

"Thought I'd enjoy it a while longer." Annie angled her arms proudly. "Wash 'em off in the sea. Release the art back into the universe."

Joanna folded her arms against the slight breeze and gazed out to sea. "Looks, er, inviting."

"Colder than it looks," said Helen, snapping a swimming cap into place.

"Your first time on Lyme Regis beach?" Annie asked Joanna as Helen headed over the pebbly beach towards the surf.

"No, Annie. Not at all. I used to come down to Devon and Cornwall all the time when Rosamund was little."

"We're in Dorset, Mum," said Rosamund.

Joanna gave a dismissive wave. "Same thing. You know what I mean. Quite a few holidays down here."

"Bit of sea swimming then?" asked Annie.

"I don't recall."

"I do," said Rosamund. "Put me off swimming in the sea for years."

"Oh?" said Annie.

Rosamund looked at her mother. "You told me I couldn't swim in the sea. You were petrified."

Joanna frowned. "Doesn't sound like me."

Rosamund sighed. "There was that thing. The boy had drowned."

Joanna clutched her daughter's arm in sudden recollection. "You're right. Must be thirty years ago. I remember it like it was yesterday. Day before your birthday."

"What happened?" asked Figgy.

"A little boy drowned. Out there." Joanna pointed to the area where the most distant swimmers were.

"Forty-odd years ago," said Annie, softly. "That would have been Simon Cromwell. Tim's son. Swam out too far. Got into trouble."

"Exactly," said Joanna. "All I could think about was what if that had been my little girl."

"Thirty years ago I was very much a teenager, Mum," Rosamund pointed out.

"Still my little girl." Joanna wagged her finger. "No way was I letting her go into that sea."

"Scarred for life," said Rosamund with a forced smile. "Speaking of going into the sea..."

"Last one in's a rotten egg," said Annie, making her way down to join Helen.

Rosamund waited while her mum stripped off her tracksuit. Joanna had borrowed one of Rosamund's older costumes. It fit her rather well. How odd to think that they were almost identical in physique. It made Rosamund worry that she might one day be like her mum in other ways.

Joanna gestured at Figgy. "Now, are you... what's your name?"

"Figgy," said Figgy.

"That's right. Now, am I correct in thinking that you are good... friends with my grandson?"

Figgy's eyes widened in what looked like panic. "Er, yes?"

"Ah, good. Let's have a look at you then." Joanna stepped back and looked her up and down.

Figgy, not the most confident of people at the best of times, froze like a rabbit in headlights.

"I must say..." Joanna began.

Rosamund's heart stopped. What was it her mum 'must' say?

"I must say, it's not typical of the younger generation to be up at this hour with us old fuddy duddies."

Rosamund replayed the sentence in her head.

It wasn't crass. Rosamund could even overlook her mum identifying her as a 'fuddy duddy' in the circumstances.

"I like the swimming," said Figgy. "My therapist suggested I should get out more."

"Therapist, see?" said Joanna, nudging Rosamund. "You should get yourself one of them."

"Yes, Mum," sighed Rosamund.

Chapter Twenty-Seven

Later that day, Annie was vacuuming the upstairs bedrooms when Rosamund arrived to drop off the LPs for Dante. A few minutes later she turned off the vacuum and heard the sound of the door closing.

"Did I miss Rosamund?" she asked Dante as she came partway down the stairs to find him with a large pile of archive boxes.

"You missed her on this journey, but she'll be back in a few minutes with the next lot. She couldn't fit them all in her car in one go."

Annie looked at the boxes. Rosamund's car was enormous.

"I don't remember there being this many when we went round there."

"No, we just looked at a few. The rest were upstairs."

Annie took a slow, deep breath. This had all the hall-marks of a situation spiralling out of her control.

"You alright?" Dante said. "You sound like Darth Vader."

Annie came the rest of the way down the stairs and

started counting the boxes. "Any idea how many of these boxes there are?"

"Yep." Dante pulled a piece of paper from his pocket. "David must have been a meticulous soul. He indexed them all. There are fifty boxes."

"Fifty." She pursed her lips and blew hard.

"You're not having a stroke or something, are you?" asked Dante.

"Not just yet, but I might when there's fifty of these boxes here. Where will they go?"

Dante gestured towards the lounge. "In there? There's plenty of room."

"But it's a room, Dante, not a warehouse. How long will they be there? In fact, what do you even plan to do with them?"

He shrugged. "I need to play them first of all. Make sure they're OK."

Annie narrowed her eyes. "Play them all?"

"Yeah."

She bent down to one of the boxes and flicked through the top. "I'm not counting them properly, but there's at least thirty LPs in this box. Do me a favour, Dante, and do a bit of maths. If there are fifty boxes of thirty LPs, each with a playing time of three quarters of an hour, how long is that going to take, eh?"

Dante's lips moved and his eyes shifted as he tried to calculate. "Ah. Five threes. Divided by three quarters. Oh, I don't know. Nine hours or so?"

"No!" Annie scowled. "It's three quarters of fifteen hundred, which is eleven hundred-odd hours. That's weeks and weeks. Are you mad?"

He gave a slow nod. "Yeah, sure, I hear you. I don't need to listen to each and every one. Obviously."

She grunted. "Back to the problem of where they're going. It's going to be quite the eyesore in there. I'm really not keen on this. Will you sell them as a job lot?"

Dante raised his hands, palms down. "It won't be so bad. Trust me. I will make them blend in."

Annie was running out of breathing exercises. She wanted to accommodate Dante as a house guest, she really did, but surely this was above and beyond what anyone should have to put up with.

She took another breath. "Right. I am going for a walk. I'll be disappointed to miss Rosamund coming back, but I need some air. When I return, I would like you to have a sensible proposal for me as to how long these records will need to stay in my house, and your exact plans for moving them along. An actual proposal – no, a plan! A plan with dates."

"Dates?" Dante looked mildly horrified.

"Yes, dates. If you can't manage that, then you and I might be about to have a slightly more serious conversation."

He leaned back. "Oh."

"Yes. 'Oh'." Annie picked up her bag and went through the front door, walking at speed, so she wasn't tempted to listen to any argument Dante might be thinking up.

Walking always lifted her spirits.

Worried about something – go for a walk and those worries often melted away.

Depressed and down in the dumps – go for a walk and let the world pick you up.

Angry about an older man-child using your home as a

record warehouse – go for a long, long walk until the anger faded.

And the deeper the anger, the longer and faster the walk needed to be.

She powered down Anning Road, through Poole's Court to Church Street and along Marine Parade. Still vestiges of her anger remained. She thought about stopping in at the lifeboat station to see Tim, maybe to tell him how much she'd enjoyed the other night.

But she'd already messaged her thanks to him, and a childish part of her didn't want to come across as too keen. Drinks and laughs with Tim were lovely, a million miles away from Dante's raucous brand of fun, but Annie wasn't sure what she wanted from a relationship with Tim.

Not yet. Best not to rush things.

She walked past the Cobb and across the car park that faced onto Monmouth Beach. On the landward side were a number of houses, many of them lodges. On the beach side was a row of static caravans where Figgy lived. This was where Figgy had spent her entire life, living with her grandparents, then just her grandma and then, in the past year or so, entirely alone.

It was mid-afternoon, a perfectly reasonable time for visiting friends. If Figgy was busy with work, Annie could give a cheery "howdy doody" and be on her way again.

She knocked on the door.

As she waited, a seagull approached her, stealthily.

"I haven't anything for you," she told the scavenger.

"Who is it?" called Figgy from inside.

"Just us seagulls," Annie called back.

The door opened and Figgy looked out. "You're not a seagull."

"Only at weekends."

"Social visit?"

"I guess. I went for an angry walk, and it brought me here."

"You're not angry with me though, are you?"

Annie smiled. "I don't think you could do anything that would anger me."

"Hmm. I'm not sure that's the compliment you think it is."

Chapter Twenty-Eight

Figgy worked from home in some sort of tech industry that Annie didn't understand. After her grandma's death, she'd become a recluse, a virtual shut-in. The swimming group had come about as a deliberate attempt to get her out of her home and out of herself. It had apparently worked.

Annie could imagine a scenario in which the young woman lived a squalid life, hoarding things and letting her housekeeping standards slip. But Figgy had always maintained a neat and tidy home.

It was still decorated in a style that Annie supposed her grandparents had chosen. The sofa and thick pile carpets had swirling floral patterns. The wallpaper was glistening silver and beige. Prints of sailing ships, old map charts and a heavy wooden barometer hung on the walls. It was all out of date, but Figgy kept it clean and presentable.

"Tea?"

"Go on then," said Annie. "I'm not interrupting work, am I?"

"I mostly make my own hours."

Annie nodded. Young people seemed to have a very different relationship to work than what she'd been used to. Good for them.

"So what's made you angry?" asked Figgy as she boiled the kettle.

"People who don't think," Annie replied.

"There's a lot of those about. Gonna give me specifics?"

Annie grunted. She didn't want to bother Figgy with her gripes about unwanted lodgers and their inability to see the grief they would cause with their half-baked plans.

"I should learn to be more tolerant," she said.

"Wise. Xandrea always talks about having the grace or serenity to recognise things we can't change and just need to accept."

Xandrea was Figgy's therapist. Annie wasn't sure she would be so willing to expose her innermost being to a stranger, but it did seem that the woman offered intelligent advice at times.

"Putting it into effect in your own life, then?" asked Annie.

"I hope so." Figgy poured water into two mugs.

"Not worried about our Juniper Brown showing undue interest in your Cameron anymore?"

"I rise above it."

"Good."

Figgy squeezed the teabag in the cups. Some people said squeezing teabags ruined the flavour. As far as Annie was concerned, tea was tea, and it tasted nice or nasty regardless.

"Did the police have to question him, by the way?" she asked.

Figgy paused, milk carton in hand. "Pardon?"

"You know. At the house."

"I'm sorry?"

"You know, because Cameron was round at Juniper's when the police discovered the break-in at Clifford Muldoon's place. You know, she lives in that little studio apartment thing at the bottom of his garden."

Figgy placed the milk on the worktop. "And Cameron was there?"

Only now did Annie realise that Figgy hadn't known. "Ah. I misspoke."

"Did you?" Figgy sloshed milk into the cups.

Annie coughed and put on her most genial face. "I heard from Tina that Cameron was round there when the police visited. I didn't for a moment think you weren't aware."

Figgy said stiffly, "Well, Cameron Winters is his own man and it's not like I own him."

"I'm sure it was all innocent," Annie added.

"Are you?"

"Not any hanky-panky or anything, I shouldn't think."

"You don't think there was hanky-panky?"

Annie wished she hadn't spoken. "No, that's not what I said."

"Maybe some rumpy-pumpy?" urged Figgy.

"That's quite a different kettle of fish, Figgy. I—"

"Maybe some slap-and-tickle?"

"I really don't think anyone says slap—"

"Or a bit of how's-your-father?"

"Now, don't be silly."

Figgy glared at Annie. "I'm silly now, am I?"

Annie floundered. "Can we rewind? Please? I've been an idiot and blurted out something I didn't mean to, even though it's true. I'm sure there's nothing going on."

The glare lasted several more seconds before Figgy

clenched and unclenched her fingers and shook the annoyance out.

"I clearly have some unresolved trust issues to address," she said, slowly and carefully. "Thank you for bringing those details to my attention."

"Um. No problem." Annie felt more than a little awkward. "Perhaps I ought to go."

"I've made two cups of tea now," Figgy huffed. "And I'm not in the best mood. I think you'd better tell me about all the cruddy ups and downs in your life just to cheer me up."

"Oh, well. If I must," said Annie. "What shall I start with? The peculiar date? Or the man who's filled my house with ten thousand records?"

"Whichever."

Annie nodded and reached for her tea. "You wouldn't happen to have a biscuit, would you?"

She returned to her home an hour and a half later and let herself in.

"Ah, there you are!" said Dante. "Come in and let me make you a cup of tea."

Annie was taken aback. Not only was she being welcomed into her own house like a guest, which was weird, but Dante was making tea.

"Good. Thank you." She drifted through into the kitchen, not quite prepared to believe that a cup of tea was being made in there without her being the one making it.

She hovered as he boiled the kettle and leaned in to watch him put teabags into mugs.

"I do know what I'm doing, you know?" he said. "I've made tea before."

She said nothing but backed off slightly.

When the tea was made, Dante put it on a tray. "Shall we go into the lounge?" He waved her ahead of him.

She saw immediately that something was very different. "Oh?"

She had a new coffee table.

It was approximately the size of four rows of archive boxes, each row five deep. It was covered in a sheet so that it didn't look like a load of boxes. It even had a plant in the middle.

She also had some new bench seating. Next to the wall, there was a long line of boxes, two deep. Cushions had been arranged on top, to make it look inviting, although Annie wasn't certain it would take the weight of an adult.

"Ta-da?" Dante said. His face was anxious.

"You are a fool, but you know that," she said.

"Yes, I am."

This would have been an excellent moment for him to apologise, Annie realised. She had softened enough that she'd probably have laughed it off and then put up with this ridiculous furniture arrangement for goodness knows how long.

He didn't apologise, though. Instead he gave her his best, most winning smile, then turned to the turntable.

"I thought we might start with some of the basics," he said. "You like Toots and the Maytals? Everybody does. Hold onto your hat, Annie."

Annie raised her eyes to the ceiling and started to take long, slow deep breaths.

Chapter Twenty-Nine

Tina sat in the garden at Naomi's house. Poppy and Louis had been so thrilled with the mud play instigated by Dante the other day, that Dougie and Naomi had built a mud kitchen. Daisy was safely out of the way of the mud, shaded in her pram by a parasol.

"Nathan's here!" shouted Naomi from inside, and a moment later he appeared through the patio doors.

"Hello." Tina gestured at the children. "You've heard about the mud kitchen, yeah? You want to taste the delights they're cooking up?"

"Oh. Yeah." DS Strunk peered at the gloop being stirred by Louis, under Poppy's instruction.

It was very much a basic mud kitchen. Dougie had carved out a small piece of turf from the lawn and loosened the soil underneath. The two children had plastic containers from the recycling, a trowel, a stick and a watering can.

"Soup of the day?" Poppy asked the DS. She had adopted the solemn demeanour of a head waiter in a fancy restaurant. Dougie had suggested the soup line, and Poppy used it at every opportunity.

The DS looked nervous.

Tina leaned towards him. "You don't have to actually eat it. Just act like you're super impressed with their cooking."

"Sounds delicious." He addressed Poppy. "What is it?"

"Eels," replied Poppy, promptly.

"Eels?" chorused the two adults.

Tina looked up at the DS from her chair. "I don't even know how Poppy knows what eels are, to be honest. Pull up a chair." She addressed the children. "Eels take a lot of cooking, because the chefs have to catch them first."

Poppy and Louis looked up in anticipation.

"Over there! Eels! I can see them!" Tina pointed.

Poppy and Louis squealed with glee and ran off to catch eels.

The DS fetched one of the wooden patio chairs and set it down beside Tina's.

"What's brought you over here?" she asked.

"I just went by the station, and Douglas said you'd want this update. We got the toxicology results."

"Oh yeah?" Tina sat up straighter. "Anything of interest?"

He raised his eyebrows. "They extended the toxicology screening, based on what Gavin found in Clifford's kitchen."

"Good. I'd hope so."

"Yeah. Well, Gavin was right. Those grains that he found were a match for one of Clifford's heart medications."

Tina thought for a moment. "Out of a capsule, yeah?"

He nodded. "Yep."

"Is there any chance one got crushed accidentally? Maybe Clifford was a bit heavy-handed?"

"Well, we can ask, but you need to hear the next part."

"Go on."

The DS pulled out his notepad. "Right, so out of all the medications that Clifford was on, his blood contained twice as much as it should have done of nearly all of them. That includes Ramipril, Bisoprolol, Amlodipine—"

"I get the picture," said Tina. Hearing him attempting to pronounce the names of the medications reminded her of Louis tackling tough multi-syllable words like 'barbecue'. "Was that enough to kill him?"

He made a seesaw motion with his hand. "Enough to lower his blood pressure way, way down, apparently. He'd have felt very poorly. I asked the lab, and they said he'd probably have collapsed, maybe died, but obviously he pitched off the edge of the Cobb before that could happen."

"Wow."

"Wow indeed," said Nathan. "There's more."

"You what?"

"Yep. Do you remember the pills we found called Madopar? Used to treat Parkinson's?"

"Yes."

"Well, that one wasn't doubled. In fact, the screening found none at all in Clifford's system."

"Oh." Tina thought through the implications of what Nathan was saying. "So, whoever did this wanted Clifford's blood pressure to drop down dangerously and wanted his Parkinson's symptoms to be untreated?"

"That's about it, yes."

Poppy reappeared, with Louis tagging along. She was wrestling an invisible eel that, judging by the exaggerated effort she was putting in, was the size of a large anaconda.

"This eel doesn't want to be soup."

"Maybe I'll have the vegetarian option?" said Nathan.

Poppy stopped struggling and let the imaginary eel go with a wave. "Fine. It's beetroot."

"Sounds lovely," said Nathan.

Poppy lifted the trowel from the pit. It dripped with mud. "Want a taste?"

"I'll wait until it's all finished, thank you." Nathan eyed his white trainers.

Tina stood up, her mind racing. "So, we think it went like this, then. I'm Clifford, I feel really ropey because my medication's all been tampered with. I might have some tremors, if my Parkinson's is going unchecked. I get up from my chair because I want to go and get help, but I'm disorientated and shaky. I cover the distance that stands between me and the edge of the Cobb..." She paced, as she imagined Clifford would have done. "What was it, about eight feet?"

"Something like that, yeah."

"What do you reckon?" Tina asked.

"I reckon that's what happened," said Nathan with a nod. "It's definitely murder. I'll retask the officers at the station accordingly. I'm popping over there now."

Tina held out a hand. "Well, I'll come, too."

Nathan pointed at the children. "Don't you have young cordon bleu chefs to supervise?"

Tina's face tightened. "Grandparent number one should be here any moment. I thought grandparent number two was going to be around, but he said he had urgent business to attend to."

"Mike's dad?"

Tina nodded. "Apparently. Mum will be here soon, though."

There was a noisy cough from behind. Both officers turned.

"Only me!" said Annie. "Came by to pick up the littlies."

Tina and Nathan exchanged a look. Had Annie heard any of their conversation?

"How are they enjoying themselves?" Annie looked at Tina. "What's wrong? Don't worry. I didn't hear any of your police-y conversation."

Tina was quite certain her mother had heard every word.

Chapter Thirty

Annie opened the door to the gallery shop on Coombe Street and ushered Poppy and Louis inside before wheeling baby Daisy through in the pushchair. A customer held the door open for her.

Helen somehow managed to make a living out of her gallery, even though there rarely seemed to be a customer in there. The fact there was one in today was a mild surprise. To see three other customers inside on a weekday morning was really rather unusual.

Thanking the customer, whose purchases were wrapped in a stripy paper bag under his arm, Annie went over to the till where Helen was ringing up the sale of a trio of art prints. Two more people were by the well-lit exhibition nook at the back of the shop.

"Busy in here," Annie said once the customer at the till had moved on.

"Madcap." Helen waved to the children. "Thank goodness Juniper's offered to help out or I'd be run off my feet."

"Juniper?"

Annie looked round and saw the Australian coming in from the back with mugs of tea.

"With her mentor and benefactor dead and the house a crime scene, she's at a bit of a loose end," Helen whispered.

"G'day, Annie," said Juniper, placing the cups on the counter. "Tea?"

"You knew I was coming?"

"Can soon make myself another if you're all right with no sugar."

"Tea with no sugar is fine," said Annie.

Juniper went off again.

"She's keeping Harper well hydrated, working in a hot workshop at this time of year," said Helen.

Poppy and Louis had found a display basket of little metal dragonflies made out of teaspoons and were sorting through them. Poppy seemed intent on dividing them into boys and girls. How she could distinguish between male and female teaspoon dragonflies was a question best left unasked.

"Your lodger's in here, by the way," said Helen to Annie.

Annie paused in her manoeuvring of the pushchair. "Dante?"

He leaned across from behind a display. "Hey, Annie."

"Funny seeing you in here," said Annie. It was true. People belonged in certain settings. It was clearly ridiculous, as he was a grown man who could go wherever he wanted. Seeing him here in Helen's gallery seemed all wrong.

"Been thinking about that place next door," he said, using his thumb to indicate the empty fossil shop.

"You and a great many other people," said Helen. Her expression suggested she didn't approve of other people thinking about the empty shop.

Dante strolled out from behind the display, hands in

pockets. "This town needs a record shop. Something that speaks to the nostalgia market without seeming old-fashioned. Casual and cool, with curated choices, all shown off in high-impact displays."

Annie was taken aback. "That's quite the vision you have there."

"There's space enough to make it a feast for all the senses," Dante continued, his hands now in the air as he walked through the imaginary space. "Some listening booths, connected up to a quality sound system. Rooms with a totally different feel for fans of different genres. Posters for albums and gigs that relate to the contents."

Annie nodded. She was starting to picture what Dante described. More importantly, she could picture all of those records moving out of her lounge and into a shop.

"Of course, there's a whole movement towards vinyl. If we could make ourselves part of the scene, get young bands to make this a stop-off on a promotional tour, then we could also cater for a younger audience."

Helen pulled a face. "Well, yes. This is all very fanciful, but have you seen the red tape associated with that shop? It's as if someone has deliberately made it challenging."

"Deliberately?" Annie asked.

"Yes! As you know, I'm not a conspiracy nutcase by any stretch of the imagination," said Helen, "but I did wonder whether your cousin Gillian might be behind it."

Annie tapped her fingers against her chin. "Hmm."

"It makes sense, don't you think? She's probably the only person in the town who can afford to weave a path through this minefield. Stands to reason that she had a hand in making it so bloody awful."

"I thought you said a solicitor was doing all the admin?" Annie asked.

"Yes. Admin. But they didn't make up these crazy rules, they're simply evaluating applicants against them." Helen folded her arms and leaned against the counter.

"They were pretty helpful, actually," said Dante.

Annie and Helen both turned to him, confused.

"Who were?" Annie asked.

"The solicitors. They even helped me fill in the application. Said I ticked a lot of the boxes." Dante strolled around the space, failing to notice Helen's furious scowl.

"I don't understand," said Annie. "What boxes are you ticking?"

"Seems as though the planning people in Lyme Regis put a lot of value in diverse businesses that serve both locals and tourists," said Dante. "A record shop scores really well, especially when you break down the demographics. It's easy to prove that there's a demand when you look at how popular record fairs have been, both here and in other local towns."

Helen was flabbergasted. "So, you rock up with a half-baked idea, and that trumps everything else? I thought a solid financial plan was key here?"

Annie thought Dante's idea was far from half-baked, judging by all the research he'd apparently done.

Dante shrugged. "The solicitor said they can hook me up with the loans I need, as long as the business plan stacks up. What can I say?"

Annie was still trying to process it all. She'd assumed Dante's record shop talk was just idle speculation on a fun idea when the conversation had started, but clearly, he'd put in some serious work.

"What is it that makes you want to run a record shop here in Lyme Regis, Dante?" she asked.

He grinned. "I like it here. I've felt like I'm a part of something here. I've seen more of my grandchildren than I honestly expected to."

"Your grandchildren don't live here, though," said Annie. "As soon as Mike and Tina have finished the work on their house, they'll be back over on the other side of Dorset."

"It's close enough. I know Mike doesn't want to see me right now, and who can blame him? Maybe with time he might want to get to know me."

Annie sighed. She'd have loved to see that, but Tina had sounded very sure about Mike's feelings towards his dad. Still, she couldn't blame Dante for trying.

"What are the next steps?" she asked.

Helen heaved a massive sigh.

"The deadline for applications is almost up," said Dante, "and they're supposed to make a decision by the end of the month. They told me unofficially that I'm a front runner at the moment. Apparently, the other applications are nowhere near as strong."

Annie glanced at Helen.

"Well, it's really nice to see you working on something that's important to you." A thought crossed Annie's mind. "Of course, there's accommodation in the upstairs of the shop, isn't there?"

"There is indeed," agreed Dante with a chuckle. "Although if I want to make the business plan stack up, I might have to rent out the flat to tourists during high season. Would you be up for having a lodger for some of the time, help me make it work?"

Annie's face fell. Having Dante stay as a short-term

favour was one thing. Shoring up his long-term plans by agreeing to host him at the drop of a hat was something else entirely.

She puffed out her cheeks. "I don't know, Dante. I'm used to my own company. I don't think I can commit to that in the longer term."

He flashed her his most charismatic grin. "We've had a blast though, haven't we? Say you'll think about it? I love stopping round yours, Annie."

"Flattery, huh? I'm making no promises, Dante. But I will think about it."

Annie tried not to look at Helen's glowering face. She didn't want this to come between their friendship.

"You'll think about it is good enough for me," he said. He waggled magic fingers at the children on the floor, whispered "Going to see a man about a bank loan," and with a wink, he slid out of the shop.

Chapter Thirty-One

As Dante left the gallery, two more customers came in. The shop was fuller than Annie had ever seen it.

"Is there a reason for the rush?" she asked Helen.

"Been like this for two days." Helen leaned forward. "It's Clifford Muldoon," she whispered. "It's true what they say. An artist's work shoots up in value once they're dead."

"Really?"

Helen's hand went to the postcards and framed prints by the counter. Annie took a closer look, and saw they were all Muldoon's wild paintings of Lyme Regis and the surrounding area.

She raised an eyebrow. "Have you been, er, capitalising on the death of a local artist?"

"Not deliberately," replied Helen. "Not really. It sort of just happened."

"Happened how?"

Helen straightened up. "A customer would come in and maybe they'd say, 'what's this?' and I'd tell them it's a Muldoon. And they'd go 'oh, the guy who drowned last week?' Of course I'd say yes and then... well, I'd make a sale. And now they're coming in specifically to look at the art of 'that dead artist who paints the seagulls', the one they'd never even paused to consider before. Suddenly, everyone looks at these rather pedestrian paintings and sees some deep philosophical meaning or some great expression of melancholy in them."

"I see."

Helen gestured at the display area. "Obviously, by that point it seemed more than a little prudent to sort of consolidate the Muldoon pieces I had into a single area so those with an interest could have a look. Someone asks about Clifford Muldoon and now I can direct them to that corner of the shop. Juniper's helped by arranging several of the pieces we have of his."

"A special little exhibition, so to speak," said Annie.

Helen ignored the lightly mocking tone. "We might have put together a tasteful retrospective of a much-loved artist's work. It's a fitting memorial to the man. And, as such, I've put a hold on anyone purchasing his original art at this time. Prints and postcards and such, fine. But we won't be selling the original oils for a few weeks."

"And pop a couple of zeroes on the end of the price when you do?" suggested Annie.

"I'm not trying to profit from the man's death." Helen exhaled sharply through her nose. "But I *am* running a business. One where the chances of making a profit vary from slim to none. So don't you be judging me."

"Not judging you at all, my dear." Annie took a slurp of hot tea. "Wow. Juniper makes a strong brew. Proper builder's tea, that."

"I believe the Antipodeans call it gumboot tea," said

Helen. "Or maybe just the Kiwis. Anyway. She's been a little godsend."

"Well, I certainly don't want to detain you while you're busy. I only came in to see if you had anything that could be added to the tombola for the Lifeboat Week."

"Ah, I see." An impish smile played at the corner of Helen's mouth. "Collecting raffle prizes so you'll have an excuse to visit Tim again?"

"I don't need an excuse to visit Tim. I'm an adult. I can do as I please. But, yes, it may come to pass that I suggest we have another evening out together."

"More painting each other's bodies."

"Not that. No. Fun though it was."

"I can certainly have a little root around for some bits and bobs for the raffle," said Helen. She eyed the customers by the paintings. "Speaking of Clifford Muldoon," she whispered, "did you know your Tina and your son-in-law were in here asking about his art?"

"Dougie?" said Annie. "You mean, as police officers?"

"Well, you know there'd been a break-in at Clifford's, probably on the day of his murder?"

"Tina mentioned something."

"They think one of his own paintings from the house has gone missing."

"Missing, as in stolen?"

"Exactly that," said Helen. "And they came to see if I could help them work out what had been taken."

"And have you?"

Helen's expression was suddenly sly, almost cat-like. "Would you like me to show you what I've found out?"

Annie took another sip of tea. "You know me, Helen. Always interested to hear what you've got to say."

Chapter Thirty-Two

There was a knock at the door to Figgy's caravan.

She had few callers. Her most regular visitor was a hungry seagull she'd named Kevin. And he didn't knock.

She opened the door. Cameron Winters stood back from the step.

"Thought I'd better come over."

"Yes?"

He held up his phone. "Cos I don't understand this."

She peered forward. It was their messenger chat. Her last comment to him was: *Why didn't you tell me about you and Juniper?*

"Oh, that."

"That."

He gave an expressive shrug.

"I just don't know if I should be worried about you and her," she said.

"And I don't know if I should be worried about you and me." His face was pinched. "Do you want to have this conversation in the doorway or what?"

She stepped back to let him in.

"I also brought cold drinks and cookie dough ice cream," he added, clearly still irritated, as he waggled a small carrier bag.

"That's very kind of you."

"My biggest weakness."

He put the bag on the counter and pulled out a can of fizzy drink. The ring pull opened with an angry 'pop'.

He took a slurp and then offered her another can from the bag.

"So are you going to start or am I?" he said.

"Start? Er, yes." She put the can down, unopened. "I know about you and Juniper."

His pinched look didn't ease. "OK. What? What about me and Juniper?"

She gestured with a hand. "I know that you were round her place the other day."

Cameron blinked. "Like, last week? Yes. I was."

"That."

His stare didn't let up. "Are you asking me why I didn't tell you about me going round to Juniper's little apartment?"

"I think I am."

"Is there a reason why I should tell you about that?" He shook his head. "You think there's something going on between me and Juniper? You do, don't you?"

"I didn't say that."

"But you thought it. You thought I was... cheating on you with Juniper. That's it." He looked away. "You're jealous."

"Am I?"

"Yes. And it's not an attractive look on you."

Figgy felt a flush of rising emotion. Guilt and embarrassment. But also anger.

Cameron was a few years younger than Figgy. Not a lot, but some. He was young. He was fit – in every sense of the word. And he was clever. They'd been going out, sort of, for little more than four months, and Figgy was forever taken by the fact that he was both way out of her league and more mature than his years. But it did lead to moments where she felt he treated her like a child.

"If you've got something going with her, you should let me know," she said.

"I spend time with another girl, and you think we're cheating behind your back? Am I not allowed to have female friends?"

"Of course you are!"

"Good. Am I allowed to go and visit other people's homes without telling you?"

She shook with annoyance. "Obviously."

"Good! And do you have so little trust in your boyfriend that this is where your mind leaps to when I speak to other women?"

She churned with hot emotions and no words to express them. She clutched the can he'd given her. It was cool to the touch. She squeezed it, but being angry, both with herself and with the world, wasn't enough to make her the Incredible Hulk.

"She's..." Figgy breathed out sharply and looked away. "She's beautiful. She's tall. She's..."

Cameron laughed.

"What?"

"You're jealous of the tall woman."

"No. Obviously." But she couldn't help thinking of her less than average five foot four height.

"Do you know what I don't like about you, Figgy?"

A tremor of fear passed through her. "What?"

"You don't believe in yourself. No. That's too cheesy. You don't have faith that you're good enough. Damn. Still cheesy."

"I do have faith in myself," she replied, not believing herself.

"I like you. I actually bloody like you. I thought you'd know that because I actually bloody tell you all the actual bloody time."

"You do."

"You and me, we have fun together."

"We do."

"And you are the person I like."

"Thank you. I mean, good. It's... I like you, too."

"Really? Because you have a funny way of showing it at times."

"I'm sorry."

"You know, it is possible to drive people away."

"I..."

A thought passed through her, the idea that by saying she could drive people away, Cameron was hinting that he wanted her to drive him away, that he wanted an excuse to be rid of her. She tried to thrust it aside, but it stuck.

"I like you very much," she said. "I'm sorry."

"Don't say sorry," he said, then closed his eyes. "I mean, yes, you should be sorry. Cos you thought I... I'm just saying, we shouldn't be these people who have bad thoughts about each other and have to worry and then have to say sorry." He stepped closer, and put his hands on hers, around the can she was holding. "It shouldn't have to be this complicated."

"No."

"Are you always going to make things complicated?"

She was hot and still a little angry and very much ashamed and embarrassed and still filled with some creeping suspicion. Too many emotions. She felt like she needed to shower them off. But here was Cameron, his hands on hers, and when he told her that he hadn't been cheating on her, she believed him. That, she did believe.

She kissed him. He was surprised, and then he kissed her back, and the negative emotions were pushed back and away.

When they parted, he said, "We good then?"

"Better than good."

"Thank God for that." He sighed. "Because I like you very much."

"Not sure why."

"And Grandma Joanna likes you very much."

"Does she?"

He nodded. "She thinks it's cool that I have an 'urban' girlfriend."

"Did she actually say that?"

"Unfortunately."

"Wow."

He nodded. "Ice cream's probably melting."

They got out the tub of ice cream and spoons and sat on the seating area with the tub of cookie dough ice cream between them. Figgy caught a glimpse of a seagull from the corner of her eye and bent closer over the ice cream.

She turned, but the seagull was gone. *Kevin, was that you?* Trust him to interfere.

Ignore him.

"So what do you like about me?" she asked.

Cameron looked at her. "You need some reassurance or something?"

"No," she lied.

"Obviously, I like the fact that you're not at all needy and emotionally insecure."

She elbowed him.

He put his arm around her waist. "What do I like about Figgy Edmunds? Apart from her interestingly retro old granny caravan home? Hmmm. You don't pretend you're something you're not."

"Isn't that just spinning my self-doubt into a positive attribute?"

"Maybe. No, more than that. You take things at face value. You appreciate things for what they are. Ice cream. Yum. A walk along the cliffs. Great. You actually enjoy life. You're not tied up in, uh, jobs and social media and owning this or that."

She nodded. "What I'm hearing here is that I'm a simple person with simple tastes."

"You're going out with me, aren't you? I like the way you smell."

"I smell now?"

"You know what I mean. And when you smile... when you smile, you mean it. Definitely. Like that."

She nodded, accepting his words. She dug her spoon into the ice cream.

"So, what were you doing over at Juniper's?" she asked.

She felt him stiffen.

"I'm just asking," she added. "I've never been over to hers. She lives with that artist guy. Lived."

"She asked me to help move some stuff," said Cameron. "She's been over here for a few years. Accumulated some junk. Keeps half her stuff in storage. She just doesn't have room in her art studio. It's not very big."

"You're talking to a woman who lives in a shoe box," Figgy pointed out.

"Her actual living space, like bedroom, bathroom, kitchen and that, is tiny. It's part of a larger studio at the bottom of Mr Muldoon's garden. Now, that's nice."

"Is it?"

He nodded. "Modern, clean. Like, it's all sort of colours but it somehow works. There are paintings hanging in it. Juniper's a really good painter. The whole place is – I don't want to say it's really cool but, yeah, it's really cool."

"Huh. Nice."

"Course, she might lose it now that Muldoon's dead. I really don't know."

"I see. So, Juniper has a really nice place..." she said, and completed the sentence in her head, *...and Figgy lives in an uncool retro granny caravan on the edge of a car park on the least popular bit of beach.*

"She does," said Cameron. "At least, she does for now. Who knows?"

Chapter Thirty-Three

With the children in Annie's care, Tina grabbed a lift back to the station with the DS.

They entered the office where Dougie and Wendy were working at their desks.

"It's time for us all to get together for a recap." Tina folded her arms. "We have quite a lot of moving parts to this investigation now."

The DS gave her a look. The same look Mike sometimes gave her. She wanted to caption it as: 'you are trying my patience'.

"As I'm here representing the senior investigating officer on this case, I think it's time we had a recap, don't you?" the DS said.

Dougie and Wendy smiled at the good-natured jibe. It was a reminder of who was officially in charge.

"Well said, Sarge," said Tina.

The DS made his way to the front of the room, where a board captured many of the key facts relating to the case.

Dougie and Wendy gathered to watch. The DS pointed to a map of the town and stabbed a finger on the Cobb.

"Let's begin with Clifford's death. We now know his medication was tampered with, so when he was here in his usual spot, he became disoriented. He got up to seek help and stumbled over the edge."

There were nods from around the room.

"Shortly afterwards, there was a break-in at Clifford's home," the DS said. He tapped the location on the map.

"Did we get anywhere looking at CCTV?" Tina asked. "See if anyone went up there from the Cobb?"

"We have cameras at several locations on the most obvious route from the Cobb to Clifford's home," said Wendy. "Those locations include the Cobb Gate car park here, several shops up Broad Street and three properties up Silver Street. We have a lot of people in the shopping areas, obviously. We tracked several individuals who walked up Silver Street during that time window. Unfortunately, the images from those particular cameras are very low quality." She walked to her desk and held up a picture that showed a grainy shot of someone wearing a red top. It looked like a person from a Lowry painting with a smudge of white for their face and a coloured smear to represent their body. "We have five pictures of people like this."

"Huh." The DS shook his head. "I can't even guess what gender that person might be."

"Bit of a dead end," said Tina.

"Yes. Now we move on to the break-in at Clifford's place. Or should I say break-ins? Two points of entry or possibly exit. The crowbar to the front door and the loose catch to the rear window."

"We haven't come across a crowbar at all, have we?" Tina asked.

Heads shook.

"And then, the evidence inside the house that Clifford's medicine was tampered with."

Dougie raised an arm. "I just got off the phone with the woman who does Clifford's cleaning. Pietra is her name."

"This is good." DS Strunk rubbed his hands together. "What do we know about her?"

"She's been in Greece for a fortnight. Just got back yesterday. Obviously, we'll check the flight manifests to confirm that, but assuming it all checks out, it rules her out of any involvement."

"We'll need to interview her, see whether she might have left her keys with someone," said Tina.

"I already asked that," said Dougie. "She never had a set of keys, they always stayed with Clifford. She only cleaned when he was home."

"Ah." Tina looked across at the DS with a shrug.

"Next of kin, though. Surely there's someone else in Clifford's life?" the DS asked.

"You'd think so," said Dougie. He flipped through his notebook. "All we have so far is a cousin in South Africa. Eighty-four years old, so quite an elderly cousin at that. Clifford had a will and we've spoken to the solicitor who prepared it. The cousin isn't even the beneficiary for most of Clifford's estate, he just gets a token legacy. It's mostly arts charities who will benefit."

"OK," said the DS. "So no one else had keys to the house, the one other person who was regularly in the house was out of the country, and there's no one obvious who stands to benefit financially from Clifford's death." He sucked his teeth and put his hands on his hips. "I suppose it's good to rule some things out."

Tina nodded. "We need to cast our investigation wider. Someone clearly wanted our man dead."

"What about this woman?" the DS said. "The one who lives at the bottom of the garden?"

"Juniper Brown," said Tina. "Clifford was bankrolling her living expenses. I gather from the grapevine—"

"This'd be your mum," said Dougie.

"—from the grapevine," Tina continued, "that Juniper is now concerned about her living situation, what with her patron being dead."

"But we do have something noteworthy on her from the CCTV," said Wendy.

"Oh?" said the DS.

"She was down on the beach when Clifford went into the water. She appears occasionally on CCTV on Marine Parade. I made a note because I thought she might be a person of interest."

"Good work. And?"

Wendy pulled a face. "She was there the whole time."

"What do you mean, the whole time?" asked the DS.

Wendy shrugged. "From the moment Clifford went in until forty minutes later. We know she swims with Tina's mum from the crack of dawn, and we've got her down in that part of town pretty much throughout the morning, on and off. If we're assuming the break-in happened after Clifford left his home that morning, there's no real timeframe in which she could have done it."

"Great," said the DS. "So, someone else to rule out."

"Indeed, sir."

The DS looked at the board again. "A fairly reclusive man. Few friends. Almost no family. And the people who knew him at all were either out of the country or down at the beach, right under our noses."

Chapter Thirty-Four

Helen had spread exhibition magazines and catalogues on the counter and brought out a laptop. Annie suspected she needed little of this equipment to demonstrate what she'd uncovered. But she supposed Helen got few opportunities to showcase the knowledge and skill that went into running a successful gallery, and she clearly wanted Annie to get the full experience of what it meant to be an art expert.

On the floor, having divided the model dragonflies into boys and girls, Poppy was now instructing Louis on how to arrange them for what appeared to be a little dragonfly wedding.

"Years ago," said Helen, tapping the printed items on the counter, "galleries produced catalogues for all their exhibitions. You wanted to know what was being produced and sold in this country? You could look through these. I've spent whole days in the archives at Bonham's and Sotheby's auction houses. The same kind of stuff can be found at the National Gallery Research Centre."

"But times have moved on, technologically speaking?" Annie prompted.

"They have," said Helen, "but we sometimes forget that the likes of you and I have lived across two eras. Go back less than thirty years – and that's very much in the middle of Clifford Muldoon's heyday – and print and paper were still king. Digitisation..." she tapped the laptop, "...has not yet eradicated the old ways. Do you know much about Clifford?"

Annie wrinkled her nose. "I'm afraid to say, I only ever thought of him as a harmless old boy sitting on the Cobb every day painting seas, skies and seagulls."

"With some skill," pointed out Helen.

Annie nodded. "With some skill."

"Clifford Muldoon was born at the tail end of the Second World War. Oxford, I believe. His parents were well-educated. His father an academic, his mother a pianist. The family made several trips to Dorset, which is no doubt where his love for the area came from. But he studied in Oxford and London, first at the Ruskin School of Art and then at the Royal College of Art."

"I see."

"His early works were sold in London galleries. I think he even worked in a gallery shop there, or perhaps a market stall. His first major exhibition was in nineteen seventy-four. He'd already built up a reputation for atmospheric land-scapes. Light, texture." Her fingers rested on the catalogues. "People were showing an interest."

"He was successful, I know."

"And that's a rare achievement for any artist, whatever the field. I'm sure you're aware. For every rock guitarist who makes the big time, there's ten thousand perfectly competent guitarists who never play a venue bigger than their local pub. Clifford Muldoon was successful."

"I get it."

"By the time he'd made Lyme Regis his permanent home, he'd made the decision to give the paying public exactly what they wanted."

Annie smiled. "Do I detect a note of criticism?"

"Not at all," said Helen. "If Status Quo could make a fifty-year career out of playing the same tunes again and again, then Clifford Muldoon could keep churning out – what was it? – seas, skies and seagulls." Her hands went to the laptop. "We should be thankful that Muldoon chose a naming convention for his works and stuck to it. Location, date, and number. And nearly all of them feature on the databases I have access to."

"Special secret databases?" suggested Annie.

"I pay a fee. And I know what I'm looking for. You ready for this?"

"I'm learning and loving it."

Helen angled the screen so Annie could see, though the web-based form on display meant nothing to her.

"As I mentioned," said Helen, "the major auction houses have their own databases of every artwork they've sold. But those databases are individual, so you have to go through all of them rather than having one collated list to search. Art UK have a private and public collections database which covers everything notionally on public display."

"So, a lot of Clifford's works are on there."

"They are. And a great deal of use it is, too. What we also have is the British Antiques Dealers Association. A lot of information there. And the Artist's Resale Right Database.

And the Art Loss Register. Very handy if you think a piece has been stolen."

"If you expect me to be impressed by all this, I am," said Annie. "Please tell me you found something."

Helen clicked on her laptop and up came a table in which works of art had been listed in one column, descriptions in another and locations in a third. Something about the simplicity of the document told Annie that this was Helen's own creation.

"Why's Lyme Regis underlined in a red squiggle everywhere?" she asked.

Helen tutted. "Silly computer thinks it's a spelling mistake."

Annie pointed at a painting entitled *Charmouth Beach – colour and tone study*. "It's also got a problem with the word colour."

"It seems to think I should be writing in American English. Probably a settings thing. Anyway, every single painting Clifford Muldoon has created is on this list, and I've filled in with a degree of certainty where they can be found."

Annie pointed at some blank boxes. "So these are the ones that are missing."

"Ones I've not yet located."

"There's a few of them."

"Ah, but here's the thing," said Helen. "Clifford Muldoon took his craft seriously, and for most of his middle career he made his own canvases."

"Yes?"

"Lots of sizes. Irregular sizes."

Annie scanned the information listed on the screen. "You know how big these pieces are."

"Most of them."

"Do the police know the size of the one that was stolen?"

Helen's eyes gleamed. "There was a space on the wall. When I next speak to Douglas or Tina, I'm going to ask them if there's an outline, or marks."

"Measure the space, identify the painting."

"One hopes."

"That is impressive," said Annie. "And I think one revelation deserves another."

"Oh?"

They had already been close together, speaking in low, conspiratorial voices, but Annie leant closer still. "I might have been accidentally eavesdropping on my Tina earlier."

"Accidentally?"

"God's honest truth so strike me dead," said Annie. "She was talking to that DS Strunk. Nathan. They've done the autopsy on Clifford's body."

"Yes?"

"They think he was poisoned."

Helen pulled back, frowning. "He drowned."

"He fell in the sea," Annie corrected.

Helen's eyes widened. "Poisoned?" she mouthed.

"I know."

"Bloody hell. This calls for another cup of tea."

Chapter Thirty-Five

Helen smiled as she watched Juniper in action. The younger woman was doing a superb job of talking to the customers about the intricacies of Clifford Muldoon's work. Juniper found something important and insightful to say about even his later works, which Helen thought lazy and unconsidered. She knew her art well and was doing a damned fine job of selling it.

Helen decided to let her get on with it and made another cuppa for herself and Annie.

Clifford Muldoon, *poisoned*! It was a shocking thought. And did that mean deliberately poisoned? Was it an accident, or did someone want him dead? Helen couldn't imagine an eighty-year-old recluse in Lyme Regis had many enemies.

While she was making the tea, ready to go back and ask Annie these vital questions, Harper came in from the rear yard. She had sweaty soot streaks on her forehead. Sweat glistened on her forearms. She put down her large tin mug.

"How goes construction of the Pegasus?"

Harper gave her a look. "I thought you had Juniper on tea duty."

"Oh, she's waxing lyrical about the great Clifford Muldoon." Helen splashed water into cups. "Obviously, she knew him, so she's turning that knowledge into a sales pitch. If this continues much longer, I might have to employ her as a gallery assistant."

Harper made a surprised noise. "Thought you said you could never afford to employ help."

"Times change, I suppose."

Beneath the sweat and grime, Harper's expression was hard and bitter.

"Sweetheart, are you still annoyed with me?"

"Still?"

"It's been a week. A woman makes some off-hand comment about being a 'free spirit' – something you've always admired in me, by the way – and you decide to take umbrage."

"Umbrage, is it?"

"Harper, you can't just keep repeating words back to me as though that's some sort of argument."

Harper growled and stomped back out the rear of the building. The back door slammed.

"Artists are too damned temperamental," Helen tutted. She finished the teas, put them on a tray with a small packet of biscuits, and went back through to the front of the shop. The numbers in the shop had swelled further and now included Rosamund and her mother, Joanna.

"If this carries on, I'll need to make it admission by appointment only," Helen noted.

"Enjoy it while it lasts," said Annie.

"I'm not stopping," said Joanna. "I'm going to the supermarket. We need some air freshener for Rosamund's place."

"We do not need air freshener," said Rosamund.

"You've gone nose-blind, dear." Joanna made for the door. "I'll be back for you in ten."

She squeezed past the pram where baby Daisy snoozed. On the floor, quite out of the way, Annie's other grandchildren played happily with Harper's teaspoon dragonflies.

"I've only made two teas," said Helen, putting them on the counter.

"My house doesn't smell, does it?" asked Rosamund.

Helen, who thought Rosamund had the cleanest, most sterile and most lifeless house in Lyme Regis, laughed the comment off. "Lord, no."

"I think if she tries to sort out my life any more, I might have to kill her."

Helen clutched Annie and Rosamund's hands and leaned in close. "Poison."

"I didn't mean it," said Rosamund. "Although I am thinking of arranging a wine and nibbles evening at home just so I can have a buffer between me and her for one evening. You'd be up for that?"

"Annie was about to give us the lowdown on Clifford being poisoned," said Helen.

"Poisoned?" Rosamund was shocked. "Was he poisoned?"

"Can we all stop saying the word poisoned?" whispered Annie.

"But was he poisoned?" said Rosamund.

"You're still saying it. Shush. What I heard was overheard in the strictest of confidence."

"She was eavesdropping on her police daughter," said Helen.

"Accidentally."

"She says."

Rosamund fixed Annie with a look. "Well?"

Annie nodded. "They think he was poisoned."

"And?" said Helen. "How? Why? Who did it?"

"I don't know. That's pretty much all I heard."

"I was expecting a bit more than that."

Annie stuck out her tongue and thought. "They tested his blood and what have you and they think he was poisoned. He ate the poison or whatever and fell into the sea. I think they're treating it as murder."

"Blimey," said Rosamund. "Who'd want to kill him?"

"And why?" said Helen.

"Did he have any enemies?"

"Not that I'm aware of," said Annie. "But the police are investigating some paintings stolen from his house."

"Painting. Singular," said Helen.

"They're worth a bob or two, then?" said Rosamund.

"Only some of them. He went off the boil a bit a few years back then got really sloppy. The recent stuff is..." She waved towards the band of customers gathered around the paintings at the far end. "It's pleasant enough, but quite pedestrian."

"But profitable," Annie reminded her. "I know I was joking earlier, but you really should make the Muldoon moolah while the sun shines."

"Are we not more interested in the fact that he's been murdered?" said Rosamund. "It's a proper mystery. A man sits at the end of the Cobb day after day and then all of a sudden – bang! – he's dead."

"Bang?" said Helen. "He was poisoned, not shot."

"I can't do a noise for poisoned."

"Glug, glug?" suggested Annie. She reached for one of the biscuits Helen had brought through from the kitchen. A dark look crossed her face.

"What is it?" said Helen.

Annie spoke slowly. "When I went to Clifford's spot on the Cobb that day, I picked up his things."

"Yes?"

"And Figgy's cake box was among his items."

"Really?"

"The little one. The one Figgy had put the cake in, for Juniper. You know, because of her nut allergy."

"Why did Muldoon have it?" said Rosamund.

"He and Juniper sort of live together," said Helen. "Maybe she gave him the cake. Maybe she didn't fancy it."

Annie's worried gaze went from one friend to the other. "Was he the actual intended victim?" she whispered.

"Poisoned cake?" said Rosamund.

"Figgy? Our Figgy?" said Helen in disgusted disbelief.

"She's not exactly Juniper's number one fan," said Annie.

As one, the three women turned to look at Juniper, chatting merrily and with confidence to potential customers.

"Flipping heck," said Annie.

Chapter Thirty-Six

The shop door opened and Joanna bustled in.

"Five air fresheners bought. Pomegranate, fresh linen and summer breeze. You can decide where to put them."

"Mum!"

"Come on, now. I'm taking you to a clothes shop. You need some new blouses."

"I really don't." Rosamund turned back to Helen and Annie. "We're doing a wine and nibbles evening on Friday. Your attendance is mandatory. And we've not finished discussing that business." She made a gesture, apparently intended to encapsulate the recent news about Muldoon's death, then left.

"This is some disturbing stuff," said Helen.

Annie nodded. "Let's not jump to any conclusions yet." She looked at her grandchildren. The dragonfly game had spread out across the floor. "I need to get my little ducklings here a bit of fresh air and exercise. Otherwise you're going to have some breakages."

A couple of minutes saw all the metal ornaments back in their display basket. There was some wheedling, along with the expected demands to buy the entire collection, but Annie held strong and ignored the unconvincing tears.

She pulled out her phone and Helen saw a smile light up her face.

"Ooh, someone's had a text that's made them happy."

"It's just Tim. We're organising a bit of a get-together. Nothing significant."

Helen winked. "I think your face tells a different story."

"We'll continue this chat later."

Annie wheeled Daisy's pram outside, and the little gang headed down the street.

Helen was deep in thought about their earlier discussion when Juniper approached with a smiling older couple. "Joan and Peter here are very interested in buying one of, er, Clifford's pieces. The June twenty-four Portland Bill. I've explained that the pieces aren't for sale while the memorial retrospective is ongoing."

Smiling Peter came forward, wallet in hand. "This young lady has suggested that maybe we could put down a deposit to hold the piece."

"I suggested we might let it go for fourteen hundred pounds," said Juniper. "A deposit of seven hundred now...?"

Seven hundred pounds was more than Helen would have got for it in total, prior to Muldoon's death. She coughed.

"Yes. Yes, I think we can do that."

She put the deposit through the till, took the couple's payment, and left Juniper to jot down contact details and delivery address while she took the tea things back through to the kitchen, where Harper sat with the look of someone who'd been waiting there a while.

Helen nodded. "Hello."

Harper took the tray from Helen, put it down on the side, then seized Helen's hand and put something in it. Helen looked. It was an elegant ring, made from strands of hand-beaten iron.

"You remember that?" said Harper.

"I do. You've taken this from my nightstand."

"You don't wear it."

"I treasure it."

Harper's eyes glistened. "We've been together for ten years. Thereabouts. Ten years of commitment."

"I know."

"Three years ago, I got down on my knees and I offered you that ring."

"You were drunk at the time, I recall."

"Doesn't matter. Dutch courage. I put myself out there. I gave you my heart and I asked you..." Harper stopped, overcome for a moment by emotion. Emotions did not come quickly to Harper, not the softer, gooier, more vulnerable ones.

"You asked me to marry you," said Helen. "I remember."

"And do you remember what you said?"

"I said no."

Harper's eyes glistened. "Your exact words. Seared in my memory, they are. You said, 'I love you. I truly do. But I can't marry. Who knows where we'll be in five years' time? In ten years' time? We're just two...' Ah, I can't remember it all. Boats in the sea or feathers or something or—"

"—leaves in the wind," said Helen.

"That! Two flippin' leaves in the wind. 'I can't marry

you. I can't tie you down or let myself be tied down.' That's what you said."

Helen nodded slowly. "I said that."

"And yet here we are!" Harper's voice rose. "We *are* settled down. We own a shop. You're thinking of buying the shop next door. You're thinking of hiring staff. That's settled down in anyone's book. Yet you cling to the notion that you're some free bloody spirit!"

Helen understood Harper's anger.

"I'm sorry. I want to make a commitment to you."

"Do you?"

"I do. I love you, Harper McCoppin."

"Except you can't make a simple commitment to me. You can't publicly demonstrate that love. You can't tell the world that you're mine and I'm yours."

Helen let out a ragged breath.

"I would marry you if I could," she said.

"But you won't."

"No. I won't."

Harper crossed her arms. "Is there a reason you won't marry me?"

"Yes."

Harper waited for more, but Helen didn't know what to say.

"Are you going to tell me what it is?" demanded Harper.

"No."

"Are you already married?"

"No!"

"Is there some woman – or man – you've been keeping secret from me all these years?"

"No. Not at all."

Harper fumed silently, waiting.

"I love you," said Helen. "I will tell you that morning, noon and **night**. Isn't that enough?"

Harper **studied** her for a second. "Apparently, it's all I'm getting," she said, and stormed off.

Helen called after her. "Please don't slam the—"

The rear door slammed.

Chapter Thirty-Seven

Dougie lifted two carrier bags of shopping out of the car and looped them onto his arm as he opened the front door.

Naomi greeted him with a kiss.

"Good day?"

He nodded. "Insanely busy, but that's July."

Naomi took the groceries from him, and he followed her through to the kitchen. Tina was in there, along with all three children. Poppy and Louis were playing with bricks in the corner by Daisy's bouncy chair.

Dougie enjoyed having the extended family round. There was something life-affirming about the chaotic energy generated whenever Poppy's cousins came to stay. Every once in a while, though, he wished things could be a bit quieter.

"Tell us all about it then," said Naomi, pulling salad ingredients out of the bag and handing them to Tina, who was on washing and chopping duty.

Dougie rolled his eyes. "We had a missing child alert this

afternoon, but the little chap had followed another family along the beach and fallen asleep by their bags. All sorted after an hour, but you can imagine how frantic the parents were."

"God, yes!"

"We've had shoplifting, but that's a regular thing when everywhere's rammed with bodies. Low value items, probably kids. Traffic issues, bad parking, bad tempers. Your basic people problems. Hot weather brings out the worst."

"People, eh?"

"Oh, and Helen's asked me to get the dimensions for that missing painting in the Muldoon case. I'll get those over to her or take her over to see for herself."

"Sounds good."

Dougie nodded. "And, Tina, on that subject, we've had another update you'll want to hear."

"Yeah?" Tina turned, a bunch of spring onions in her hand.

"A fingerprint match from a cup at the Muldoon residence."

"A match from the database?"

"Yes." He looked at both Naomi and Tina. "Now, you can't share this detail, obviously. But the match was for Dante Legg."

Both Naomi and Tina put down what they were holding and stared at Dougie.

"Say that again," said Naomi.

"We've found Dante's fingerprints in Clifford Muldoon's house."

"Our Dante?" said Tina.

"Our Dante. Your father-in-law."

"Wait, so our mum's lodger has a criminal record?" Tina asked.

"He does."

"I know we can't share details with her, but I'd very much like to know what he's done. He's staying in her house, for crying out loud!"

Dougie lifted his hands. "I wouldn't get too agitated. It's from a few years ago."

"Yes?"

"He... Look, he's got form. That's all I'm saying with Naomi here."

Naomi scoffed. "Pretend I'm not here."

Dougie leaned closer to Tina and lowered his voice. Naomi was humming to herself.

"He was convicted for a burglary in London," he muttered.

"Convicted?" Tina whispered. "Guilty, then?"

He nodded. "Suspended sentence. Nothing else on the database."

"Christ on a bike, that's enough, isn't it?" Tina growled. She glanced at Naomi, who was still humming.

Dougie swallowed. He hoped he wouldn't regret telling Tina. She was on maternity leave, after all, and Dante was her father-in-law...

Tina thought for a long moment before speaking. "I don't think it would be appropriate for Mike to hear about this."

Dougie felt bad for Mike. The two of them were estranged, and Mike had made it clear that he didn't want to see Dante when he'd visited Tina and the kids. But Dante was still Mike's dad. If their roles were reversed, Dougie would want to know about this.

Tina was looking at him sternly. "I mean it, Dougie. Mike is not to hear of this. At least, not for now."

If Dante was implicated in the murder of Clifford Muldoon, there would be no way of keeping the news from Mike. But they'd cross that bridge when – and if – they came to it.

He nodded. "Yes. Of course."

"We can interview Dante tomorrow," said Tina. "I'll text Nathan and let him know that you and I will do it, yeah?"

Dougie nodded. It wasn't for him to point out that Tina wasn't supposed to be working.

He sat on one of the kitchen stools and looked over towards the children. Poppy and Louis continued to play with Lego. As usual, it seemed to be a game in which Poppy steered the rules and the scenario, making sure that Louis was able to join in, but very much on her terms.

Each of them held a tiny figurine, and they were each jigging along a pathway between half-built towers.

"Go on, Louis. You're the police and I'm the burglar," said Poppy.

Dougie wasn't sure whether this was part of an ongoing narrative, and he'd just tuned into it, or whether Poppy had only just started chattering.

He glanced up and saw that Tina and Naomi had both frozen in place, watching the children. They'd also heard Poppy's words. All three adults in the room seemed suspended for a long moment, waiting for the next part of Poppy's childish monologue.

"No! Stop it, Louis, you can't catch me, because I am your granddad Dante and I can run really fast."

It struck Dougie that he'd made the rookie parenting

error of forgetting that kids would hear and repeat any small detail, particularly if you really didn't want them to.

Naomi was staring at him, wide-eyed. Tina was looking his way as well, but Dougie didn't want to turn to see the expression on her face. He heaved a sigh, knowing he'd messed up, but lacking the words to make it better without digging further into the hole he'd already made.

He fell back on the most English of all techniques when it came to diverting attention and negotiating a crisis.

"Can I get anyone a cup of tea?"

Chapter Thirty-Eight

The evening sky glowed red over Lyme Regis. In her caravan, Figgy adjusted her laptop on the small kitchen table. A chime from the screen heralded the connection, and her therapist's face appeared.

"Hi, Figgy." Xandrea's voice was steady, soothing. "How's the world looking from your little corner of England?"

England had three syllables – 'In-ger-land'.

Figgy shrugged, glancing towards the curtains. "Same as always. The tide comes and goes and the caravan's still standing."

"Sounds like things are holding steady. And how are you feeling?"

She brushed her fingers along the edge of the table top. "I guess... fine. Not great, not awful. Somewhere in the middle."

"A very human place to be," Xandrea said with a nod. "So, where are we at with the *Shipping Forecast*?"

"I forgot to listen to it earlier this week."

The therapist clapped her hands. "Wow. That is progress!"

"I know."

Figgy's granddad had died at sea many years ago, his boat capsizing during a winter storm. Her grandmother had kept on listening to the *Shipping Forecast* as if it formed some unbroken connection to him. Figgy had picked up the habit herself, though for her, it was less about comfort and more about continuity, as though she was carrying on the ritual in her grandmother's place.

"Worth celebrating, surely."

Figgy tried to smile.

"Or have we got our minds on other things?" said Xandrea.

She exhaled, tucking her hair behind her ear. "It's Cameron," she said. "And Juniper."

"Juniper." Xandrea nodded, leaning forward.

Figgy recounted the whole saga, at least those bits she hadn't already told the therapist in earlier sessions. She tried to gloss over the embarrassing parts, but she could feel Xandrea watching her closely, her gaze calm but probing.

"And then he told me I don't believe in myself," Figgy finished. "Which is fair, I suppose. I don't believe in myself enough, and maybe I don't believe in what I have to offer, either."

Xandrea nodded. "Go on."

Figgy looked around the caravan. The old-fashioned linoleum floor, the faded wallpaper above the sink, the sagging cushions on the bench seat. "I mean, it's not like I have much to offer, is it? Juniper's got this fancy studio with art hanging everywhere. And me, I've got this... this. You can see it. You can see what kind of place I live in."

Xandrea's brow furrowed. "Do you think Cameron values you for the space you live in, or for who you are?"

Figgy gave a dismissive wave. "I know, I know, it's me he likes."

"Do you, though?"

"He's said it, and I believe him. Mostly. But... Maybe I could become more. You know?"

Xandrea sat back slightly. "When you say 'become more,' what does that mean to you?"

"Well..." Figgy glanced at the cupboard doors, imagining them painted in a clean, bright colour. "Maybe it's time for a change. You said I'm always growing. Developing. Maybe I could start with the caravan. Like, give it a bit of a makeover. New curtains, maybe. Fresh paint."

Xandrea smiled, but there was concern in her eyes. "Figgy, growth doesn't have to mean change in a material sense. When I said you're always becoming, I meant you're evolving emotionally and mentally. You're learning how to trust, how to navigate relationships, how to feel confident in yourself."

"Oh, I know," said Figgy quickly, her mind racing ahead. "But wouldn't it help to show that? Like, if I'm becoming a better version of myself, shouldn't my surroundings reflect that? I mean, I bet Cameron would notice. He said how cool Juniper's place is – colourful this, modern that. Whatever. And this caravan..." She gestured broadly. "Wherever cool lives, this is at the far end of that street."

Xandrea leaned forward, her tone calm but firmer now. "Figgy, do you really think renovating your caravan will make you feel better about yourself?"

"Er, yes."

"Or is this another way of trying to measure up to someone else's standards?"

Figgy paused. Her gaze flicked to the corner of the room, where the faded curtains pooled against the floor.

"I think it would help," she said. "Not just for Cameron, but for me, too. I mean, who wouldn't feel better waking up in a nice, bright space instead of... this?"

"Figgy," Xandrea said gently, "I want to make sure we're not mixing up external changes with internal growth. Renovating your caravan might be a fun project, but—"

"Exactly! This place could use some love."

Xandrea hesitated. "Listen, it's important to ask yourself why you want to make these changes. Is it because you think Cameron will like you more, or because you think it will genuinely make you happier?"

"Yes. Them. Those things. Both of them."

Xandrea opened her mouth but seemed to decide against pushing the point. Instead, she said, "If it's something you want to do for yourself, then I think it's worth exploring. Just remember, Figgy, that real growth comes from within, not from paint or curtains."

"I know that," Figgy said with a nod. But even as the call wound down, her mind was already spinning with ideas. She could get fabric swatches online, maybe ask Helen for advice on upholstery. Rosamund might know someone who could help with the DIY stuff. She'd repaint the cupboards, replace the worn-out cushions, and maybe even add some fairy lights.

If she was going to make improvements, she might need to check out the competition, see exactly what kind of 'cool' interior design she was up against.

Chapter Thirty-Nine

Tina chatted to her husband on the phone as she walked into town from Naomi's. She'd wanted to stretch her legs and have a conversation. Mike might be fifty miles away, trying to repair his DIY catastrophe so Tina and the children could return, but these phone calls were as close to private time with him as she was getting.

"How's it going?" she asked.

"Not bad. I had a go at some plastering."

Tina stopped in her tracks. "You what?"

The situation with their house had been made worse by Mike's attempts at DIY. They'd agreed that the time had come to leave things to the professionals. Surely he wasn't trying to cut corners at this late stage?

"Yeah, I got a tube of that Primula cheese, and I plastered it right across some crackers. Best snack ever."

"Oh, you idiot! You had me worried."

They both laughed.

"My dad still acting like a decent grandparent, is he?"

The question was casual, but Tina could hear the tension in his voice.

"He seems smitten with the kids. I mean, who wouldn't be, eh?"

Mike grunted. "Yeah. They are adorable. How's the case?"

Tina didn't want to mention Dante's fingerprints. Not yet. "Coming along. We know how Clifford was killed now. We just need a whole bunch of other stuff."

"Like a suspect, a motive, that sort of thing?"

"Yes, exactly." Tina sighed.

She was in the town centre now, wondering whether to get a cup of tea or a cold drink from somewhere. She scanned Broad Street, considering the possibilities. Then she spotted Dante, coming out of Tesco.

"Hey, I'd better go," she said to Mike. "Speak later."

"Love you."

"Love you."

She moved towards her father-in-law.

"Dante," said Tina. "How are things?"

He held up the Twix he'd just bought. "Sugar boost time. Always had a sweet tooth, me."

"Yeah? Not seen that with Mike. I guess it's not in the blood."

Dante was in the middle of taking another bite, but at the mention of Mike's name, his hand drifted from his mouth.

"It's good to see you exploring the town," Tina said. "Mum says you walk a fair bit."

"It's good exercise, and in a beautiful place like this, it's no chore." Dante spread his arms wide.

"Who doesn't like being by the sea, eh? Get up on the Cobb?"

"Of course. I don't think you can claim to have been to Lyme Regis if you haven't taken a walk along the Cobb."

"That is true. I bet you came across Clifford Muldoon, didn't you? He seemed like someone who'd like to chat."

"Think I might have seen him. Just from a distance, like."

"Not met him, then?"

"No."

Tina nodded, as if that was understandable.

"Any chance I might get to see him while I'm around?"

"Sorry?"

"Mike, I mean." Dante looked older as he spoke. Lines etched anxiety across his face.

"No, Dante." She had to be completely clear on this. She'd promised Mike she would be. She turned to face him. "Mike doesn't want to see you."

Dante gave a small nod. "Yeah. Get that." He looked at Tina. "You could talk to him?"

Tina raised her eyebrows. "Talk to him? Am I going to fix all the stuff that's between the two of you by *talking* to him? Am I going to mend his broken childhood?"

Dante made a flapping gesture with his arms. His face was contorted with an ugly mix of raw emotion. "Nah. Nah. His childhood. It wasn't—"

"Don't you dare try to say it wasn't broken, Dante." Tina's voice was low and hard. "Mike's mum was an amazing woman, but she couldn't fix a thing like his dad abandoning him. I'm sorry you have to hear this from me, but you do need to hear it. Mike won't see you because he still feels the pain. Even now."

Dante looked at her, his eyes brimming. He opened his mouth, closed it again, and then turned to walk away, dropping his Twix onto the pavement as he went.

Chapter Forty

Annie felt it was a fine balancing act, preparing her home for Tim's arrival. This evening was another step on that careful path towards... what should she call it? Romance? A special friendship? Companionship? Whatever it was, this evening was the next piece in the puzzle.

On the other hand, Tim was ostensibly coming over to prepare the tombola prizes for Lifeboat Week fundraising.

So, it was a date but not a date.

Because it was a date, she'd got a couple of bottles of fizz in. But, because it wasn't a date, they were in the fridge, out of sight. Because it was a date, she was wearing a nice top. But, because it wasn't a date, she'd coupled it with her comfy jeans. Because it wasn't a date, she'd laid out potential prizes, presentation baskets and cellophane wrapping paper on the table. But, because it was a date, she'd dimmed the lights in the dining room and put on some gentle music.

Most importantly of all, she had sent Dante Legg out a couple of hours ago. If there was to be a bit of Annie and Tim Time – wherever that might lead – then a chatty granddad with no social filter hanging around the house would be the mother of all obstacles. She'd sent him round to Tina's to see the grandchildren and suggested he might want to eat out that night at one of the town's many fine restaurants. She'd even pressed twenty quid into his hand and, with a wink, told him to enjoy his evening out on her.

The doorbell rang. She glanced at the clock. It was ten to seven. Tim was a bit early.

She checked her appearance in the mirror in the hallway, told herself that Tim probably didn't care one bit what she looked like, and opened the door.

"Lost my keys," said Dante, and walked in.

Annie stepped back.

"I thought you were going out."

"No one wants me."

"What do you mean?" There was a slur in his voice and a stagger in his step. He'd been drinking. "Couldn't you find anywhere to eat?"

"No one wants me," he repeated with a growl.

"Don't you take that tone with me, Dante."

He looked instantly contrite. Childlike.

"You don't want me," he said, miserably.

Annie didn't want him. She certainly did not want him right now. She peered out of the door to see if Tim might be coming up the path.

"Of course we want you," she lied. "Who doesn't want you?"

"My boy, for one!" He headed through to the kitchen.

"Mike? Is that true?" It probably was true.

"Mike hasn't forgiven me for... for..." Dante started opening cupboards. "I didn't run out on them, you know!"

"No?"

188

She went into the kitchen. Dante was inspecting the interior of the fridge.

"He has so much anger, you know?" he said, fists clenched. "And Tina's made it clear, that's the situation. Mike isn't going to come here while I'm here."

He took out a box of eggs and sniffed a pack of ham.

"What are you doing?" asked Annie.

"I'm just trying to be a good granddad, you know? Just trying to..." He made a wild pumping motion. "Trying to reconnect."

"No. I meant, what are you actually doing, right now?"

He looked at the eggs and ham and seemed surprised to find them in his hands. How much had he managed to drink since leaving the house?

"Making dinner?" he suggested.

"You're making yourself some dinner?"

"Nobody wants me."

"You said."

"I've been a solitary... what are those things? I want to say tortoise. Do I mean tortoise? Are they solitary?"

"Could be," said Annie.

"I've always had to fend for myself. It's not easy, you know. People look at me. I'm a man. They look at me and they have expectations. And I don't always meet them, so I've had to fend for myself."

Annie wasn't sure what he was going on about. She wasn't sure it was a good idea for this rambling, incoherent man to make himself dinner, either.

He seemed to read her expression. "I know what I'm doing. Cooked for fifty years, I have. I won't cause a gas explosion."

"It's an electric hob, so that'd be unlikely," she agreed.

189

The doorbell rang again.

"Promise me you'll keep the noise down and not hurt yourself on the hob," she said.

"It's electric," said Dante.

"It is." She closed the kitchen door and went to answer the doorbell. This time it was Tim.

"Ah-ha! It is you!" she said.

"Expecting someone else?" Tim had a pull-along trolley stacked high with potential tombola prizes.

"An unexpected caller."

There came some scat singing from the kitchen, warbling, yet tuneful in its own way. She held up a finger to indicate the unexpected caller.

"Oh. I thought you said your lodger was going out for the evening," said Tim.

"I thought he was, too. Come in, come in."

Chapter Forty-One

"Did you haul that lot up from the town by yourself?" Annie asked Tim.

"Bit of exercise never hurt no one."

With much manoeuvring over the doorstep, the trolley made it inside, and the two of them wheeled it into the dining room.

Tim surveyed the scene. "Blimey." His eyes scanned the neatly laid-out prizes, baskets, and rolls of cellophane. "You're better organised than I thought."

Annie nodded. "We've got a lot to get through, haven't we? And I didn't want us tripping over each other."

She busied herself arranging some of the smaller prizes – a bottle of bubble bath here, a box of chocolates there – into a basket. Tim unpacked his own haul with care: a bottle of wine, some novelty socks, and a small, boxed game, among other odds and ends.

"I'm not sure if these are tombola gold or charity shop rejects," he said, holding up a jar of pickled onions.

"Somebody will want them. It's all part of the charm."

The sound of Dante's singing grew louder, a strange mix of jazz scatting and what might have been a sea shanty. Tim raised an eyebrow.

"Lively chap, isn't he?"

"Lively is one word for it." Annie tied a neat bow on her first completed basket.

"You two always keep things this... entertaining?"

"Only when you're here."

Annie had put together several groups of prizes. Tim looked at them with a questioning eye.

"Everything all right?" she asked.

"Just thinking."

"Yes?"

"Are you trying to create groups of prizes where each group looks of approximately equal value?"

"I was aiming for a sort of story with each basket. Like a picture, every basket should tell a story."

"Oh?" he said. "Do tell."

She presented one basket. "Here we have bath bombs, a flannel and a scented candle."

"Yes?"

"This is clearly a prize for a person who owns a bath. Not a given in this day and age. And this person – it's probably a mum, isn't it? – fancies relaxing in the bath with a candle burning nearby. Bit of atmosphere. Just a bit of 'me' time."

"I see. That is indeed a story. And this one?" he asked.

Annie gestured over the basket. "Pickled onions, socks and a board game. This is the man package."

"Oh, is it now?"

"Or a woman. But definitely someone who could do with

new socks, appreciates a tart savoury snack, and could enjoy this 'Enchanted Forest' escape room game."

"That sounds like a whole lot of fun right there."

"Indeed." She put her elbows on the table and leaned closer. "What would you have in your perfect prize basket?"

"Me?"

"You're the only other person here."

He hummed. "Can always appreciate a new pair of socks. Good cotton ones, mind. A bottle of something nice to drink always goes down well."

"And?"

"And..." He pulled a face. "I don't know. I've never been one for things, really."

"Things."

"Things. Stuff. Materialistic stuff. Look at me. I'm an old crusty man who lives in a pokey house and spends his days keeping the lifeboat station and the area around it neat and tidy. I don't need stuff."

"Less of the old. You're the same age as me, Mr Cromwell."

He gave her a warm look. "You know what I mean. It's people, not things, that make life worth living. Relationships."

She nodded. "Bit hard to wrap up relationships and raffle them off in a tombola."

"I never claimed to be easy."

"But," she said, getting up, "I can get us a bottle of something nice to drink."

As she moved across the room, the kitchen door opened and Dante came through. He had an open bottle of fizzy plonk in one hand and a mug in the other.

"Ah! We're in here!" he said.

"We *did* have something nice to drink," Annie said to Tim.

Dante looked at the bottle and topped up his mug.

"I thought you were making dinner," Annie said.

"Really? What were we having?"

Annie turned to Tim. "I do apologise. Dante is a little worse for wear."

"Not a problem."

She tried to steer Dante away. "Tim and I were having an evening together. We've got packages to wrap up for the tombola."

"No one wants me," said Dante.

"No one wants him," Annie explained to Tim. "I'll get rid of him."

"Please. Don't worry on my account."

She wanted Dante out. This was going to be a pleasant and moderately special evening with Tim. Didn't he want that, too?

Dante drank from his mug and pulled a face.

"Maybe tea is what we need," said Tim.

"Tea?" said Dante.

Tim reached through the pile of prizes. "And some golden crunch cream biscuits?"

Annie saw the hesitation in Dante, and the tiredness, too.

"I'll put the kettle on," she said, taking the mug and bottle from Dante.

In the kitchen, she expected to find smashed eggs on the floor, maybe a slice of ham stuck to the wall, but Dante hadn't even got that far in his drunken culinary exploits.

"My boy doesn't want me," she heard Dante moan from the next room. Tim made soft comforting sounds in response.

Annie made a pot of tea in the large teapot she'd bought from Chapman's Pottery by the mill. She carried the teapot, three mugs, a jug of milk and sugar bowl into the dining room. Dante was much quieter now, and it was Tim doing the talking.

"He was only eight years old," he said. "The mother of a school friend was meant to be watching them but..." Tim shook his head. "He drowned. That was how it happened. No one even saw it. Well, almost no one."

"Man. Oh, man," said Dante in a low, weary voice. "I'm so sorry."

"Oh, long time gone now," said Tim. "Course, it still hurts. Every single day."

"It does. It does."

"But I can't spend my life thinking about that day. We can't be people just filled with regrets, can we? No. That kind of negativity would kill us."

"But it hurts," said Dante.

"We can't spend our lives worrying about our past mistakes or wishing ill on those who wronged us. That's no life. We have to take those bad memories, cut them out if we can. Burn them out if we can."

"I can't do that."

"You can always try." Tim looked up. He smiled at Annie, a sad smile. "And look. There's tea. How many sugars, Dante?"

"Three."

Annie put the things down and poured.

"I reckon," said Tim, slowly, "that we might all enjoy a cup of tea and then Dante here might fancy a bit of a lie down."

Dante was struggling with the packet of biscuits, and didn't seem to hear.

Tim chuckled as he caught Annie's eye. "Wait for the kids to go to bed and then pick up where we left off, eh?"

Annie liked the sound of that.

Chapter Forty-Two

For much of the week, Figgy had been thinking about embracing change. Choosing to adapt to one's circumstances was like charting a course through turbulent seas. It was an analogy that brought her granddad to mind, and she smiled at the notion that, like him, she was a trawlerperson, steering the good ship Figgy. She could get all seasick and petulant, or she could ride those waves and sail away to a location of her choosing. She was filled with a restless energy at the idea. She knew that was what she wanted to do, but where should she start?

She decided to start after her morning swim on Friday.

After coffees and a good natter, everyone prepared to leave, to carry on with their days.

Rosamund reminded them all that it was wine and nibbles evening at her house that night. Her mother, Joanna, seemed oblivious to the notion that the event had been invented purely to create a social buffer between the two of them for just one evening.

Rosamund and her mum headed off towards home.

Juniper accompanied Helen in the direction of the gallery. Figgy sidled over to Annie.

"Annie, can I ask for your help with something?"

"Course you can, Figgy love."

Figgy cast around for a way to lead into the idea, but she couldn't see one.

"What is it?"

"I need someone to help me break into Juniper's place, so I can see how she's decorated it."

Annie pressed her lips together.

"You might need to run that by me again, Figgeroni. It sounded like you wanted to break into Juniper's place."

"I do."

"Because...?"

"I want to update my caravan, and I need some inspiration."

Annie opened and closed her mouth several times before she finally replied.

"At the risk of being really dull, had you thought of just asking Juniper?"

Figgy had expected the question. "I did think of asking, but I don't want to."

Annie didn't argue. She looked up at the sky, seeking inspiration.

"Fair enough."

Figgy blinked. "Really? You heard what I asked?"

"I did. And it's quite mad."

"And yet...?"

Annie waggled her eyebrows. "Shall we go now? Strike while the iron's hot, and more importantly, while Juniper's at the gallery."

And that was that. Annie and Figgy walked up to Silver Street.

"We shouldn't take long," said Figgy. "I just want to see for myself what Cameron liked about Juniper's décor."

Figgy caught Annie's sideways glance. "And this is a good idea because...?"

"I want to embrace change in my life. It's a healthy, healing thing to do."

"Riiiight?"

"And in order to do that, I need to be in possession of all the relevant facts," said Figgy.

"And the relevant facts includes what Juniper's place looks like?" Annie asked.

"Yes." Figgy heard the defensiveness in her own voice. "Obviously, I don't want to copy what she's done."

"Obviously."

Figgy clamped her lips shut. Every time she said something, she sounded less sure of her motivations.

"Right, let's go and see, shall we?" said Annie, as they walked up to Clifford's impressively large home, and down the side into the garden.

"Have the police finished here now?" whispered Figgy.

"I believe so," said Annie. "Certainly hope so. Actually, that gives us a decent excuse for mooching around. I can say I'm looking for Tina."

"Would anyone believe that?"

They were now approaching the studio, which nestled at the bottom of the long garden behind an old drooping tree. Figgy could see why Cameron might draw comparisons between the studio and Figgy's caravan. They were about the same size.

She went straight to a window and tried to peer inside. "I can't see much."

"Let's go in then, shall we?" said Annie.

"How will we... oh!" Figgy saw that Annie had the door open.

"Not locked."

"Really?"

Annie shrugged. "Maybe she forgot to lock it. Maybe Australians don't lock their doors. Whatever."

The two of them went inside.

Figgy took a moment to absorb her surroundings. "Is there a name for this kind of style?" she asked Annie.

One end of the room was a cosy living space, with the other dedicated to art, easels and materials, all on display. Somehow the two portions of the room blended seamlessly, with riotous colour somehow performing the trickery of making it look intentional.

Annie shrugged, still gazing at the room. "I have no idea. I can see all of the colours and all of the patterns. Is it a style, or is it just everything? I feel as if someone was given a catalogue of choices, and they slapped their thigh and declared that they would take them all. And yet somehow, it works..." Annie stood shaking her head, looking round in confusion.

Figgy pondered the room. "It's chaotic and fun. I do like it, although I'm not sure I understand it."

There were so many things adding colour to the room that it was hard to know where to start.

"We need to find labels, so I can see where it came from," said Figgy. She lifted the edge of a rug, searching for a tag.

"I thought you didn't want to copy what she's done?" Annie said.

"Oh no, I probably won't do that," said Figgy. "Probably."

"Maybe you need to absorb what's here in a more general way," said Annie.

"How can I do that?" Figgy asked. "There's too much."

She knelt down by a chair, wondering if there might be a label underneath it.

"Oh no!" She realised she had knelt on a paintbrush. Where had that come from?

"Oh lord, Figgy. We need to get that stain off the floor."

"And my trousers!" She tutted. "It would have to be black, wouldn't it?"

"You'll be taking your trousers with you. You can deal with them later. We can't leave the place like this, though. I've got a tissue for the floor."

Annie swooped in and rubbed at the floor with a tissue. Fortunately, the paint had missed the rug.

"That looks better," said Figgy. She put the brush on a nearby easel, from where she must have knocked it off. There was an open tube of the same paint next to it. Oil paint.

"Do oil paint stains come out easily?" she asked.

"I rarely dabble in oils," said Annie.

Figgy decided she'd seen enough. There was no doubt that Juniper's place had a unique style, and she could see why Cameron had mentioned it. But she definitely needed to leave before she made any more mess.

She and Annie shut the door behind them as they left.

"You're right about the bright colours," said Figgy as they walked swiftly down the road. "I've been living with brown and beige for too long. It's time to embrace change."

"And, just checking, Figgy, you do mean in decoration? Not going to make a habit of breaking into people's homes?"

"You hardly protested," Figgy pointed out.

"True," agreed Annie. "But I'm easily led."

Chapter Forty-Three

When she returned home in the late morning, Annie found a hungover Dante.

He sat at the little kitchen table, head resting on his hands as he stared into a cup of black coffee.

"Where you been?"

"Out and about. A bit of swimming. A bit of snooping." She put a hand on his shoulder. "How we feeling?"

"Full of remorse." His voice was croaky.

"A night of drinking will do that to you."

"A lifetime of bad choices."

"Oh, we can't go around thinking like that."

"It's true. I was a terrible dad to Mike."

"There's no rulebook for parenting. We all have to learn."

"Be there. That's rule number one, isn't it? But I couldn't even manage that." He moved the handle of his cup but didn't pick it up. "I've always had big plans."

"I can imagine."

"The seventies, eighties. I was always working, always doing music. Moody Blues, The Specials, the man Bowie.

I've worked across the board. Always doing a bit of buying and selling and jobs on the side to actually make ends meet. Ran a stall in Camden Market for a time." His face twisted. "But it's not easy."

"Is that so?"

"Some of us are never given a chance, and..." He shook his head. "We use that as an excuse for all the bad decisions we make from then on."

Annie brightened. "If I can steer this conversation in a more practical direction, you and I are going to be helpful people this evening."

"We are?"

"We're going to Rosamund's for wine and nibbles."

He chuckled weakly. "Do I look like a wine and nibbles kind of guy?"

"I think Mr Dante Legg can move smoothly in any social situation. Rosamund's got her mum staying with her—"

"A nice woman."

"If you say so – and I think she's more than a little tired of handling her house guest by herself. If you can imagine such a thing. So, we're going over to cheer her up and create a little social buffer."

"I don't know, Annie." He sighed. "I'm kind of done in, today."

"Nonsense! Straighten yourself up, Dante! Drink your coffee. Get some rest. And tonight, we will sparkle."

Annie didn't know if her forthright words had shocked Dante from his self-pitying funk or if – more likely – he had always been the sort of man who could turn from remorseful drunk at dawn to party animal at dusk. But whatever the reason, by the time evening came round, Dante was ready in the hallway in a crisp white suit, a thin tie and pork pie hat with a colourful hat band.

The two of them walked over to Rosamund's house across the hill.

"Oh, good," said Rosamund, glass of Cava in hand, as she ushered them in. "The more the merrier." She spotted the LPs under Dante's arm. "Trying to sneak some back?"

"Some party tunes, fair Rosamund."

Dante strutted into the lounge and loudly greeted the other guests.

"And how are things with Mother?" enquired Annie.

"Hmmm." Rosamund tilted her head, the elegant earrings she was wearing swinging with the movement. "Well, we've cleaned my already clean house. Revamped my wardrobe so I can dress like a slightly disreputable version of my own mother. And, I think – God help me – my mum's trying to set up a Tinder dating account on my behalf."

"Wow."

"Apparently, the best thing for me is to 'get onto a new horse'."

"And was your husband a horse?"

Rosamund's mouth twisted into a childish smile. "David was many things. A horse was not one of them."

Soon, Annie had a glass of wine in hand and was mingling with the others. Many of the early morning swimmers were there. Sally and Peg were sitting on the sofa, side by side, one with a tall cocktail, the other with what appeared to be a small glass of sherry. Helen was holding forth with some of Rosamund's neighbours about the importance of small businesses to the town. Helen's girlfriend, Harper, was talking in a quiet corner with Figgy, it looked like a little introverts' club.

Annie was impressed that Figgy was even here. When the young woman had joined the swimmers several months back, she'd been driven by the motivation to get out of her caravan more. She had been quite open regarding her fear of both the sea swimming and the social aspect of the group. And now here she was, a few months later, willingly coming to a party.

Dante was reintroducing himself to Rosamund's mum. Annie could see him taking Joanna's hand and gently kissing the back of it.

Annie wasn't sure how Dante managed it, because such a move should have seemed both weird and creepy and, coming from any other man, it almost certainly would have been. But he made it look gentlemanly, almost chivalrous. He spun an LP in his hands and gestured to the stereo.

Annie drifted over to Figgy and Harper.

"It wouldn't be much of a bother," Harper was saying. "You literally saw off the roof, put in some RSJs as support, lift the whole thing up, put the roof back on, and fill in the upper floor."

"Oh, I see," said Figgy.

"What are you talking about?" asked Annie.

"Double-decker caravan," said Harper.

Figgy was nodding. "I suggested I might want to make some renovations."

"Double-decker caravan," Harper repeated.

Annie gave the concept some thought. "And if you've ripped the roof off and put it on – what is that, some sort of steel girder stilts? – then aren't you going to need walls?"

"Options," said Harper, putting her beer down on a French polished table to explain. "Corrugated iron. Very brutal, very chic. My choice, wrap the whole thing in a sheet of moulded clear acrylic. A caravan with a three-sixty panoramic upstairs window."

"So people could see in?" said Figgy.

Harper shrugged. "Curtains."

There was a crackle, a faint burst of harmonica, and then the staccato drum intro to a song by The Specials. Dante clicked his fingers and single-handedly tried to get the party dancing vibe going. The way some of Rosamund's neighbours looked at him, there seemed to be a good chance he was actually going to succeed.

Annie saw a text on her phone. It was Tina.

Where's Dante?

She sent a reply, explaining that he was with her at Rosamund's. She had no clue as to why Tina might suddenly have an interest in her father-in-law's location.

As Annie put her phone away, she saw Joanna approaching, wine glass in hand.

"Good evening, ladies," she said.

"Evening to yourself," said Harper.

"Thought you'd be with my grandson," Joanna said to Figgy.

"He's watching a livestream at his friend Joel's house."

"A livestream, I see. You young hip Gen Z types. It's a whole new language, isn't it?"

"I struggle to keep up, too, if it helps," said Annie.

"Well, it's so much more acceptable in this rural setting," smiled Joanna. "But I do like to think of myself as urban and up to date."

"Never seen myself as particularly rural," said Annie, thoughtfully.

"Feral, more like," said Harper. Annie nodded in agreement.

"Back in my day..." said Joanna, then caught herself and laughed. "Back in my day? Dear me. It's like I've put myself out to pasture already. In decades past, we were in much more of a hurry to settle down. Get married, have children."

"Some people don't want to get married," said Harper. Annie noticed her glancing sharply at Helen.

"And having children's not for everyone," Annie pointed out.

"Oh, but children are a gift," said Joanna.

Annie agreed wholeheartedly, but felt compelled to say, "And an expensive one at that."

"I can't even imagine how people afford to look after them," said Figgy.

"Oh, true, true," said Joanna. "If I had my time again..." She glanced towards Rosamund. "I used to have a fine figure."

Annie looked at Joanna, who was as slender a seventy-something year old as one might expect to meet. She said nothing.

"But what were we talking about?" asked Joanna.

"Double-decker caravans," said Harper.

"Figgy is thinking of doing some light home renovations," explained Annie.

"Of course. You're a home owner," said Joanna. "At your age that's very impressive. What are you going to do?"

"Oh, I don't know," said Figgy. "Paint a bit. Change things. Bright block colours. Maybe something a bit more artistic and..." She shrugged. "Avant-garde."

"A double-decker caravan is avant-garde," said Harper.

There was a knock at the front door, followed by a ring of the bell. It was quite insistent. Rosamund went to answer it.

"I don't think we're going to be having double-decker

caravans," Annie pointed out. "There's the planning permission, for one. You can't just go messing about with caravans."

"Well, you must let me come and help!" said Joanna, putting an excited hand on Figgy's wrist. "I used to help John Stefanidis pick out fabric swatches."

Annie looked at Figgy. Clearly Figgy had no idea who John Stefanidis was, either.

"I might just get some paints..." said Figgy.

"You must let me come round, and we'll look at it together," insisted Joanna.

Rosamund came back into the room. With her were Dougie and Tina. Dougie had his police uniform on. Tina met Annie's eyes, her expression pained, and then she looked away.

Rosamund crossed to Dante, who had got one of the neighbours dancing. It took Dante a moment to realise his attention was required. He looked round in confusion. Tina inclined her head to indicate he should come outside.

"Excuse me," said Annie, passing her drink to Figgy. She followed Dante out into the hallway.

"What's going on?"

"We need to talk to Dante," said Tina.

Annie saw the police car out on the driveway and the stiff attitudes of her daughter and son-in-law.

"What? What's he done?"

Dante took her hands in his. "Don't worry, Annie. A man gets used to this. I'll be back before the party's over, I'm sure."

Given the look on Tina's face, Annie wasn't so confident.

Chapter Forty-Four

Tina had mixed feelings about interviewing Dante Legg. It was a collision between her personal life and her professional life that bordered on the uncomfortable. She hadn't mentioned to Mike that Dante was a person of interest in Clifford Muldoon's murder. It would have been both inappropriate and unhelpful.

DS Strunk had insisted that she couldn't interview Dante, or anyone else. So Dougie would be leading. But she had managed to get the DS's approval to be an observer. She just had to remember to keep her mouth shut.

Tina carried three cups of tea into the police station interview room.

"Here we go. Over to you, Dougie."

She sat back but kept her eyes on Dante.

"Thanks for agreeing to talk to us, Dante," said Dougie. "We're recording this conversation, just so you know."

Dante tipped his hat to the recording device.

"Am I under arrest?"

"Not at all, no. You're free to go at any time, but we have

cautioned you, as you'll recall, and we'd be very grateful if you'd answer a few questions."

"Delighted to help." Dante smiled. "Anything at all for family."

Tina tried not to react to the jibe. Surely Dante knew she'd be on edge?

"So, Dante, can you please tell me if you knew Clifford Muldoon, the artist?" asked Dougie.

"The dead guy?"

"Yes."

Dante gave a tight smile. "You know I'm new in town, right? I don't really know anyone here."

"Can you tell us if you ever met the deceased?"

"You asked me that before." Dante turned to Tina. "And, like I told you, I didn't meet him."

Dougie continued. "You saw him, though. On the Cobb."

"Course I did."

"How many times?"

"How many times what?"

"How many times did you see him there on the Cobb?"

Dante threw his hands in the air. "Man, I don't know. I go for a walk most days. Not always the same walk. Maybe I saw him three, four times."

"Walked past him? Is that all?"

"Yes."

"Would it surprise you to learn that your fingerprints were discovered on an item in Clifford's possession?" Dougie asked.

"Ahh." Dante leaned back in his chair. "My fingerprints."

Tina studied Dante's reaction. He had an excellent poker face, but he clearly hadn't been expecting that.

Dougie said nothing.

"What was it you found my fingerprints on?" Dante asked eventually.

Dougie met Tina's eye, and she gave a small nod.

"It was a cup," he said.

"Ah. Little plastic cup. I remember now. He dropped it one time when I was walking by. I picked it up and handed it to him."

Dougie waited for a moment more, but Dante remained silent.

"What were you doing there on the Cobb?" Dougie asked at last.

"Going for a walk. I said that already."

"Can you tell us what time it was?"

Dante pulled a face. "I don't remember. Maybe late morning?"

"And was there a conversation between the two of you?" Dougie asked.

"Let me think. If there was a conversation, it would have been something like I said, 'here you go' and he said, 'thank you'. Not a big deal at all."

"I see. Was that last Saturday?"

Dante frowned and shook his head. "Don't think so, no. I reckon it was two or three days before that."

"Which was it? Two or three days? We need to be sure of the date."

"Two." Dante shook his head again. "Two days before."

Dougie wrote in his notepad. "And was there any other interaction between the two of you at all?"

Dante shook his head. "We barely spoke, like I said."

"Think hard, please. Now we know that cup incident

211

slipped your mind, it's important that you remember anything else."

Dante stared at the ceiling, making a show of thinking hard. "The cup thing. That was the only time we spoke."

"Thank you, Dante."

Dougie turned to Tina. "Do you have anything you'd like to ask?"

She shook her head. "No, I think that's everything."

Dante smiled at the two of them. "Does that mean I can go now?"

"Unless you have anything further that you'd like to add?" Dougie said.

"There is one thing. A question."

"Ask away," replied Dougie. "Obviously, if it relates to the case, we might not be at liberty to share information."

"Obviously."

"So, what's your question, Dante?"

"My fingerprints are on file because of my old burglary conviction." Dante turned his gaze to Tina, suddenly stony and challenging. "Will you be telling my son about all of this?"

Tina felt colour rising in her cheeks. The question, while it felt unfair, was reasonable.

"That depends," she said. "He's in a different team, so there's no need to specifically tell him. But we do work closely across the two teams, so..." She licked her lips. "It's likely that he'll find out eventually, yes."

Chapter Forty-Five

"And that's all I know." Annie downed the last of her morning coffee.

Even this early, the sun blazed down. She twitched her dry robe aside to catch some sun on her legs.

"So, basically, you don't actually know anything," said Rosamund.

Annie shrugged. "The police wanted to talk to Dante about something to do with Clifford's death or the burglary or some such. Dante came in late, face like a wet weekend. He wouldn't say anything, except that the police were dredging up things from the past."

"Then perhaps we shouldn't speculate," said Helen. "People have pasts and deserve to be treated with respect."

Annie grunted. "You're as nosey as the rest of us, Helen Cruickshank. Don't pretend otherwise. I'm sure if you had some titbit about this funny business you'd be tantalising us with it straight away."

Helen's grunt was even more pointed than Annie's. "Actually, I do have a little titbit."

"What?" said Figgy.

"I've worked out which of Clifford's paintings is missing from his house."

"How'd you do that?"

"It's a good piece of detective work," said Juniper, towelling off her legs.

Helen nodded. "I whittled down the list of paintings of his that were unaccounted for, focusing on his more popular period, then asked the police to compare the sizes of those missing ones with the space in the house it was stolen from. Which they did."

"And?"

"It was a piece from the mid-nineties. Lyme Regis Bay, eighth of January nineteen-ninety-four. I've got the details on my little spreadsheet at the shop."

"And?" said Annie.

"And what?"

"And how much is it worth?"

Helen pulled a face. "So vulgar. Art is about more than its crude value."

Annie looked at her. "Obviously, art is about more than that, but apart from saying it's a pretty picture, what most of us want to know is how much it's worth. You know that's pretty much the only reason people watch *Antiques Roadshow* and *Flog It*."

Helen harrumphed.

"Given the period of the painting and the price similar pieces went for," Helen tilted her head, "it would be in the ten to twenty thousand pound price range."

Rosamund whistled.

"All depends on the buyer and the mood of the market," added Helen. "Obviously."

"A nice morning's work for any thief," said Annie.

Figgy was frowning.

"What is it, Figgaroon?" asked Annie.

"How big was the painting?"

"I've got the details at the shop," said Helen.

"But roughly. How big?"

Helen held out her hands in a square.

"Not that big, then," said Figgy. "And were there other paintings like it elsewhere in the house?"

"There were," said Helen. "PC Anderson gave me a list."

"He had them everywhere," added Juniper.

"So," said Figgy, "if they were that size and they were all worth that amount... OK, some of them were worth that amount, why didn't the thief take two of them? Or five? Or ten?"

"Ten would have been hard to carry," said Helen.

"But two would have been as easy as one."

"She's not wrong," said Rosamund. "The thief took only one painting. Bit odd, isn't it?"

"Maybe they really liked that one," suggested Juniper.

"Maybe they should be looking for someone who's doing a bit of home refurbishment," said Annie, giving Figgy a nudge.

"I didn't steal any pictures of Lyme Regis," said Figgy. "There's enough in the caravan as it is."

"Ah, yes," said Rosamund, "my mother is very keen to come and help you with your decorating, Figgy."

"Is she?"

"She mentioned it last night, didn't she?"

"I didn't think she was actually going to come over, you know, to my actual home, and actually do things."

Rosamund smiled sweetly. "I think it would be lovely for her to take up a little project while she's here."

"You mean get her out of your house and into mine," said Figgy.

Rosamund maintained the sweet smile.

While Figgy tried to explain that she really didn't need Rosamund's mum's help, Juniper tied her towel at her waist and sidled round to Helen. She spoke in a low voice, but loud enough for Annie to hear.

"Speaking of selling art, I wonder if you would consider putting a couple of pieces of mine on sale in the gallery."

"Really?" said Helen.

"I think they might be popular, and I could do with the money."

"Honestly, dear," said Helen. "I'm quite cluttered as it is. The Muldoons are proving to be a big draw. I do appreciate you helping out while there's this resurgence of interest."

"I'm not asking much. Just take a look at a couple."

Helen shook her head. "I'm sure they're lovely. But right now, we should be focusing on selling what's popular. I'm looking to print up some more Muldoon postcards. Maybe you could knock up a couple of new Muldoon paintings. Joke, obviously. No, no. I don't think I have time for that at the moment."

"Please. I'm going to be homeless soon."

"I understand. I thought I was paying the going rate for your time..."

Juniper nodded and backed away.

Chapter Forty-Six

Figgy was ready to get cracking on her caravan. Since she'd decided to make changes, she was seeing it with new eyes. Even newer, since she'd seen Juniper's place.

She was anxious about the offer of help from Rosamund's mum, who'd arranged to come round after swimming. But she wasn't about to be rude.

She welcomed Joanna into her tiny living space.

"Gracious! Isn't this fun? A caravan on the beach. Very Enid Blyton."

Figgy shrugged. "It's a nice place to live."

"I can see why you felt the need to make some changes. I don't mean to be judgemental, but it's ghastly, isn't it?"

Figgy hadn't expected to feel defensive about the décor, but Joanna's blunt language seemed like a direct attack on her grandmother. "It was very much a product of my grand-mother's tastes."

"Of course it was, darling, but times move on. Now, let's sit down and discuss your scheme, shall we?"

Joanna plonked a pile of magazines and books on the

table. They had titles like *Chic Homes* and *Rural Living*. "Plenty of inspiration here!"

Figgy made tea and then sat down to flick through a magazine. It showed a smug-looking woman sitting on an enormous settee in a room that surely belonged in a castle.

"Hm, probably not that one." Joanna leaned over. "This one here has ideas for smaller spaces." She riffled the pages until she found an article about storage solutions on a houseboat.

"Yeah, the space itself is fine," Figgy said. "I just need the décor to reflect who I am a bit more."

"Of course you do! I see you as tasteful. Timeless. Classic. We could use neutrals, perhaps? A subdued palette with a few astonishing highlights, yes?"

Figgy pursed her lips. "To be honest, I don't see neutrals at all. I want a riot of colour."

"Colour? Yes. I can see that you might want to inject a little colour."

"No, a lot of colour."

"A lot. Yes." Joanna looked as though she wanted to argue, but she clamped her lips together. "Let's see what we have here, shall we?"

Joanna flicked through her magazines and books, pausing occasionally when she came to a picture that showed pale interiors. Was Figgy imagining things, or did she emit a small sigh each time she saw something that she thought was more appropriate?

"You know how when you get a new box of crayons, it's really exciting?" Figgy said eventually. "That's the look I want."

Joanna opened and closed her mouth a few times before speaking. Presumably it had been a long time since she'd considered crayons. "Is that the excitement that comes from the potential, rather than the actual colour combinations?"

Figgy was beginning to feel her way into this now. She recognised a streak of stubbornness in herself, but it felt right.

"Yeah, no. It's definitely the colours."

Joanna dipped a hand into her handbag. "I've also brought some swatches and colour charts. Show me the ones that you like."

"Ooh!" Figgy picked up the cards. "Now this is what I'm talking about."

They were paint shades, with outlandish names like Dewy Sapphire, Molten Caramel and Rusty Spade. She made a pile of colours that she liked and those that she didn't.

"There."

"Interesting," Joanna said.

Figgy thought her face suggested otherwise.

"I see what you're thinking here, and I would urge caution."

"Caution?"

Joanna held up a hand. "Not that I want to crush your creative spirit at all, but you have selected many different colours in many different tones. I would suggest that you attempt to select colours that support each other."

Figgy's face must have given her away, because Joanna blinked and huffed before she tried to explain.

"So, you could go about this a couple of ways. Maybe you really like blue? So, you get some different shades of blue and combine them. Now, I know that you want multiple colours, so you need to do something slightly different. Perhaps you choose a range of colours, but they are all of a similar tone?"

"Similar tone?"

"Like if you had a packet of Opal Fruits?" Joanna threw

her hands up in the air. "Different colours, but all quite vibrant, yes?"

"Opal Fruits?"

"Oh right. Yes. They have a new name, don't they? Starburst?"

"Oh, yeah," Figgy said. "I like the idea of decorating based on sweets. How about Jelly Babies?"

Joanna pulled a face, then rallied. "That could work. Yes."

Figgy pulled up a picture on her phone. "These are my colours, aren't they? Shall I get a can of paint for each one?"

"I'd suggest you use just one of the colours for the painting. Apply the others in some other form," Joanna said. "Rugs, cushions, curtains, perhaps?"

Figgy sorted through the colour cards, searching for a match for the Jelly Babies on her screen. "This is brilliant! I bet I could scan some actual jelly babies with my phone and do a colour match on them online. Imagine the cupboard doors, each one painted in a different colour."

Joanna smiled weakly. "A bold choice, to be sure. Why not try out one of the colours, see how you like it?"

Figgy nodded politely, but in her heart of hearts she now knew she wanted to lean into this mixed colour idea full-tilt. She was in a rush to get out and buy Jelly Babies.

"Will you have the seating re-upholstered?" Joanna asked, prodding the cushion she was sitting on.

"Hm." Figgy hadn't really thought about the logistics of changing the seats, but it was true that together with the old-fashioned curtains, they were responsible for a good part of the granny vibe. "Maybe I could get covers for them, or paint them, even?"

"I do believe it's possible to paint fabric," Joanna said, in much the same way she might have conceded that it was possible to eat lard or shop in Poundland.

They sipped their tea. Figgy was preoccupied with thoughts of Jelly Babies while Joanna looked as though she was thinking hard about how best to change Figgy's mind.

"Where do you think you might start?" Joanna asked eventually.

"Jelly Babies," Figgy told her, with a grin. "I have research to do."

Chapter Forty-Seven

Tina was in Lyme Regis police station.

She and Dougie sipped tea and flicked through the case notes on Dougie's screen.

"I guess there's nothing to follow up with Dante," Tina said. "Picking up Clifford's cup for him would explain the fingerprints. Did you believe his version of events?"

Dougie thought for a moment. "He didn't look like a man who was lying. If anything, he was more worried about Mike finding out about his past."

"Yes. He was." Tina peered at the photos from the crime scene. "That cup wasn't there on the Cobb on the day Clifford died. Looks like he had two or three different ones that he took along to wash out his brushes."

Dougie nodded.

Tina went to some other pictures. "Or maybe he used it to wash down his pills? He had all that medication to take."

"I reckon you'd take a bottle of water. Put some in the cup for your brushes, and take a swig from the bottle if you needed a drink, wouldn't you?"

"Yeah. That makes sense."

"Was there a cup of water by his easel on the day he died?" Tina asked.

They scanned the photos and considered what they'd seen. There was no sign of a cup that contained water, just an empty one.

"I guess it's possible that it got knocked over when Clifford stumbled to his feet," said Tina. "It would have evaporated quickly in the sunshine."

"Yes. Or maybe he hadn't needed to wash any brushes at that point."

"Possibly." Her knowledge of how artists worked was mainly limited to Louis and Poppy, who sploshed watercolours onto paper with abandon, stirring the colours into a brown sludge.

"The paints he was using were acrylics, yeah? He'd definitely wash the brushes between colours, wouldn't he?"

A brief Google search confirmed that he probably would.

Tina zoomed in to examine the rest of the evidence collected from the Cobb. "Can you even see a paintbrush that's got paint on it?"

Dougie stared at the screen. "They do all look clean, don't they?"

Tina looked at the list of pills, and the narrative the CSI team had written at the side of each one. Many of them were for his heart condition, and then there was the Madopar for Parkinson's.

"Can you imagine being an artist and having Parkinson's?" she asked Dougie. "It would be the worst thing imaginable, wouldn't it? It would be so frustrating if tremors affected what you could do."

She pulled her hands back from the mouse she'd been

using to scroll through the pictures and drummed her fingers on the desk.

"What are you thinking?" asked Dougie.

"You know what this feels like?" Tina said slowly. "This is going to sound a bit crazy."

"Go on."

"It feels like those stories where someone loses their job, but they keep going out every day, because they can't bear to admit it, either to themselves, their families or the world."

Dougie stared at her. "You think Clifford was only pretending to paint?"

"He had Parkinson's. His paintbrushes were all clean and dry. Maybe the tremors came on really badly because his medication had been messed up, but on the day he died, I don't think he was painting at all. He was just going through the motions."

"That's both sad and strange."

Tina scoffed. "Strange doesn't even cover half of it. We have a painter who dies in plain sight on the Cobb, a man who essentially had no friends, with no one who would benefit from his death. We have a break-in at his house. A break-in and a break-out via the rear window for some reason. A single painting, stolen in a house full of equally valuable paintings. And now we discover it's possible – likely, even – that he hasn't painted a single painting for months. Years, maybe. He's just pretending and living off his back catalogue."

"It is strange when you put it like that," said Dougie.

"And the closest thing we have to a lead is a fingerprint from my father-in-law for which there's a perfectly rational explanation." She tutted and stared into her cup. "I need another cup of tea."

Chapter Forty-Eight

Joanna returned from Figgy's full of chatter about the colour scheme Figgy had settled on.

Rosamund was only half-listening. It was approaching the time when families would be vacating their rental cottages, and she needed to prepare them for the new arrivals.

She'd been looking forward to escaping her mother for a few hours at work. It seemed odd to view the prospect of cleaning holiday cottages as a treat, but right now, it was up there with a mini-break to Antibes.

"Darling, did I mention that I might come with you?" Joanna swept down the stairs as if accepting an Oscar.

"No." Rosamund's eyes widened. "That wouldn't really work."

"Nonsense!" Joanna held up a pair of Marigolds with a faux fur trim. "I even picked up some gloves so I can lend a hand."

Rosamund thought hard, searching for a solid reason to

stop her mother coming along. "You must have something better to do with your time, surely?"

"Time supporting my daughter is always time well spent, wouldn't you say? Besides, I can help you look out for opportunities for improvements. Another pair of eyes."

Rosamund wasn't sure whether her mum wanted to check up on her cleaning skills or find ways to climb the career ladder of cleaning. Either possibility sounded absurd.

"Fine. I'm doing the changeover on three cottages on Silver Street. I need to do it quickly, so you can't get in the way."

Joanna gave a little clap. "You won't even notice I'm there."

At Seaview Cottage, Rosamund retrieved the key from the key safe and opened the front door.

"If you wanted to be helpful, you could go upstairs and gather all the bedlinen and towels into a laundry bag," she said, unlocking the cleaning supplies cupboard.

"Oh, I'm not sure I can do that." Joanna frowned. "How about I check through the kitchen instead?"

Rosamund shrugged and hauled the Henry hoover up the stairs with the huge laundry bag.

She gathered the linen and dragged the bag towards the stairs. Her mother was coming up, a pair of bottles in her outstretched hands.

"There are two open bottles of extra virgin olive oil. Where do you recycle them?"

Rosamund frowned. "I normally leave those, so the next people can use them."

"Surely not? They could be contaminated."

"How do people contaminate a bottle of oil?"

226

Joanna ignored the question. "There were two open tubs of Himalayan rock salt, as well."

"The condiments get left alone. The next people might appreciate them."

Rosamund knew the salt was already in the bin.

Joanna pulled a face and went back down the stairs, holding the oil at arm's length as if it were toxic waste.

Rosamund huffed and trotted down behind her.

"Don't throw stuff away! It's wasteful."

Joanna went into the kitchen, tutting loudly. "There's even milk left in the fridge. That can go down the sink."

"No! I take that home. Cameron gets through a lot of milk."

Joanna turned, aghast. "You're reduced to this? Eating leftovers from holidaymakers?"

"I'm not reduced to anything, Mum. I don't like waste, that's all."

Joanna delved into her handbag. "Here's a fiver. Get uncontaminated milk for Cameron. Tell him it's on me."

Chapter Forty-Nine

By the time Tina reached her mum's house on Anning Way, she'd convinced herself that Clifford Muldoon hadn't been painting for some time. If the man, almost crippled by Parkinson's, had only been pretending to paint, any sales he'd made must have come from the stockpile of artwork still in his house.

She rang the doorbell and, while she waited, messaged Helen Cruickshank at the gallery asking for the date on the last Muldoon painting she'd received. That would tell them when his condition had reached the point at which it prevented him from creating more works. It wouldn't help solve the mystery of his death, but it would add some colour and shade to their understanding of the man.

Annie opened the door.

"Mummy!" squealed Louis, reaching up with grasping hands.

"Whoop! Whoop! It's da sound of da police!" sang Poppy.

Tina frowned.

"A certain granddad might have been giving them an education in modern music," said Annie.

Tina peered past her. "Is Dante here?"

Annie must have seen the wariness on her face. "OK, you have to tell me," she said.

"Tell you?"

Annie turned and went down to the kitchen. "Tell me why you arrested Dante at the party the other night."

Tina ushered the children back in and followed her mum. "First of all, we didn't arrest him. He was just helping us with our enquiries."

"Potay-to, potah-to," said Annie, putting on the kettle.

"Secondly, you know I can't tell you about any police business."

Annie got the cups out. "Either you tell me, or I wangle it out of Dante."

"You are welcome to do that."

"You're not even supposed to be working at the moment. Do the Lyme Regis police really need your help?"

Tina couldn't directly answer 'yes' or 'no'. Neither was wholly true. Of course, the police force could cope without her, but at the same time, there was a baffling investigation to be unravelled in this town.

"We are still looking into the events surrounding Clifford Muldoon's death, if you must know."

"I do know. It's poisoning, isn't it?"

"How do you know?"

"I overheard you in the garden on Thursday."

Tina tutted, at herself as much as anything.

"Actually," said Annie, the kettle now coming to the boil, "about that poisoning thing..."

"Yes?"

"I'm wondering if maybe no one intended to poison Clifford, like it was accidental."

"What makes you say that?"

"Well, I might have a teeny confession – I mean, it's not a confession, just a bit of, I suppose I'd call it conjecture, to share with you."

"Yes?"

Annie picked up the kettle to pour the teas but put it down again.

"I took something from the crime scene," she said. "No, that makes it sound too deliberate. I was by Clifford's things after he'd fallen in the water."

"Yes. I remember."

"And you see, Figgy had baked cakes for us a day or so before that. And Juniper is allergic to nuts."

Tina nodded, hoping this was going somewhere.

"So, she'd baked Juniper a separate cake that didn't have any nuts in it, even though Figgy is currently not Juniper's biggest fan. A bit of jealousy going on there. You really shouldn't have told me Cameron was round at Juniper's when you were over there investigating the break in. Do you know how the thief got in, by the way?"

"Crowbar to the front door. Mum, can you just say what you've got to say?"

"I found the little cake box Figgy had put the cake in next to Clifford's things. And I picked it up to return to her. I was just being tidy."

Tina tried to put her mum's words into the context of the picture as she understood it.

"You thought that maybe Figgy had baked a poisoned cake in order to poison Juniper Brown, and that Juniper had perhaps given it to Clifford because they know each other and sort of share a house, or parts of one...?"

"I'm not for an instant suggesting that Figgy is the sort of person to set out to poison a love rival, Tina."

"But that's exactly what you're thinking."

Annie made an uncomfortable face as she poured hot water into the cups.

"Let me put your mind at rest, Mum," said Tina.

"Yes?"

"Clifford's death seems to have been caused by alterations to his medication. Someone changed the contents of some of his medicine capsules. Caused a heart attack or seizure which, probably by accident more than design, led to him falling off the Cobb."

"Oh, I see."

"It certainly wasn't some random poison in baked goods."

"Well, that's a relief."

Tina felt her phone vibrate with a text. It was a reply from Helen.

See screenshot. Last painting produced by Clifford dated 6/12/25. Hope this helps.

Tina couldn't help a small bark of laughter.

"What's the matter?" asked Annie.

"I just had the most nonsensical text from your friend at the gallery."

"Helen?"

"Yes. I asked about Clifford's most recent painting. She has it dated on the sixth of December this year."

"In the future?"

"Yeah. Exactly. No idea what that's all about."

"Show me," said Annie.

Tina held up the phone and showed her mum the screenshot.

Annie puffed out her cheeks. "Maybe Helen was looking at some other thing? You'll probably get a 'whoops!' text in a few minutes with the correct info."

There was the sound of the front door.

"Hello!" came a call.

"Granddad!" yelled Louis.

"Time for me to go," said Tina.

Chapter Fifty

Annie watched Tina's face as Dante came in. Whatever had gone on between them, a woman should never look so utterly mortified to be in the presence of her father-in-law. Dante stepped into the kitchen, young Louis in his arms, and stopped at the sight of Tina.

"Tina."

"Dante." She swallowed. "I've got to go."

"Not on my account."

"No. I really must." She stood. "Naomi's cooking dinner for us all tonight."

She took Louis from Dante's arms.

"Your cup of tea..." Annie began, but it was no good.

Within a minute, Tina had rounded up her own children and her niece, Poppy, and was gone.

Dante let out a huge sigh.

"Oh dear. This seems quite a mess," Annie said.

"Huh. Story of my life."

He made to leave, but Annie tapped one of the mugs of

tea with her fingernails. "I'm willing to listen if you want to tell me."

He tried on a smile. It didn't fit. "No one wants to hear my side of things."

"I do. I really do."

He hesitated, then sat down at the kitchen table. Annie placed two mugs on the table in front of them.

"I'm not gonna pretend the world's had it in for me from the beginning," he said. "There were good times. You know, I've told you. Session musician at every studio in London. Seventy-nine, I recorded on *Armed Forces* with Elvis Costello's band. Don't think I've mentioned that one. That was Eden Studios in Chiswick. Brilliant times."

"You've been about a bit."

Dante grinned. "Yeah. Not saying anyone ever remembers me, but I was in the mix and that was enough. The music didn't pay for everything. Had to run the stall in Camden Market to make ends meet. Life moved fast and so did I. By the time I was thirty I was still hustling, chasing the dream, but I'd also met Carmen, Mike's mum."

Annie held her mug in both hands. "What was she like?"

Dante's smile softened. "Oh, she was smart. Smarter than me. She was a... a steadying influence and, yeah, she was too good for me. I don't know what she saw in me."

"Oh, I've seen you waggle your snake hips, Dante."

He laughed. "We certainly clicked. She got pregnant. We weren't ready, but I thought, *Time to grow up, Dante.* I tried to make it work. I really did. I worked the stall. I took every gig. I wanted to provide for them, but I wasn't really there. And the world doesn't give men like me many chances."

He took a sip of tea and gasped.

"Brixton riots, Broadwater Farm riots. To be black in London, particularly in them days, it was an open invitation for the police to harass you on the street, arrest you for no reason, maybe have you fall down the police station stairs in a little 'accident'. Man, things aren't fixed now but back then..." He sucked his teeth. "I had my reckoning when I was thirty-five."

"Reckoning?"

"I was working in the market one morning when the police came over and said I'd been identified as the suspect in a burglary in Kentish Town. I knew nothing about it."

"Wow."

"Case of mistaken identity. All black guys look the same, right? I wasn't there. I even had an alibi. I was with a mate, Degsy. But, no, the witness, who knew he had it wrong but didn't want the embarrassment of admitting his mistake, he doubled down in court, swore in front of the magistrate that it had been me he saw outside the property."

"Oh, heck."

"Mmm-hmmm. Convicted on that coward's testimony alone. A suspended sentence, and a criminal record for life."

She reached across the table and squeezed his hand.

"We don't get many chances in life," said Dante. "And your daughter seems a real nice girl. But the police, they take one look at this face and just glance at that criminal record. Employers, too. And I spend my life paying for a crime I didn't commit."

"Oh lord, Dante, what a story. I'm so sorry."

Dante sagged over his tea.

"But you know what?" she continued. "If you want my opinion, there's never anything to be gained by wallowing."

"A man gets to a certain age, all he can do is wallow."

235

"That's rubbish and you know it. You've had some time to feel sorry for yourself, now you need to move forward. Is it sharks that die if they don't keep moving forward? Like that."

"I'm a shark?"

"Snappy dressers, sharks," Annie replied.

"What does moving forward look like?" Dante asked.

"Right now? You could always go and lend a hand with Figgy's caravan. Practical stuff sounds like just the distraction you need."

Chapter Fifty-One

Figgy was taken aback when Joanna turned up at the door of her caravan with Juniper in tow.

"Figgy, I've had the most genius idea." Joanna beamed. "Your ideas for combining colour seem so ambitious that I thought we might enlist the help of an actual artist. Juniper has an hour now, before she's due for her shift at Helen's gallery."

"Oh. I see."

"Tell me I've overstepped the mark and that I'm a dreadful old busybody, if you like."

Joanna threw on that charming smile that seemed to fix everything.

"No." Figgy sighed. Complaining wouldn't help. "I would be really grateful for the help. Come in, Juniper."

Juniper was drawn instantly to the big bay window at the end of the caravan. "Wow, Figgy. What a view!"

"Thank you." Figgy wasn't sure why she'd said that. It wasn't as if she was responsible for the view.

"I do hope it's forming a feature in your remodelling plans?" Juniper asked.

"Um?" Figgy hadn't even considered the idea, but now that Juniper had said it, it seemed obvious. It was the most noticeable feature of the whole caravan.

"Figgy wanted a riot of colour," said Joanna. Her voice suggested that Figgy was wrong to want such a thing and that she'd brought Juniper along to confirm this.

"Good on ya, Figgy! I wish there was more appetite for colour in this country. People here like to play it safe."

"How would I do that, though?" Figgy asked. The whole thing was making her head spin, especially now she'd Googled some of the things Joanna had mentioned. "It seems as though there are loads of rules that relate to colour."

"Yeah, there are, but we can look at those. What can we use as a test bed? Is there anywhere in here where we can try out some ideas?"

Figgy shrugged and pointed to the wall cabinet where she kept her teabags. "This door? Let me just grab the tea things and put the kettle on."

Figgy made drinks while Juniper plonked a canvas bag on the counter and pulled out some brushes and small pots of paint. She opened the door, angling it away from Figgy, so that it wasn't visible while she worked.

"Just playing around, so we can see what appeals."

Joanna was sitting in a position from where she could see Juniper working. She kept making excited little 'squee' noises and scrunching up her face.

After fifteen minutes, Juniper put down her brush. "Right, I'm done. We can always paint over this if it's no good."

Slowly, she closed the cupboard, so that her work was visible to Figgy.

"Oh. My. Goodness. It's Van Gogh's Starry Night!" Figgy gasped.

"A very rough and ready approximation," agreed Juniper. "Look, maybe I should explain how I see it working. Loads of blue in this picture, right?"

Figgy nodded. The swirling dabs of paint were world famous, and now she had her very own version! Juniper hadn't even copied a reference picture. The whole thing had come straight out of her head. Figgy found a copy of a Van Gogh on her phone and saw what a close match it was.

"But also, some yellows and greens," continued Juniper. "It might be a night sky, but there's no black in it. Black is a lazy term for a range of dark and beautiful colours."

"I guess."

"I never use black in my art, Figgy. Like I say, it's lazy. Now, as well as colour we need lots of movement and shading, too. How about you continue some of the colour across the wall? You can do this painting yourself."

Figgy followed Juniper's outstretched hand as she pictured the colour drenching her living space.

"You make it look so easy," said Figgy. "I'm not sure I could do that."

"Sure you can." Juniper picked up a piece of chalk and drew a bold shape across the remaining three cupboards, like a capital 'S' lying on its side. "Follow that line with some dabby little brush strokes. Try it now."

"Can I?" Figgy asked, incredulous.

Juniper put the brush in her hand. "Yep."

"Can I do some?" Joanna asked, her smile wide.

Juniper gave her a brush, too, squeezed some acrylic

239

paints onto a palette and set it down between the two of them. "Use the full range of those colours as you go."

Figgy made some tentative dabs, afraid that she might make a terrible mess.

When she glanced over and saw the speed of Joanna's painting, she sped up. If it was going to be a mess, at least it would be her own mess.

Juniper stood by, sipping her tea and nodding. "Going great."

Figgy and Joanna stepped back when they had created a broad swirl across the cupboards. It was bold, definitely. Figgy grinned at Joanna.

"Look, I need to get to Helen's now. Has that helped at all?" asked Juniper, starting to pack away her materials.

"It really has, thank you," said Figgy. She meant it, too.

"So you need to choose one of those shades of blue to paint the wall," said Joanna. "A pale one, I'd say."

"No," said Figgy. "All of the shades. So I can make more swirls along the wall."

"Surely Juniper meant that you'd just continue one of the colours across the wall. Not the whole design. That would be too much. Just too much."

Figgy smiled. She was very much of the opinion that too much was exactly what she wanted. Bold choices were what she needed in her life.

"I will have a think about it," she said.

In truth, she'd already thought about it. Now she'd learned how to make the swirly patterns, the entire caravan was going to be covered in them.

Chapter Fifty-Two

That evening, Rosamund and Joanna shared a couple of glasses of wine in the kitchen. Rosamund eyed the to-do list on the fridge. Since her mum's arrival she hadn't added to it, for fear of inviting further criticism and uninvited help. She missed the little boost of ticking off her minor achievements.

Joanna picked up a pen. "I know something that needs to go on your list. A manicure. It will do you the power of good to get your nails done."

Rosamund gave a tight smile. "I'm not really a manicure kind of person."

"Nonsense! Everyone's a manicure person. It's basic personal grooming."

"I swim in the sea every day and I clean holiday cottages."

"Oh darling! You're like Cinderella. Let me be your fairy godmother."

Rosamund rolled her eyes. "Even before I did those things, I didn't paint my nails."

"Well, your cuticles are red raw, I can see that from here. You should wear gloves while you're cleaning."

"Uh huh."

"And of course, you're looking out for something better, aren't you, darling?"

"Something better." Rosamund raised her eyes to the ceiling.

"Than cleaning. Yes."

Rosamund whirled. "You know what? Cleaning's better than a whole bunch of alternatives."

"I don't think—"

"Things like not being able to afford to live in this house."

"I hardly think you're destitute. Surely David's—"

"David has not been in touch. He has stopped paying for everything and closed our joint accounts."

Joanna frowned. "Disgraceful behaviour."

"So you see, it's sink or swim, really." Rosamund thought of her friends in the Lyme Regis Women's Swimming Club and smiled. She felt them at her side as she squared up to her mother. "And I choose swimming."

Joanna gave a small nod. "Good for you, sweets. Tell you what, though, I do still worry about your cuticles. Shall I rub some almond oil into them when you get home from work tomorrow?"

Chapter Fifty-Three

Figgy stared at the swirls on the inside of her caravan. Her head buzzed with the riot of colours.

It was possible, she thought, that the buzzing was caused by sleeping in a caravan full of paint fumes.

She'd woken that morning from strange dreams in which Juniper instructed her on which colours she must and must not use to decorate her home, telling her off every time she got splodges of paint on her clothes.

She needed a swim to clear her head.

When she returned, she considered her decorating project anew. It had ceased to be a matter of redecorating. It was now an extended playtime, where she could daub paint wherever she pleased. She hadn't had so much fun since she was a child. She was eyeing up the ceiling when there was a knock at the door.

"Figgy, you have two helpers today!" It was Joanna, with Dante at her side.

"Aren't I lucky?" Figgy stepped back. "Come in."

"We stopped at the hardware store and got some paintbrushes. We thought you might need more, and Dante here has some strong ideas about painting."

"I always go large." Dante waggled a wide paintbrush. "That extra inch makes all the difference."

"Oh, you are simply awful!" Joanna tapped his arm. "Isn't he awful, Figgy?"

Figgy had no idea how she was supposed to respond. Was this how flirting worked for seniors? She'd been to a pantomime once and found it irritating. In her mind, Dante's joke belonged in the same pigeonhole.

"I'll make tea, shall I?"

"I like what you're doing here," said Dante, taking it all in. "Crashing waves. Swirling turbulence. Yin mixed up with Yang. It's like life, isn't it?"

Figgy thought about that. "I suppose it is, yes."

"No suppose about it," said Dante. "Life would be dull if it was all good, safe stuff. It's the blending of the epic moments with the awful ones that makes it interesting. Gotta have a bit of rough with the smooth."

"Never was a truer word spoken," added Joanna.

Figgy turned to look at the two of them. There it was again, the weird flirting thing. Figgy wasn't always swift when it came to reading the unspoken mood of an exchange, but this particular mood was being telegraphed loud and clear.

"Tell me about some of your amazing moments, Dante," said Joanna.

Figgy handed them both a tea and let them get on with it.

"Let me think," said Dante. "I was on *Top of the Pops* a couple of times. That was neat."

"You were not!" said Joanna. "How did that happen?"

"Some of the bands needed extra session musicians when

they played on there. I got the gig if I was in the right place at the right time."

"Anything I might remember?"

Dante gave a small nod. "'Lip Up Fatty'. Remember that one?"

"Not Bad Manners, no!"

To Figgy's horror, Joanna commenced an inexplicable prancing dance involving high knees and garbled shouting. Dante joined in with an invisible trumpet. They carried on for several minutes until they both collapsed in laughter.

"Buster Bloodvessel was hilarious," said Joanna, bent over and panting.

"I'd see him sometimes in London," said Dante.

"Wait, what was that thing you just did?" Figgy asked. "Was that an actual song about fat people?"

Joanna chewed her lip. "I suppose it was, yes. But it was a fat man singing about himself, really."

"Singing," echoed Figgy. It hadn't sounded very melodic, but perhaps the original was less shouty.

"Different times," said Dante. "I think it was an attempt to challenge convention. Buster was more about celebrating his body shape, in his own way."

Figgy picked up her paintbrush. Could she tune them out? She had no idea what they were talking about, and she lacked the energy to Google their twentieth-century references.

She decided to paint the area around the large bay window so she could work at the other end from Dante and Joanna. She found herself making larger and larger swirls as she concentrated on not listening to their nonsense, but it wasn't working.

"How many instruments can you play, Dante?" Joanna asked.

He shrugged. "Never met an instrument that I couldn't get a tune out of."

"I would love to hear you play some time."

Figgy rolled her eyes. She pulled out her phone, planning to complain to Annie and Rosamund, but then she sighed and put it back again. They just wanted a couple of hours without their annoying house guests. Surely, she could suck it up if she tried hard enough?

"Good to know. I think Annie's getting fed up of me being tuneful around the place," said Dante.

"Oh, tell me about it. My Rosamund won't listen to a word I say. I have a lifetime of experience to draw on. A lifetime! If I say there's a better way to fold towels, I can tell you now, I've done the research. I know what I'm talking about."

"Impressive stuff," said Dante.

Figgy tried to sneak a look at him to see if he was being serious. The man either wasn't paying any actual attention to Joanna's words, or he had a great poker face. Figgy wasn't sure which.

"So," she asked loudly. Dante and Joanna both turned to her, as if they'd forgotten she was there. "Swirls across the ceiling or not?"

"Definitely," said Dante.

"Definitely not," said Joanna at the same moment.

They looked at each other and fell about laughing again.

Figgy sighed and moved the stepladder into position. She'd do the ceiling on her own.

Chapter Fifty-Four

Helen kept the gallery space pristine. Clean space to allow the artworks to speak for themselves. Calming white space to soothe the eye, encouraging customers to relax and linger.

Today, though, was an emergency. She couldn't afford to take time away from the gallery, so the messy stuff had to come in there with her. She'd taken over a corner and installed a table with the equipment she'd be using. Annie was coming to help in a short while.

She wore an apron as part of today's outfit, partly to protect her long skirt and partly because it was a rather sweet design all on its own. It tied at the waist and had generous ruffles all around the edges. Helen was partial to a ruffle or two.

Harper came in, her cheeks flushed from the heat of her workshop. "Here's the frame you asked for." She handed Helen a wooden frame with fine plastic mesh fastened across it.

"Darling, that's perfect." Helen held it up and inspected it. "Thank you."

"What's it for?"

"I'm screen printing some Clifford Muldoon merch. Tea towels with a seagull."

Harper frowned. "Is that legal? Surely you can't just make things and put his name on them?"

"Oh, no. I can't do that, obviously. These tea towels will simply be in the *Muldoon style*. There's such an appetite for his work at the moment, I can't let an opportunity like this pass me by."

Harper gave Helen a long, hard stare. "True enough. Fickle creatures, humans. Something else will capture their attention soon enough."

Helen sighed as Harper went back outside. Was that another of her angry swipes? It felt that way.

She returned to the task in hand. She'd acquired a huge roll of pale blue fabric and some hastily-scribbled calculations.

Cut 18" from roll & cut in half. This will make 2 tea towels. Make sure you leave at least 1" around each edge for hems.

Helen took her scissors and prepared a large pile of rectangles from the roll. Once she started printing, she'd want to keep going.

She'd also strung a line around several of the walls so that she could peg out the printed rectangles. It would detract from the appearance of the artwork on display, but she hoped it might also satisfy the Muldoon-mania while it lasted.

The Muldoon seagull was a simple enough shape to cut out as a stencil. She'd also need a border. Helen worked on the stencil, referencing the Muldoon paintings on the wall.

First, she sketched, then she cut with a scalpel. After twenty minutes, she was happy that she had captured the Muldoon seagull in a way that would look good on a tea towel.

The decorative border would need to complement and frame the design. That took a little longer, but when Helen stepped back to look at the finished article, she was pleased with her effort. It was all cut out from the stencil paper so that she could lay it on top of the frame Harper had made.

Carefully, she taped it onto the frame and held it up to the light, checking that she could only see through the parts that would take the ink.

"Morning, Helen! What are we doing today, then?"

Helen looked up to see Annie enter the gallery.

"Screen printing."

Annie walked over, rubbing her hands. "Sounds fun. I don't think I know how it works, mind."

"I'll show you. Mostly your job will be to hold this frame nice and firm while I add the ink."

"Sounds like something I can do. Let's crack on."

"Thanks. It does mean we're both likely to get covered in ink, you realise that?" Helen gave her a wink.

"All in the name of art?" Annie looked at the screen. "A seagull?"

"It is. A Muldoon seagull."

"Great idea. These look as if they could be tea towels?"

"Yep. I wanted something else to sell to the people who crave a piece of the Muldoon story." Helen eyed Annie, in case she showed signs of disapproving.

"Great idea. Play up to the legend of the man. Why not?"

Helen nodded as she smoothed a piece of fabric underneath the screen. "You hold this down. Lean hard on it."

Annie pressed the sides of the frame down onto the table while Helen squeezed a generous line of white ink across the top.

"Here we go!" Helen picked up the squeegee and dragged it down the stencil. The ink flowed smoothly onto the design. She put the squeegee down and out of the way.

"Looks good. Shall we take a peek?"

Annie nodded and relaxed the downward pressure, leaving Helen to lift the frame gently away from the fabric.

Helen held up the fabric and they both admired the finished article. The pale blue fabric worked well as a background for the stark white seagull. The border was a more detailed design, loosely based on crested waves, rippling around the edges.

"That looks fantastic!" said Annie. "So simple, but so Muldoon."

Helen pegged the fabric onto the line to dry.

"One down, ninety-nine to go!" she said.

Annie eyed the pile of rectangles and shrugged. "We are the dream team. How are these getting finished?"

"I have a woman who will sort them out. I'm hoping she might come and do it here, so there's less delay."

The bell rang as a woman entered the shop. Helen shimmied over, but Annie caught her eye and pointed to her face.

"Paint!" Annie mouthed.

Without thinking, Helen reached for her face. Annie shook her head.

"You've made it worse."

Helen tutted and approached the woman. "Welcome! And apologies for my warpaint."

The woman turned to look with interest at the table in the corner. "Are you running a workshop?"

Helen ran through the possible answers. She could see an opportunity, but did she want an extra pair of hands getting in the way?

"Ah, no. It's an installation. A work in progress, if you will. A tribute to the late, great Clifford Muldoon."

"Good lord, so it is!" The woman clapped her hands in delight. "The seagull pennant is simply astonishing. I must have one."

"Pennant. Yes. It's a pennant. Of course you can have one." Helen nodded. "It won't come with the, um, hanger, though."

"That's fine. I'll take it now," said the woman.

Helen smiled and went over to discreetly check how dry the paint was before ringing up the sale.

When the customer had left, Helen beckoned Annie over. "Want to see the picture that went missing from Clifford's?"

"Oh yes!" Annie hurried over.

"It's just a thumbnail from a catalogue. See here? Eighth of January, ninety-four."

Annie peered at the tiny image. "Wow. Here it finally is. It's actually making me cold thinking about Clifford, sitting out there on the coldest days of winter. Can you imagine?"

"Madness," agreed Helen.

"It doesn't look all that wintry though, does it?"

"Hard to tell. I guess the weather looks pleasant enough, but you get that sort of day in January sometimes, don't you?"

"You don't get folk swimming that far out in the sea, though." Annie tapped the thumbnail.

"Oh, there is a figure there, I think you're right."

"Think about us lot in January," said Annie. "We go in

251

for the Lyme Lunge on New Year's Day, but nobody spends too long in there, do they?"

"Very true. That's because we're all thinking about getting out and having a big breakfast."

The two of them laughed.

"Oh, take a look at the poster I designed for these tea towels," said Helen.

"Pennants," said Annie with a grin. "Oh, clever. You're calling them an homage. That's a nice touch. I guess it means you can use his name but not be accused of using his name for commercial gain."

"As if!"

Chapter Fifty-Five

Tina sat in the chair she'd begun to think of as hers. Wendy Sharman was on the phone, running through details of police involvement in Lifeboat Week. Dougie was doing paperwork.

Tina's phone rang. Mike.

"Hey! How are things?"

"We very nearly have a house a family could live in," said Mike. "Although I'm learning that plaster dust has weird magical properties."

"Oh yeah?"

"I do the dusting and then there's loads more dust. How is it even doing that? Where does the dust keep coming from? Am I going to have to dust every day forever?"

Tina laughed. "Keep going! It will be *so* good to come home. I'm having a great time here, but it's not home."

She glanced sideways at Dougie. Would he be offended by her saying that? He and Naomi had been kind enough to have Tina, Louis and baby Daisy to stay for weeks now, but surely they'd like to have their house back to themselves.

"Ah, but there's the case," said Mike.

"Clifford Muldoon."

"I've heard my dad's a person of interest."

Tina waited.

"Is it likely that he did it, do you think?" Mike asked. His voice was light, casual.

"We interviewed him," said Tina. "And honestly, no. I don't think he did it. He talked about just walking past Clifford while he was painting and picking up the cup that he'd dropped. That was how he explained his fingerprint."

"So, he's calling it a coincidence?"

"Yep. Maybe it is a coincidence. They do happen."

"Yeah. Sure."

Tina got up and walked away from Dougie and Wendy. "Do you want to talk about all this stuff with your dad? It must feel strange."

"No. I really can't be bothered. He walked out on us, and I've come to terms with that, over the years. I heard about the burglary conviction ages ago when I joined up. Didn't surprise me one bit. A rubbish human does a bad thing. I guess I'd be more surprised if he didn't have some sort of conviction."

"It was a long time ago. Who knows what was going on in his life? He seems like an old guy who knows he's messed up and just wants to connect with his family."

She could hear the clattering of a keyboard.

"Are you looking up the old case?" she asked.

"I am."

Tina smiled. If Mike didn't want to discuss his dad directly, maybe they could just talk shop and deal with it that way. "Come on then, you're the one with the systems access. Talk me through it."

Mike laughed. "I bet you're driving them mad over there, trying to work around the fact you're on maternity."

Tina tutted. "What do you mean, 'trying'? I have ways and means."

"You certainly do. Right, so this incident took place on April the fifteenth, nineteen eighty-nine."

"Over thirty-five years ago."

"The break-in was to a property on Kentish Town Road, where around fifteen hundred pounds worth of valuables were taken. There was no forensic evidence involved in the conviction. The only evidence the prosecution had was the testimony of a witness who saw Legg inside the property and recognised him three days later, when he saw him on the street operating as a market trader. The witness alerted the police and then picked Legg out of a lineup."

Tina heard Mike release a long, slow breath.

"What is it?" she asked.

"I'm guessing you guys over there didn't read all the details of the case."

Tina thought. There was a summary document. She'd read that, but it sounded as though Mike had found something else. "Tell me?"

"Guess who that witness was? The one whose testimony got my dad convicted?"

Tina held her breath. "Not Clifford Muldoon?"

"Bingo!"

Tina turned to Dougie, wide-eyed. "So, Dante did have a motive. A pretty big one. Damn."

Over the line, Mike released a long sigh. "I think you need to revisit my dad. Sounds like you need DS Strunk over there and..." Another sigh. "You're going to have to arrest my dad."

Chapter Fifty-Six

F iggy opened the door to her caravan.

"I came as soon as I could," Cameron said. "It sounded like you were having a bit of a crisis." He frowned. "Also, why are you wearing sunglasses indoors?"

"Come inside. You may wish you had some sunglasses on yourself in a moment."

Cameron went inside.

"Sit down, and we can talk about how some of my recent choices have not been my wisest," said Figgy. "Kettle's on."

Cameron glanced around. "Come on. Tell me. What's on your mind? I'm here to help."

Figgy lifted her shades for the first time since he'd arrived. "Looking back, I can see that this makeover had three phases. The first phase was me not knowing what I wanted, but knowing I wanted something to change. The middle phase was being inspired by Juniper."

"Inspired by Juniper?"

"Yes." Figgy pointed to the original set of swirls Juniper had painted. "Juniper painted this, and I loved it so much that it led me to phase three, where Figgy makes all the swirls."

Cameron nodded, taking in the swirls that covered the walls, ceiling, cupboards, seating and carpet. It was like being inside a kaleidoscope.

"Are you thinking it's a bit much?"

Figgy waggled the arms of her sunglasses, so that they jiggled on her face. "It's actually giving me a headache."

"I see."

Figgy sighed. "I might have got carried away. No, I definitely got carried away."

Cameron nodded. "I honestly had no idea you could paint carpet. Or curtains."

"Don't forget the cushions," said Figgy, bending over the teapot. "In fact, you should probably avoid sitting down for the—" She turned as she spoke. "Ah, never mind."

Cameron sprang up, twisting around to check whether he had paint on the back of his trousers.

Figgy glanced down at her own trousers. She'd been unsuccessful in getting the paint out before it dried. She wondered briefly if she should paint all over the trousers, so that it looked intentional, but then realised that sort of thinking was exactly how she'd got her caravan into its current state.

"I think the question is not so much can you paint carpet. It's more like *should* you paint carpet."

"Is there any chance some of this is reversible?" Cameron asked. "Like if you washed the curtains, might it come off?"

Figgy looked at the deep, inky blue that covered the pale curtains. "I suppose it's possible."

"And I can see zips on the seat covers. Are they removeable?"

257

"Yes, they are."

"Then why don't we take all of those things to the launderette and wash them?"

Figgy nodded. She felt a warm glow, hearing Cameron use the word 'we'. "It would feel good to be doing something. Thank you for offering to help."

"And if we feel like doing more after that, the launderette hires out those carpet shampooing machines."

Figgy laughed. "They do, don't they?"

"Why are you laughing? I'm trying to help."

"You have no idea how much you're helping. I've just gone from despair to laughing at what an idiot I've been. This is massive."

"It's good to see you laugh."

"I've been such an idiot about all this. I'm sorry."

"Life makes us all weird sometimes. I get it, I really do. My mum and my granny are making each other so miserable right now, it's unbelievable."

"Oh crumbs. And you've been right in the middle of all that, too." Figgy reached out and squeezed Cameron's hand.

Cameron squeezed back. "Come on. No time for mushy stuff right now. We need to get this lot into a washer as soon as we can. You find some bin bags, I'll start getting the covers off. We can do this!"

Chapter Fifty-Seven

Rosamund let herself in through the front door and sighed with relief. She was glad of the work that high season brought. Making holiday cottages beautiful for the next guests was fulfilling.

She tried to ignore the less savoury aspects. Just that morning, she'd dealt with broken wine glasses and suncream stains on natural stone flooring. Then there'd been a new contender in the Most Disgusting Bathroom Hall of Fame. She got through it all with a pair of extra-long rubber gloves, a bit of tutting and the occasional burst of 'Roar' by Katy Perry. She always felt proud when she'd restored order and left a property gleaming.

She closed the door behind her and tried to place the sounds she could hear inside. It was definitely Joanna, but she sounded as if she was talking to someone. No, not talking exactly...

The door to the lounge was closed, which was not how Rosamund usually left it. She walked over and listened for a moment, until she could place the voice.

It was Dante in there with her mother and they both sounded giggly.

"It's possible that you're leading me astray, Dante," said Joanna.

Rosamund rolled her eyes.

"I've only known you for a short while, but I think you're a woman who knows her own mind. If I am leading you astray, it's because you want to go there," said Dante.

"We've both been around long enough to dispense with pretending, don't you think?"

"You're so right."

There was a long silence. Rosamund frowned. Then it dawned on her that they'd stopped talking because they were doing something else. Were they snogging in her lounge, like horny teenagers?

She crept upstairs, not wanting to alert them to her presence.

She texted the Lyme Regis Swimming Club.

Dante is round here with my mum. They don't know I'm here. I think they might be getting friendly in my lounge.

Figgy replied almost instantly.

OMG they were doing this weird flirting thing in my caravan earlier!

Rosamund grimaced.

What do I do? I want a cup of tea and a sit down, but it's all a bit awkward. I can't just go downstairs, can I?

Want me to come round and 'visit'? Cameron's here.

Rosamund thought for a moment.

Yes please! Probably not Cameron, though. Could get awkward.

Rosamund crept back outside and waited for Figgy.

When she appeared, the two of them exchanged a look,

and then Figgy leaned on the bell, rapping the door hard as well for good measure.

"We leave it a couple of minutes," said Rosamund, "and then I'll 'arrive' back myself."

They waited, and then Rosamund opened the door and the two of them went inside, chattering as loudly as they could.

"Oh goodness, hello, darling!" Joanna emerged from the lounge, her hair in disarray, her lipstick smudged. "Hello, Figgy."

"Hello, Mum. How was your day?"

"Oh, you know. Keeping busy. Thought you'd be out for hours yet."

"Only a half day today. That's why Figgy popped over, she thought I might be back. The two of us arrived at the same time. How funny is that?"

Figgy laughed. Rosamund and Joanna joined in.

Dante emerged from the lounge. His hat was nowhere to be seen, and his hand went to his head in search of it as he looked at them all, confused. "Why are you all laughing like you're in a competition?"

They all laughed even louder. Rosamund was conscious of how manic they sounded, so she stopped. "Just about to put the kettle on. Ha ha!"

Figgy followed her into the kitchen and pulled the door shut behind her. "Is this what older people are like when they decide to get together? Someone should have the talk with those two!"

Rosamund exhaled sharply. "Honestly! I didn't know where to put myself."

Figgy smiled. "Did you put your mum in that exact situation yourself when you were young?"

"Of course I didn't!" Rosamund paused. "Actually, maybe I did."

Figgy blew out a thoughtful breath. "Well, it's nice that they've found each other."

Rosamund paused. "Yes. I suppose it is. What happened to Cameron, by the way?"

"He is very kindly looking after some laundry of mine while it washes in the launderette."

Rosamund smiled. "He has a heart of gold."

"He really does."

Figgy glanced down at Rosamund's extra-long cleaning gloves. "How's the job going?"

"I really quite enjoy it." Rosamund paused. "I know it sounds crazy to say that I find it satisfying, but I do."

"Not crazy at all."

"I just wish it paid more. I put in a lot of care."

"It's the same for most young people. The world of work has changed a lot."

"Has it really, do you think?" Rosamund was thinking of Cameron.

"Yes. Take Juniper. She has such a talent, but she can't seem to make any money from it."

A message appeared on the group chat from Annie.

Lawks! Sorry, been up to my neck in it here at Helen's. I need to hear all about this. Stop by and tell me all.

Rosamund and Figgy read the message on their phones at the same time.

"Annie's going to die laughing at all of this," said Rosamund. "We should pop down and see her."

Chapter Fifty-Eight

If there were two options available, Annie always took the one that looked more fun. But this mantra was over-ridden by a simple caveat: 'If you don't work, you don't play.' Or, in this case: 'If you make a mess, you must tidy it.'

After twenty minutes of helping Helen clean up the mess left by the tea towel printing operation, she was begin-ning to think another cup of tea was required. The shop doorbell rang and in stepped Rosamund and Figgy.

"Ah, just a moment too late to help with the tidying up." Annie raised an eyebrow. "How convenient."

"What's been going on here?" Figgy asked.

"Screen printing Clifford Muldoon tea towels," said Helen. "In memoriam."

"Your sign has a spelling mistake," added Rosamund, gesturing to the window.

"Does it?"

"Inspired by 'favorite' Clifford Muldoon paintings. You've got the American spelling. It's missing a 'u'."

"Oh, fiddlesticks." Helen frowned. "Bloody spellchecker. It's this blasted laptop. Thinks it's living on the other side of the Atlantic. I thought we'd fixed this, Juniper."

"I thought we had, too." Juniper sighed. "I'd best stick to making tea."

"Let me take a look," said Figgy. She drifted over to the counter where the laptop stood and started clicking.

Annie wiped the last residue of paint from her hands. "So, Rosamund, did you come here to escape from Joanna and Dante getting well-acquainted at your place?"

Rosamund rolled her eyes. "I thought my mother couldn't get any more embarrassing. I mean, I suppose I should be glad she's found some distraction while she's here."

"Maybe you misunderstood what you heard."

"Oh, no. Figgy tells me there had been a frisson during the caravan redecorating."

"A frisson?" asked Helen.

"A frisson. Isn't that right, Figgy?"

"I don't know what frisson means," said Figgy, who was busy with the laptop settings. "But, yes, they were doing old-people flirting."

"What's old-people flirting?" asked Helen.

"It's like modern flirting except you do it out loud and not via messages. It's really cringe to hear."

"I'm somewhat surprised," said Helen. "I would not have put those two together."

Annie shrugged. "They're of a similar age. Both have a London background. She probably thinks the disreputable musician aspect makes Dante seem bohemian, even exotic."

"And his attraction to her?"

"Oh, he's happy to charm his way into the heart or bedroom of almost any lady."

Rosamund pulled a face. "Ugh. You don't think he's going to use her and leave her?"

A wry grin. "Tell me honestly, Rosamund, which of the two of them should be most wary?"

"Oh, Dante. Absolutely. Any man trying to tangle romantically with my mum should be wary, if not downright terrified."

"Done!" declared Figgy, tapping the laptop.

"Sorted?" asked Helen.

"Yes. Your universal settings were for the US. Spellcheckers, currency, even the date format. You know, how Americans do the date and month the other way round?"

Something struck Annie. "Ah! That makes sense!"

"What does?"

"Tina was moaning about how you'd said the last painting he'd produced was, oh, something like, yes, it was the sixth of December this year. Which is impossible because that's the future. But if you swap the month and date – twelfth of the sixth, so June, that makes much more sense."

"Moaning, was she?" said Helen, an eyebrow arched.

Annie ignored the comment. A thought had occurred to her.

"Oh, flipping heck!"

"What is it?" asked Rosamund.

"The date. The date was wrong."

"What date?" said Figgy.

"The date on the painting."

"Which painting?"

"I said it looked too sunny."

"What was too sunny?"

Helen made an irritated noise. "I really do feel that this

isn't more of a monologue than a conversation at the moment. Is there any chance you could make a bit more sense, Annie Abbott?"

But Annie didn't answer. Thoughts and ideas, mostly conjecture and half-notions, were whizzing through her mind. None of them made sense by themselves but, when put together, they built up a picture that seemed conclusive.

"I think I know..." she began.

"Know what?" asked Figgy.

"Don't encourage her," warned Helen. "Annie needs to start speaking in whole sentences or she should learn to keep her thoughts to herself."

Annie blinked and looked at her friends in turn.

"Full sentences then, Helen. I know who stole the painting from Clifford Muldoon's house. I think I know why it was stolen. I think I even know when it was stolen. Yes. And, if I'm even half right, I know one person who had a solid motive for murdering him."

"You do?" said Juniper, who had just come in with a tray of tea things.

"I do!" declared Annie. "And I'm going to confirm it now."

She turned to the door and, as Rosamund made to follow, Annie held up her hand. "No. Please. This might be something I need to do by myself. Tactfully."

"You're going to confront a thief and a murderer. You shouldn't go alone."

"If I'm right," said Annie, "then this is a matter of revenge. And the revenge is complete. I'm just going to the Cobb. There'll be nothing to fear."

She stepped outside and pulled the door closed behind her.

Chapter Fifty-Nine

Annie strode across the road, through the Cobb Gate car park and along Marine Parade. The seafront thronged with holidaymakers enjoying the sunshine. High season was upon the town and the roads and pavements were crowded, but Annie marched with such conviction that the crowds simply opened before her.

Her phone rang. Her friends, with more questions? But it was her daughter, Tina.

"What is it, love? I'm busy at the moment."

"Mum, do you know where Dante is?"

"No." A half-truth at best. "Why?"

"We need to talk to him." There was something in the way she said 'we'. Tina in professional mode.

"What's he done now?"

"We just need to talk to him again."

"Is it about that business with Clifford and the fingerprint?"

"I'm at your house and he's not here. I've tried phoning him. Mum, there's a lot going on here that you don't know."

"I might know more than you reckon."

"Yes. Including Clifford Muldoon. Did you know that?"

Annie slowed. "Clifford?"

"Damn it. Forget I said that. But, yes, Dante knew Clifford of old. He's been lying to us all along."

"He's your own father-in-law."

"I know. Granddad to my grandchildren. He's Mike's dad, Mike the policeman. I know exactly how bad this is going to be. But we need to talk to him."

Annie thought for a moment, then made a decision she hoped she wouldn't regret.

"I don't know where he is. I'll ask around."

She ended the call and immediately phoned Dante. It went to voicemail. She tutted and then looked in her group chat messages. Rosamund's mum had been added to one of them. She clicked on the account and phoned Joanna.

It rang three times before it was picked up.

"Hello?"

"Joanna, it's Annie. Is Dante there?"

There was a murmur, a man's voice.

Joanna's voice went up an octave. "What on earth makes you think that man is here?"

"If he's there, put him on. It's a matter of life and death." Annie wrinkled her nose at herself. "Well, almost. But it's really important."

There was muffled conversation on the line, and then Dante's voice.

"What is it, Annie? Are the family OK?"

"Dante, the police are after you."

"Story of my life," he chuckled.

"No. They're really after you. That thing you told me—"

"What thing?"

"About you getting convicted because of mistaken identity, and the witness doubling down on their false statement. That was Clifford Muldoon, wasn't it?"

There was a long pause, and then Dante swore. "Who knows?"

"The police know. You saw him during this visit. You interacted with him."

Another long pause. "I didn't mean to. I didn't even know he was here. But then I saw him. I... Where are you?"

"Me? I'm down at the front. I was at the shop. I didn't tell Tina where you were, but you need to talk to her. If you've any intention of staying part of this family, then you have to."

"Yeah, yeah." He sounded drained, exhausted, more like an old man than ever. "I will. Look, stay there. I'll come down."

She was about to disagree when the call ended. She thought about phoning back but no, Dante had as much information as he needed or deserved. If he had some link to Clifford's death – and she strongly doubted it – then she was going to have to trust him to be adult about it and come clean to his police officer son and police officer daughter-in-law.

Annie had her own thing to deal with.

She walked round the harbour and into the lifeboat station shop. Tim Cromwell was nowhere in sight. She gestured to the volunteer at the till, over the heads of the children looking at the keyrings and toys, and mouthed, "Where's Tim?" The woman gestured through to the boat-shed and station proper.

Annie nodded, gave her a thumbs up and went through a door marked 'staff only'. Inside the boatshed, the station's main lifeboat stood on a steel-grey launch trailer. Tim was alone in there, sorting through a wooden chest of bright orange life vests and ticking them off on a clipboard sheet.

"Hey," said Annie.

He looked up. He hadn't noticed her enter. His thin, melancholy mouth broke into a smile.

"Annie. Did not expect to see you here." He came forward. "A genuine sight for sore eyes. To what do I owe this pleasure?"

Annie wasn't sure how to phrase what she needed to say. But he must have seen the worry and conflict in her eyes, because he asked, "Is there something wrong?"

Nothing left to do but spit it out.

"Tim, you stole the painting from Clifford Muldoon's house, didn't you?"

His mouth formed an 'o' shape, ready to say, 'What do you mean?' or 'Why would you say that?' but he stopped himself and took a deep breath.

"I knew someone would come asking one day," he said. "I'm glad it's you, Annie."

Chapter Sixty

A car pulled up, mounting the pavement outside the gallery. Rosamund looked round, ready to offer some pithy comments about tourists not knowing how to drive in this small town of narrow streets. Then she saw it was her own car. Dante Legg leapt out of the passenger side with no small amount of athleticism for a man of his age.

He burst into the shop.

"Where's Annie?" he gasped.

Dante appeared quite dishevelled. The usually dapper man had his shirt untucked and one cuff unbuttoned. He looked, Rosamund thought, like he had just dressed in a hurry, and then she gave a little shiver as she realised what that implied.

Her mum was getting out of the car in a more sedate manner.

"Where's Annie?" he demanded again.

"Not here," said Helen bluntly. "Would you care to explain what the emergency is?"

"She said..." He was panting now. "She said something. I need to know what people know. She said she was here."

"She was here," said Figgy.

"But she's gone down to the Cobb now," said Juniper.

Dante looked at Juniper as if, in all the excitement, he was having a hard time processing what people were saying.

"Right! Right. The Cobb."

Rosamund reached and gently took hold of his arm. "Dante. Just take a moment. Breathe. Why don't you and I walk down to the Cobb and see if we can spot Annie together?"

He resisted a moment, then gave a terse nod. "Yes. Thank you."

As Rosamund stepped outside with him, Joanna came round the car she had abandoned on the pavement. A car beeped as it tried to squeeze past.

"Not here?" asked Joanna.

"On the Cobb," said Dante.

"I'll drive!"

"You'll do no such thing," said Rosamund.

She looked at the queue of traffic coming down the narrow road and the additional obstacle Joanna had created by parking here.

"Mum," said Rosamund in her most forthright voice. "You will get back in the car, circle round, find somewhere sensible to park and then you can walk down to the Cobb and join us."

"But Rosamund—"

"No buts, Mum. Treat this town and its pavements with some respect." She stuck her arm through Dante's. "Dante and I are going to stroll along the front, to the Cobb, where I'm sure you will join us."

Joanna's mouth hung open, but she did as she was told.

Rosamund steered Dante around the car, crossed the road to the Cobb Gate car park and only then, as they began to walk along the front, did she ask, "So, what's going on?"

Dante raised his eyes to the heavens, mouth wide, as though the world and everything in it was all far too much for him.

"I'm a fool," he said eventually.

Rosamund squeezed his arm. "OK, so we know that. You're a fool. All men are fools. Women, too. We're fools. Different fools."

"Oh, but I'm the biggest fool there is," he said. "Here I am, at the gateway to happiness..."

"You talking about my mum?"

There was a sly, embarrassed smile on his face. "Apologies, fair Rosamund, but your mum is a wonderful woman."

"She is many things," said Rosamund diplomatically.

"And I thought... I came here to reconnect with my family, and the grandchildren are such wonderful little people..."

"Your love for them is obvious."

"And Annie has both put me up and put up with me. And Tina. Oof, she is a formidable young woman. And fair-minded to boot, at least, as far as a copper can be fair-minded."

"Yes?"

"But maybe, I thought, I needed to move on. And Joanna and I were talking about going... well, we talked about going to all sorts of places."

"You're thinking of taking my mum away somewhere?"

Dante gave her a concerned look. "I don't want you to think I'm going to steal your mum from you."

"Oh, no! Please, steal away, Dante."

He seemed to find that amusing, but his momentary smile was overtaken by a sad look. "But I've messed it up. I messed it up years ago, and I've messed it up again now."

"How so?" she asked.

They were passing Breaststrokes café bar now. The harbour was on their left, and not far beyond it, the sweeping stone arm of the Cobb.

"I don't know what you've heard," said Dante, "but I got a criminal conviction years ago thanks to some false testimony provided by a certain artist." He wagged his finger at the Cobb.

"Clifford Muldoon?"

"He wrongly identified me as a man he'd seen carrying out a burglary back in London. And even when he knew he was mistaken, he persisted. He'd rather sacrifice my good character than his own pride."

"I'm sorry to hear that."

"I tried to put it out of my mind. For years, for decades, I tried not to think about it. Some days, I succeeded. And then I came here, and who should I see sitting at the end of the wall there with paintbrush and easel? Clifford Muldoon. The decades might have passed, but there was no mistaking that man, and suddenly the anger came rushing back. I couldn't let go without confronting him, without wringing some sort of apology out of him. I was so angry that day."

Rosamund felt her throat tighten.

"Tell me what happened," she said.

Chapter Sixty-One

Tim sat on the wooden chest in the lifeboat shed and did not speak. Annie gave him the time to find his words.

"We all want to blame someone for the things that go wrong in our lives, don't we?" he said at last. "Whenever anything bad happens, we want there to be a person we can hold responsible."

"We do," said Annie.

"I don't know if society has changed, or if we've always been like that."

Annie tilted her head. "Hard to tell."

"But that's how we are. When we send the lifeboats out to help those in trouble. If it's a kid on an inflatable drifting out, someone caught in a rip current, or a ship in trouble out at sea, when everyone's back on shore, wrapped up in blankets with a cup of hot chocolate, people start asking whose fault it was."

"It's natural," she said.

He looked at her sharply. "Is it? Is it, Annie? The older I

get, the more I think that blaming people for the bad things that happen only leads to bitterness. Bitterness eats you up inside. It gnaws away at you. It destroys you."

She nodded. "When my Brian died, I did look for someone to blame. Maybe the GPs could have spotted the signs sooner. Maybe if hospital waiting times weren't so long. I deluded myself into thinking that if only they'd done X or Y then he'd still be here. But of course, that's not how it is."

"No, it's not." Tim's voice was quiet. "Once upon a time, I had everything. A job here by the sea, as satisfying a job as any man could hope for. A wife. I loved her and she loved me. And we had our boy, Simon. I had everything. I was king of the world. I knew I was lucky, but I didn't know how lucky I was. I want to go back in time, more than forty years now, and shake my younger self, make him see *exactly* how lucky he was."

He stood and stared at nothing.

"Cos then I lost it all."

He walked down the shed towards the beach end. The big doors there were open a crack, spilling hot white summer light onto the floor. There was a tidy, if uneven stack of boating equipment and supplies in the corner. Tim moved some floats tied together with rope aside and pulled out a large rectangle of wrapped plastic. He lifted it free, and holding it with one hand, unwrapped it with the other.

The painting was unframed, a simple canvas, an image of Lyme Regis seen across the sea from the end of the Cobb.

"I lost it all, the day my boy died," said Tim. "Here. Take a look."

He passed it to Annie.

For a moment, she considered the fact that this Muldoon

painting was worth tens of thousands of pounds. But the significance of this painting transcended money.

"How did you know it was me?" said Tim.

"We would have known much, much sooner if it wasn't for Helen Cruickshank's stupid laptop," said Annie.

"How so?"

"Helen turned art detective. The police provided her with what was known, and she trawled through various art databases to work out which paintings might have been unaccounted for. Problem was, when she put the information on her computer, it turned all the British dates into the American format. She thought she was looking for a painting from the eighth of January nineteen ninety-four. But even as a tiny thumbnail picture on her computer, I could see this wasn't a winter picture."

She turned it over in her hands and looked for Clifford Muldoon's scrawl on the back of the canvas. There it was.

"First of the eighth. First of August nineteen ninety-four. That was the day."

"The day my Simon drowned."

She turned it back the other way and studied the picture. She both knew and didn't know what she was looking for and felt a solid sense of completion and sorrowful understanding when she saw it. Right there in the centre of the picture.

Tim stood close to her and brought his finger in until it hovered above the textured paintwork.

"There he is," he said, barely more than a whisper. "There's our Simon."

Chapter Sixty-Two

The door to Helen's gallery flew open again.

"We're popular today." Helen turned to see Tina Abbott, her brother-in-law PC Douglas Anderson, and their colleague, DS Nathan Strunk. "Don't suppose you've come to buy some Clifford Muldoon memorial tea towels?"

Tina looked around. "Has Dante Legg been here?"

"Why?" asked Figgy.

"Has he?" demanded the DS.

"Indoor voices, please," said Helen.

"They were here earlier," said Juniper.

"They?"

"Dante was here with Rosamund's mum," said Figgy. "He was looking for Annie."

"Annie was with Dante?" said Tina.

"No. Annie rushed off because she thinks she knows who stole the painting from the house."

"Thanks to my detective work," added Helen.

"And Dante rushed off after her," said Juniper.

"With Rosamund."

"Where have they all gone?" asked Dougie.

"Down to the seafront." Helen waved airily out of the window.

"Why is my mum always in the thick of it?" muttered Tina.

"I'm sure they can't have gone far," said Figgy.

"We should head down there," said the DS.

"Are they in trouble?" asked Helen.

Tina looked pale. "It's my mum."

Figgy's eyebrows were knotted. "We should come," she said.

"This is police business, madam," said DS Strunk.

"We can help you look." Helen grabbed the keys to lock up the shop front. "We're all coming."

Tina tutted and rolled her eyes. "We're going to look for Annie and Dante. No silliness, you hear?"

"Clear as crystal," said Helen.

Chapter Sixty-Three

Annie followed Tim's pointing finger.

In the broad expressionist strokes of Muldoon's artwork, far from the indistinct shadows that made up the people on the beach, she could see a dot in the sea, rendered in the palest yellow, and a line of black. A head and an arm, raised. Almost nothing but a blob and a line, but it was a human being, a boy, caught in an absolute moment of life, a hand raised as though to give a cheery wave to the viewer, to the painter.

"He was too far out," whispered Tim.

"And not waving but drowning," Annie whispered back. Tears pricked her eyes.

Tim gave an involuntary sob. "That..." He tried to regain control of himself. "Clifford Muldoon watched my boy drowning, and that, that bastard, he painted him."

"Tim." She wrapped an arm around his waist and held him.

Tim sniffed hard and noisily, tears flowing. Annie found a tissue in her pocket and pressed it into his hand.

"Clifford showed me that painting, months later, after the funeral, after everything." Tim wiped his eyes. "I don't know why. No, I *do* know why. He needed to ease his conscience. He needed to know that I knew." He gripped the painting tightly. "He showed me and said that he'd had no idea Simon was in trouble. Said he'd even waved back. But he needed me to know that he hadn't known, hadn't understood. He wanted my forgiveness. He wanted my... my permission."

He stepped away from her, taking the painting in both hands.

"I told him to destroy it. I told him to burn it. It was an offence to the memory of my son. It was a permanent dagger in my heart. And Clifford looked at me with big, sad eyes like I was a poor, stupid yokel who didn't understand, and he told me that he sympathised, but he wouldn't be destroying it. And that was that." He exhaled loudly. "Until the other day."

Annie felt her shoulders slump. "The day Clifford died."

"Yes. You were with me. The shout went out, there was a man in the water. We mustered a rescue boat, but he was beyond saving. And then the police and the paramedics were there. And I looked at Clifford's body and I thought, weird though it was, I suddenly thought, 'I'm free of him. I'm free of him now.'"

She nodded. "You went to his house right then."

"I did." Tim went to a tool rack on the wall and pointed at an orange-painted short-handled crowbar. "We use these to break into doors and portholes if we need to. I came in here, took it, walked up to Silver Street. I must have been moving like a robot. Walk here, walk there, door jemmied open, into his house. Didn't take more than a minute to find this painting and then I brought it back here." A smile passed over his face. "I didn't even really try to hide it. I just carried it. No one noticed. Some master criminal, I am."

"But you didn't destroy it," said Annie. "Wasn't that the whole point of stealing it?"

"It was," he admitted. "But then I had it here, and I looked at it." He angled the painting so she could see it again. "He's there. That's my Simon there. Just there. I want to..." He raised a shaking hand. "I want to reach into the picture and save him. Madness, I know. But he's there. If only I can reach him. Does that make sense?"

"It makes perfect sense," said Tina from the doorway that led back to the shop.

Annie turned. She hadn't even heard the door open.

Tina stood with Dougie and that detective sergeant, Nathan Strunk. Annie saw Helen, Figgy and Juniper in the open doorway behind them.

Nathan moved past Tina and approached Tim.

"Mr Cromwell, I am arresting you in connection with the murder of Clifford Muldoon."

"I didn't kill him," said Tim. "I had cause to hate him, with all my heart, but I didn't kill him."

Tina looked past Nathan at Annie. "We actually came looking for Dante."

"You think he did it?"

Tina shrugged. "The evidence is there."

"Unless Mr Cromwell here wants to confess to the break-ins at the Muldoon house," said Nathan.

"Break-ins?" said Tim. "Plural?"

"In through the front door and out through the kitchen window."

Tim frowned. "Why would I do that? No, I never went into the kitchen."

"There were two separate break-ins," said Dougie.

"I think we need to find Dante Legg," said Nathan.

"He came down to the Cobb," said Figgy.

"With Rosamund," said Helen.

"The Cobb!" said Tina. She ran outside.

Chapter Sixty-Four

Rosamund and Dante had walked right to the end of the Cobb without encountering Annie.

The Cobb, paved all the way to its end, stood high above the water. Waves splashed against the rocks with a mid-level energy that seemed to say: 'Yeah, I can crash and bash with the best of them, but it's a sunny day and I can't be bothered.' Even though there were tourists wandering along much of the length of the Cobb, it was quieter out here, away from the crowds on Marine Parade and down on the beach.

"So, what I'm hearing," Rosamund said, "is that you saw Clifford Muldoon, the man who wronged you all those years ago, and decided to give him a piece of your mind. That was all."

"Yeah, I guess," said Dante. "When you put it like that, sure, that is what happened, but you don't understand the anger I felt."

"I can imagine." Rosamund frowned. "You were dragged through the courts for a crime you didn't commit. That kind of thing would burn inside anyone. When was this, anyway?"

Dante put his hands on his hips and looked out to sea. "Maybe a day or two before he died. Not long after I arrived here. I came for a walk out here. You know, everyone who comes to Lyme Regis has to go for a walk along the Cobb."

"They do."

"It would have been one of my first days here. I walked out and there he was." He turned and threw his arms down to the spot on which he was standing. "The man was right here. I dunno. Maybe the surprise of seeing him after all these years provoked my anger. You get me?"

"I do." Rosamund was distracted by activity further back down the Cobb. A group of seven or eight people was hurrying towards them. The most obvious was Douglas Anderson in his police uniform. And there was Tina Abbott right beside him, apparently carrying a painting for some reason. Annie, Figgy, Helen. Rosamund's own mum was a short distance behind them, walking at speed for all she was worth.

"Er, Dante. Seems we're about to have some company."

"Huh?" Dante put his hand to his brow to see against the sun. "Oh, hell. Looks like the cops will have me after all."

"What are they going to arrest you for?"

He laughed hollowly. "Anything they like. That's my experience."

Rosamund thought the approaching police officers seemed to slow as they neared. Was that cautiousness? Were they really treating Dante like some dangerous criminal?

"Afternoon, Dante," called Douglas. "You've been giving us a bit of a runaround today."

Dante gave Rosamund a sideways look before addressing

Douglas. "Me and my friend Rosamund here have just been walking."

Rosamund nodded. "Just walking and talking."

"We need you to come back to the station," said Tina.

"I think I've said all I need to say," said Dante.

"You can come voluntarily, or we can arrest you," added DS Strunk.

"On what charge?"

"Murder. The murder of Clifford Muldoon."

Dante scoffed, giving the detective a hard look. "Really? You have no evidence."

Tina took a step forward. "I'm sorry to do this, but we know Clifford was the man whose false testimony led to your burglary conviction. We know you spoke to him when you came to Lyme most recently. We have your fingerprints on a drinking beaker in his house."

"You think I went to his house?"

Tina glanced back at Annie and Tim, then returned her gaze to Dante.

"There were two break-ins at Clifford's house. One was after he'd died, when a painting was stolen. But the other one was earlier, when his medication was tampered with to provide him with a fatal cocktail of prescription drugs. I believe you wanted to kill him."

Dante looked at Rosamund. "See? This is how it happens." He looked out to sea. A gull cawed overhead.

"OK," he said, loudly. "You want the truth? You're right. I did."

Chapter Sixty-Five

A nnie held Tim's hand and watched as Dante, at the very edge of the Cobb, offered his confession.

"It's true. I wanted to kill Clifford Muldoon. As soon as I saw him here, I recognised him. I knew I had to give him a piece of my mind."

"Dante, you can tell us at the station," said Nathan.

Dante wagged a finger at him. "No, man. You need to listen. I came here and I saw Clifford Muldoon, that sanctimonious coward of a man who would rather see an innocent man have his name and reputation ruined than admit he was wrong. One of those people. Cultured, successful, peddling his art to the fawning public for top prices while other creatives..." He tapped his own chest. "Toiled in the gutters. When I saw him that day, he didn't even recognise me, let alone remember what he'd done."

He turned to indicate the spot in which Clifford had always sat.

"I spoke to him here, maybe a day or two before he died. I introduced myself, I reminded him of who I was. Hell, it took him long enough to remember. I was filled with this restless rage, you know? If I was going to kill him, I'd have done it there and then. I'd have pushed him in his chair off the end. Simple as. The man was frail. Would have weighed nothing."

"But you didn't kill him," said Tina.

Dante shook his head. "That vile little man. He tried to argue with me. He put on his posh airs and graces and tried to tell me why I was wrong."

Annie felt Tim's hand grip hers a little tighter.

"He tried to act all nonchalant and cool," said Dante, laughing now. "Picked up his cup for a little casual sip and dropped it."

He followed the path of the dropped cup with his hands and his mind's eye.

"His hands were shaking. Uncontrollably. Little more than claws they were."

"He had Parkinson's disease," Tina said.

"He was old," said Dante. His voice was hard.

"We're all getting old, love," called Joanna from the rear of the group.

Dante looked over at her. "Yeah," he said, "we're all getting old, and no one deserves to be afflicted with a disease like that but... but that wasn't the point. As I bent to pick up the cup, I looked into his eyes, and I saw it."

"Saw what?" asked Juniper.

"He was old. He was alone. And he was afraid."

There was disgust on his face as he let go of the imaginary cup.

"You can paint a thousand cold dark landscape paintings and sit on a great big pile of cash, but without people, without love..." Dante shook his head. "I think he came down here to paint because painting was the only thing he had left.

Death would have been no punishment for that man. The fear I saw and the knowledge that I'd looked him in the eye one last time was enough. I washed my hands of him. I walked away. That was the last dealing I had with the man, in this world and hopefully the next, too. God's honest truth."

"He didn't even have painting," said Tina.

Nathan looked to her.

"Come on, we know it," she said. "His Parkinson's meant he couldn't hold a paintbrush. He might have been sitting down here, day after day, but we know full well that he didn't even have a cup to wash his brush in. This sitting at the end of the Cobb had been an act for God knows how long."

A thought occurred to Annie. "The three canvases," she said.

Tina frowned at her.

"When I came down here, when he first fell in, I looked for medication in his bag," said Annie. "There were two canvases in there, as well as the one on his easel. All three were of the same scene, but at different stages of completion. I suppose he would whip them out during the course of the day. Beginning, middle, end. Make out he was getting the work done."

"Pride, you see," said Dante.

"No, that's not possible," said Helen. "I've been selling Clifford Muldoons all year and all last year. He's been selling them to me. Maybe twenty, thirty pictures in total."

"Maybe he's been sitting on a stockpile of them," suggested Dougie, "doling out the last of the paintings."

"But they're dated."

"Post-dated, perhaps?"

No one seemed sure what the answer might be.

Chapter Sixty-Six

Dougie turned to Nathan. "So, are we arresting Tina's father-in-law or not?"

"For what?" Dante asked. "Staring into that man's dead black soul and not killing him?"

Nathan frowned.

A titter of laughter escaped from Figgy. The others turned to stare at her.

She slapped her hand over her mouth. "I'm so sorry!"

"I'm glad someone's finding this funny." The DS scowled.

"I really am sorry," she said, "but I think I've just worked it out."

"Worked what out?"

She blinked. "Everything."

"What do you mean by 'everything'?" asked Juniper.

"I mean, everything." Figgy straightened. "I think I know why Clifford was here, painting when he could no longer paint. I know why he died. I'm fairly sure I know who killed him."

Tina sighed. "Really? We appreciate your interest in the matter, but we don't have time for everyone to give us their pet theory."

"But I really think I have it. It's about paint. We've been decorating my caravan. Made an absolute mess of it – apologies to everyone who tried to assist – and we got paint everywhere. And there's the paint stain."

"What paint stain?"

Figgy tapped her trouser leg. "The one that proves it. Because it's not just about paint. It's about money. This is all about money and it's like you said, Rosamund."

"Is it?" said Rosamund.

"Yes. When you said Juniper can't seem to make any money from her painting." Figgy straightened. "What do we know? We know that Clifford painted landscapes. The same old landscapes, year after year—"

"They're a bit more nuanced than that," Helen argued.

Figgy shook her head. "But he painted them, and people bought them, and they might not sell for as much as they used to, but each one still made him a big chunk of cash." She took a breath. "Except, he started suffering with Parkinson's and knew he couldn't paint for much longer. But still, somehow, right up to the day he died, he was out here, pretending to paint."

"He was," agreed Tina.

Figgy nodded. "What we also know, if I've been listening correctly, is that there were two break-ins at his house. On the day he died, Mr Cromwell here broke in and removed that painting, a hurtful thing that should have been tossed in the sea long ago. But at some other point in time, someone came in through the kitchen window to mess with his medicine. Since the medicine must have been messed about with before the morning on which he died, I'm guessing they didn't have to smash the window or anything like that."

"There was a loose latch, if you must know," said Tina.

Another nod. "A loose latch. Good. Yes. Because that makes sense. The murderer slipped in and out. They were familiar with Clifford's house just as they were familiar with Clifford's art. Was he a good artist, Helen?"

Helen looked surprised. "Good?" she said after a pause. "He captured the mood of the art scene briefly in the nineties, and he understood the desires of the market."

"But was he any good?" Figgy asked her.

"Not exactly to my tastes, if I'm to be honest."

"And his use of black paint?"

"I beg your pardon?"

Figgy's tone was more urgent now. "He used black in his paintings, didn't he?"

"He... he did." Helen looked around the group as if hoping someone else would tell her why Figgy was asking her all this. "I'm not sure what that has to do with anything."

Figgy pointed at the paint stain on the shin of her trousers, a splodge of black paint. "Because I was told that a good artist, a great artist, never uses black," she said. "Isn't that right, Juniper?"

Juniper's mouth opened, then closed. "Er, that's correct, Figgy. Well remembered."

"But I picked up this stain in your studio."

"How? When?"

"Very good questions," said Figgy, looking at the other young woman. "But they don't change the facts. You killed Clifford Muldoon, didn't you, Juniper?"

Chapter Sixty-Seven

"I'm sorry, mate," said Juniper. "I must have skipped a page. I killed Clifford"

Figgy stared at her. "I think you did."

"Because you've got black paint on your trousers?"

"This has all confirmed it for me. There was black paint in your studio, when you were quite vehement about not using it."

Juniper shook her head. "I can have it and not use it. I was talking about artists not using it and—"

"But you did paint Clifford's pictures for him in recent years, didn't you?"

"No!"

Annie narrowed her eyes at Juniper: she'd denied it too fast. And Juniper's look of shock told her that she realised the same thing.

"You're an excellent artist," said Figgy. "That Van Gogh you did in my caravan. I suppose you can turn your hand to anything. Even copying a hackneyed old painter like Clifford Muldoon."

"I'm not sure I'd call him 'hackneyed'," put in Helen.

Figgy smiled at her friend. "If I'm not mistaken, Helen, you were willing to sell Muldoons painted by Juniper, but not willing to sell Juniper's own work."

"Don't try to ensnare me, Figgy," Helen shot back. "The value of art is always what people are willing to pay for it. And I wouldn't participate willingly in frauds and forgeries."

Some of the things Figgy had said now struck Annie. "How much did Clifford pay you for your work, Juniper?" she asked.

Juniper's face tightened. Her cheeks reddened.

"Not enough," Annie went on. "Several thousand per painting for him. Maybe a fraction of that for you?"

Figgy clicked her fingers. "The trunk you asked Cameron to move, the reason he was there. Was it full of Muldoon pictures? Ones you'd painted?"

Juniper pulled her shoulders back. "What if they were?" she said. "They were mine. Whether in my own style or Clifford's, they were still mine."

"Are we just throwing ideas around here?" said Nathan. "This is not how a police investigation works."

"And yet," said Tina, "that thing with the latch in the kitchen always bothered me."

He looked at her. "In what way?"

"That loose latch in the kitchen. If Tim admitted to breaking in through the front door, then the second break-in, or rather the first one, in which someone tampered with Clifford's medication, pretty much relies on the culprit knowing the latch was loose. They had to know the house. They had to know that Clifford was on medication."

Nathan scoffed. "We could start speculating that the

culprit also needed a medical degree to know how to tamper with the medication."

Tina shrugged. "Or they could just have looked it up on the internet." She took a step towards Juniper. "Do you have a phone, Miss Brown? You wouldn't mind us checking your search history, would you?"

Juniper put her hand to her pocket.

"If you're innocent, you've nothing to fear," said Tina.

Juniper stepped back, pulled her phone from her pocket and hurled it into the sea.

Tina gave her a tight smile. "We don't need your physical phone to look up your search history. I mean, it would have been easier, but we can liaise with the phone company and..." She sighed.

"Juniper?" said Helen.

Juniper shot her a foul look. "You refused to sell my art, Helen. You've been selling it for months. Months!"

"I... It's true?"

Juniper's gaze swept round all of them. There was panic in her eyes, but anger, too.

"Everyone wants to take advantage of you," she spat. "I worked with that selfish old miser for so long, and how did he reward me? He made out that I should be happy just to be allowed to work beside him. A hundred pounds a week and free lodgings! Like I should be grateful!"

"Juniper," began Nathan. "Miss Brown..."

"I asked him. I asked him! Pay me what I'm owed. Pay me and we can carry on." Her lips curled into a snarl. "He just laughed at me like I was a child. He stole from me. He stole my labour and my skill, and he didn't care. I just needed to get away, with paintings I'd made myself and I could sell myself once the heat had died down."

"Did you have to kill him to do that?" asked Tina.

Her voice dropped to a harsh whisper. "Oh, but I wanted to. I wanted to."

"Juniper Brown, I am arresting you for the murder of Clifford Muldoon..." said Nathan, pulling out handcuffs.

Chapter Sixty-Eight

On Sunday, Naomi and Dougie held a barbecue as a farewell party for Dante. Annie had asked if she could bring Tim along as her 'plus one'.

"Of course." Dougie had smiled. "The more the merrier."

Naomi had asked: "Does this mean you two are a couple now, Mum?"

"Don't be so embarrassing," Annie had replied.

She and Tim walked up together to the house on Blue Waters Drive, and coming round the side of the house, found the party in full flow.

Dougie was tending the barbecue. He wore Bermuda shorts and a stripy chef's apron and seemed happy flipping burgers. Tina sat in a deckchair beside Naomi, bouncing Daisy on her knee.

Louis and Poppy were dancing with Dante in the centre of the lawn. An up-tempo song Annie didn't recognise, all brass and drums, was playing from somewhere. Granddad Dante and the young ones bounced along, grinning.

Rosamund's mum, Joanna, stood close by, a glass of wine in her hand, swaying but not quite dancing.

If Annie had heard right, Joanna was leaving, too.

Rosamund, sitting in a deckchair by the hedges separating the garden from Mrs Fournier's next door, looked relaxed and happy. There was no doubt that she loved her mum, but there was also no doubt that the prospect of Joanna's imminent departure played no small part in that happiness. Next to her sat her lad, Cameron, and Figgy.

"Burger, Tim?" called Dougie. "Or I've got grilled vegetable skewers?"

Tim squeezed Annie's hand. "Well, let me take a look."

Annie drifted over to Rosamund. Figgy was attempting to bite into an enormous hamburger without getting relish everywhere. Cameron wiped her cheek with a napkin.

"Nice afternoon for it," said Annie.

"Glorious afternoon." Rosamund sipped at her glass of fizz.

"No Helen here?"

Rosamund shook her head. "Busy filling in the application form for parties interested in the shop next door to hers. There might be stiff competition."

Annie gestured at Dante. "But no application from Dante. All just a pipe dream, then."

Despite the music and the chatter, Joanna had heard the conversation and took a step towards them.

"He's had a better offer, ladies."

A look passed between Annie and Rosamund. Annie couldn't quite interpret the expression on Rosamund's face. A little embarrassment, a huge slice of relief, a sizeable chunk of indifference given that the day was warm, they were in good company, and she had a glass of something cold and fizzy in her hand.

"You and Dante got big plans then?" asked Annie.

"We're going on a romantic road trip to visit the dance halls and clubs he used to know. First stop, Wigan Casino."

"Oh." Annie nodded. "Sounds lovely."

"An adventure." Joanna's eyes were wide.

"And you don't need to hang around to help put your girl's life in order?"

Rosamund scowled at Annie and waved a hand at her to stop.

Joanna smiled contentedly. "I think I've given her enough pointers."

"Pointers," said Rosamund dourly.

"And I can see that my grandson is a mature and grounding influence on her."

Cameron looked up. "What's that?"

"I said you're the sensible one, darling," replied Joanna.

Chapter Sixty-Nine

As a song ended, Dante gave a loud 'hoo!' and backed away, encouraging Poppy and Louis to keep dancing.

"You look exhausted," said Tina.

"Just need to get my breath back." He grinned. "And we have to be hitting the road soon."

Tina caught a twitch of discomfort on his face. She knew what it meant.

"Mike made no promises about coming along today," she reminded him.

"I know."

She stood, lifting Daisy. "You sit with your granddaughter for a bit. Rest. Let me get you a drink."

"A soft drink," he said. "I'm doing the driving."

He took Daisy from Tina. The baby burbled, and he planted a noisy kiss on her cheek that had her burbling even louder. He sank into a deck chair beside Naomi.

Tina went to the table they'd set aside for drinks and poured a coke for Dante. He took it with thanks and then she made a circuit, making sure all the guests were being catered for.

Tim had his plate piled high by Dougie. There was a burger, a hot dog and a mountain of grilled vegetables. Annie was helping him out by eating chunks of mushroom and pepper from his plate.

Tina couldn't help hoping that whatever was going on between Tim and her mum, it might continue for a while. In many ways, he was everything that Annie wasn't – sensible, cautious, purposeful – and he seemed to be nothing but a force for good in her life. Watching the pair of them resolved something in Tina's mind. She went over to them.

"Mum. Tim."

Annie gave her a kiss on the cheek.

"Thanks awfully for inviting us," said Tim. "Lovely spread your family put on."

"I'm glad you're here. I wonder if I could borrow you both for a moment."

Annie raised her eyebrows, and they followed her into the house.

"I'm not usually one for breaking the rules," Tina began.

"What have you done?" asked Annie.

"It's been a busy and confusing few weeks. I'm not even officially back at work yet."

"As everyone keeps telling you."

"Yes." She went round the back of the dining table and stood in the space between the shelving unit and the wall. "Anyway, Juniper Brown has admitted to Clifford's murder, and the Crown Prosecution Service have no interest in pursuing the breaking and entering charge against Tim here. For something so complicated, there aren't many loose ends left to tie up. And in all the confusion..."

From the space behind the shelving unit she took the painting she'd hidden there.

"We forgot to log this into evidence," she said.

Tim hurriedly set down his plate of food and took the canvas from her. His fingers traced the specks of paint in the centre of the image that represented his lost son.

"I know you're not going to sell it," said Tina. "One way or another, it seems best that this painting be... lost. You might put it somewhere or—"

Tim's intake of breath was sharp. "Dougie mentioned... he mentioned that he'd be lighting the firepit later. Keep the party going into the night."

"I believe so," said Tina.

Tim looked to Annie.

"It's time to let go, isn't it?"

"Are you sure?" she asked.

He nodded. "Sometimes we have to make that leap. Can't live in the past forever. Can't hold onto bad feelings."

There were tears in his eyes as he looked at Tina. He reached out and gripped her hand.

"Thank you," he said.

"Don't," said Tina. "You'll set me off."

There was a cheer from outside. Tina went out into the garden. Dante and Joanna were hand in hand, baby Daisy still resting in the crook of Dante's arm.

"Time for us to go!" Joanna declared. "Don't want to be driving in the dark. And we've a dinner reservation at a lovely place in Chipping Sodbury at eight."

Tina went over to relieve Dante of Daisy. Dante gave his granddaughter a final kiss and then gave Tina one, too.

"You have been too kind to me," he said. "And your

mother, too," he added, looking round for Annie. "I've never been an easy man to live with."

"I'm glad you came," she said.

"I wouldn't have missed it for the world."

Their bags were already in the car they'd come over in. Tina had no idea how well Dante and Joanna would fare together, on the road, in the real world, with only each other for company. It would be an adventure. That much was certain.

To a flurry of cheery farewells, they made their way through the house to leave. Tina and Rosamund, daughter-in-law and daughter to the unexpected couple, accompanied them.

"And you drive carefully," said Tina.

"Give us a ring when you get there," added Rosamund.

"You'd think I was the child and she was the parent," said Joanna, heading towards the ancient Renault Scenic Dante had purchased.

Another vehicle had drawn up in the cul-de-sac. It was Mike's Nissan. Dante didn't spot him until the door opened and Mike, still dressed for work, stepped out.

Dante straightened up. Joanna had never met Mike before and didn't yet understand.

"Everything all right, Dante?"

"Excuse me a second." Dante stepped aside to the edge of the pavement.

Mike stood by his car and looked across the residential street at him.

"Dad."

"Son."

Chapter Seventy

Helen Cruickshank stood at the counter of her gallery and re-read the question on the form out loud.

"How will your venture contribute to the long-term goals of the Lyme Regis development programme?"

It wasn't any clearer on a second reading.

The form to apply for ownership of the vacant shop beside her own appeared to be some devilish work of bureaucracy, devised by the most warped minds in the local council. Dante Legg might have withdrawn his passing interest in the shop, but there were plenty of other people keen to take over a retail property so close to the sea.

The form had over twenty pages, and she'd had to go through her little security box of documents to find her HMRC tax reference number, her council tax details and proof of residency in the town. The box, usually kept safely in her chest of drawers upstairs, sat on the counter close to hand, just in case she needed it again.

She read the question on the form yet again.

"Well, I suppose I need to know what the Lyme Regis development programme is," she muttered.

"Talking to yourself," said Harper, coming into the shop from the rear with a tray of tea things. "First sign of madness."

"Only way of getting a sensible answer, sometimes." Helen regarded the teapot and cups gratefully. "I thought you were busy making your... What are you making at the moment?"

"A life-size wild boar out of old tractor panels and repurposed garden forks."

"Of course you are."

Harper poured the teas.

"I thought you were still hiding from me," said Helen.

"I'm not hiding from you."

"Or sulking with me."

"Sulking is a negative word. I've been angry with you."

Helen nodded and waited for Harper to put a blob of milk in her cup.

"Are you still angry with me?"

Harper huffed. "I don't know what I am. I'm... I'm resigned to..." She flapped her arms between the two of them. "Whatever this is."

"That's very romantic," said Helen sourly.

"Every time I see you doing work on expanding the business, it hits me that I'll always come second," said Harper. "You can commit to this place, this shop, this town. You can go crazy printing hundreds of knock-off Clifford Muldoon commemorative tea towels. But the idea of committing yourself to the woman you live with..."

Helen came round the counter and took Harper's hands. Harper resisted for a moment, but Helen seized hold of her.

"I, Helen Cruickshank, love you, Harper McCoppin. With all my heart. Though you infuriate me and leave greasy tools in the sink and come to me smelling of soot, I love you."

Harper looked at her levelly and then gave a little grunt. "OK, that was sweet. Cheesy. But sweet."

"Thank you."

"But the point is, I sort of want us to do it publicly. Make a declaration to the world. I do want to get married. It might seem odd and alien to you, and I certainly didn't grow up with girly ideas of a fairytale wedding, but somewhere inside, I ache to be your wife. I want to hear you say, I, Helen Cruickshank, take you—"

Helen kissed her, partly to stop her talking. "I would do anything for you, Harper, but I, Helen Cruickshank, will never marry you. But I do have something..."

She pulled away and went to the Clifford Muldoon display. She took one of the screen-printed tea-towels and presented it to Harper.

"Oh, yay, a tea towel," said Harper sarcastically. "This is exactly what I want."

"Look at the border," said Helen.

Harper glanced at the border pattern, a narrow strip of two lines with something like waves in between them.

Harper shrugged. "It's a border."

"Look closer. Read between the waves."

Harper gave her a funny look and inspected the border again. She squinted and saw that the infill for each wave was formed from lettering. "Helen Cruickshank loves..." She looked up at Helen. Helen gestured for her to keep reading. "Helen Cruickshank loves Harper McCoppin more than the moon, more than the stars, more than..."

She looked up, a disbelieving smile on her face.

"Over two hundred tea towels printed," said Helen. "More than fifty sold so far. Every single one of them a declaration of my love for you."

"Oh, you are a soppy so-and-so," said Harper, and kissed Helen firmly on the lips. "A real soppy so-and-so."

Helen shrugged. "I try. In my own way. Is that enough love for you, for now?"

Still clutching the tea towel, Harper picked up her tea.

"Aye, yes. I suppose it is." She took a sip of tea and gasped. "Must get on with my work. That giant metal boar isn't going to finish itself."

Helen watched her go, feeling both relief and a cosy warmth inside her. She went back round the counter. Like metal boars, this application form wasn't going to finish itself.

But she didn't return to her work immediately. She put her cup down and opened the security box. On the top level were key documents from the Inland Revenue and council, her paper driving licence and utility company records. She lifted the insert tray aside and examined the items below. She looked at them so rarely, but she couldn't discard them.

In the bottom compartment of this lockable box were several letters, some handwritten, some printed with now-faded ink. Underneath those were further documents, old bank details and an old-style British passport.

Glancing to the rear door to make sure Harper had truly gone, Helen flicked open the passport. There were stamps for countries across Europe and beyond in there. At the back was the ID page.

A young woman looked back at Helen. So bloody young, thought Helen. People sometimes said that their younger selves were unrecognisable to them, but Helen thought no such thing. The woman was obviously her. There were just a few more lines drawn permanently onto her face – around her eyes, her brow, her cheeks and chin.

Next to the image was the name: Genevieve Cartwright-Jones.

The sight of the name made Helen's breath catch. It still did every time she saw it. And it touched her with sadness, too, as if this woman had been lost, taken from the world.

Helen looked at it for a full minute before she forced herself to close the passport.

Helen Cruickshank could never marry Harper McCoppin, no matter how much she loved her.

Because Helen Cruickshank didn't exist.

* * *

We hope you enjoyed reading *A Brush with Death*. We have another mystery for you, *The Dorset Cream Tea Mystery*, which you can get for free as ebook or audio from our book club or you can buy in paperback from book retailers. Read it for free at: rachelmclean.com/creamtea.

Happy Reading,
Rachel and Millie

Read a novella, The Dorset Cream Tea Mystery

When one of the members of The Lyme Regis Women's Swimming Club takes on a new job cleaning holiday lets, she expects her biggest challenge to be working her way through six cottages before the next guests arrive.

She doesn't expect a mystery.

Why is a picture in one of six identical cottages very slightly different to the others? Who is the mysterious woman who let herself in and cleaned before Rosamund got there? And what's that awful smell in cottage number one?

As Dorset Police investigate two murders they suspect of being connected with organised crime, Rosamund's mysteries may be more serious than she thinks. Will she and her swimming buddies be about to solve a double homicide?

Download the ebook or audiobook of *The Dorset Cream Tea Mystery* for FREE at rachelmclean.com/creamtea or buy in paperback from book retailers.

Also by Rachel McLean

The DI Zoe Finch Series – buy from book retailers.

Deadly Wishes

Deadly Choices

Deadly Desires

Deadly Terror

Deadly Reprisal

Deadly Fallout

Deadly Christmas

Deadly Origins, the FREE Zoe Finch prequel

The Dorset Crime Series – buy from book retailers.

The Corfe Castle Murders

The Clifftop Murders

The Island Murders

The Monument Murders

The Millionaire Murders

The Fossil Beach Murders

The Blue Pool Murders

The Lighthouse Murders

The Ghost Village Murders

The Poole Harbour Murders

The Chesil Beach Murders

...and more to come

The McBride & Tanner Series – buy from book retailers.

Blood and Money

Death and Poetry

Power and Treachery

Secrets and History

The Cumbria Crime Series by Rachel McLean and Joel Hames – buy from book retailers.

The Harbour

The Mine

The Cairn

The Barn

The Lake

The Wood

The Port

...and more to come

Also by Millie Ravensworth

The Cozy Craft Mysteries – Buy now in ebook and paperback

The Wonderland Murders

The Painted Lobster Murders

The Sequinned Cape Murders

The Swan Dress Murders

The Tie-Dyed Kaftan Murders

The Scarecrow Murders